MW01135113

Cygnus Arrives

Humanity Returns Home
Cygnus Space Opera
Book 3

A Tale in the Free Trader Universe
By Craig Martelle

Humans and the Intelligent Creatures

The Hillcats
Mixial – Tandry's bonded 'cat, a small, long-haired calico
Lutheann – bonded with Cain, all white
Carnesto – bonded with Ellie, all black
Brutus – the newest 'cat who keeps Cain honest
Tobiah – the largest Hillcat of the era, bonded with Spence

The Humans
Cain – Great-great-grandson of Free Traders Braden & Micah
Aletha – Cain's true love who wants to stay home
Ellie – Engineer aboard the Cygnus-12 & Cain's ex-wife
Tandry – Sensor operator
Dr. Johns – clone of the Cygnus VI survivor. In charge of the SES
Captain Rand – captain of the Cygnus-12 Deep Space Exploration ship
Spence – a small man, huge in spirit, a squad leader of Marines
Jo – a Marine, she is a gifted marksman
Starsgard – a professor of Astrophysics, Marine Corporal
Pace – a flight lieutenant, pilot of the Cygnus-12
Foucault – called Fickle, an academic and Marine

The Mechanicals
Cygnus-12 - also called The Olive Branch, the only space fleet interstellar ship capable of flying itself through the heliosphere and into the gravity well of a solar system
Holly – the artificial intelligence on Cygnus VII
Jolly – the artificial intelligence that Holly created for the Cygnus-12
Graham – the artificial intelligence on Concordia in system IC1396

The Hawkoids
Chirit – Crew member on Cygnus-12, sensor operator
Ascenti – Marine, stand-in sensor operator

The Tortoid
Daksha – Third Master of the Tortoise Consortium, son of Aadi, Commander of the Cygnus-12 exploration mission

The Lizard Men (Amazonians)
Peekaless – nicknamed "Pickles," Lieutenant of Marines
Zisk – a Marine

The Rabbits
   Brisbois – called "Briz," technical genius, Chief of Engineering
   Allard & Beauchene – gardeners assigned to the Cygnus-12

The Wolfoids
   Black Leaper – nicknamed "Stinky," Lieutenant of Marines
   Night Stalker – Sergeant of Marines
   Bull – much larger than the average Wolfoid, squad leader of Marines
   Grace – a squad leader of Marines
   Razor Fang, Aurochs Ring, Bounding Shepherd, Gray Streak, Black Shadow, Silent Tracker, Hidden Slayer, Lightning Flash, Dark Forest, Tan Mountain, and Shades Racer – the Marine Recruits

ACKNOWLEDGEMENTS

   I want to thank the Just In Time readers who did an incredible job making sure this was a clean manuscript, that the story continued without a hitch from the past two which were written over six months ago. Since then, I've written eight other books and four short stories, so I got confused.

A lot.

THANK YOU!!

Beck Young
Lori Hendricks
Thomas Ogden
James Caplan
Leo Roars
Theresa Barber
Norman Meredith
Diane Velasquez
Dorene Johnson

Table of Contents

Debriefing

"Crap!" Cain yelled.

'Really,' Brutus told him in his thought voice. *'I should hold the title of general, but it would only be honorific, of course. I have no intention of giving orders to this mob.'*

Cain rolled his eyes and shook his head. His senior staff tried not to look at him. The major's conversations with his Hillcat were colorful, to say the least.

Brutus was sitting on the conference table and licking his fur.

"Would you go somewhere else to lick your butt?" Cain asked out loud, having little hope the 'cat would acquiesce.

'No. I think you're jealous, that's all. Your team is waiting, dumbass.' Brutus continued his personal grooming without pause.

Cain looked at the faces around the table. His lieutenants were there, Black Leaper and Peekaless. It was time for the after-action review of their fight on Concordia. He used a simplified process, but it was all they needed to improve from one action to the next.

"Each of you, tell me one thing we did well and one thing we need to do better," he prodded.

The Wolfoids sat on the floor, but their muzzles were well above the level of the table, keeping them engaged in the conversation. Black Leaper was next to Night Stalker, and Stinky went first while Stalker watched him closely.

"They couldn't match our speed and agility," Stinky said through his vocalization device. He had thought they'd done well, despite the injuries and the loss of Hidden Slayer. They thought they had lost Tracker, but we hadn't. The Wolfoid survived thanks to getting back to sick bay as quickly as he did. The med bots worked a miracle on him, bringing him back from what seemed a sure death.

They Cygnus Marines had routed a determined enemy from a fortified position. Stinky continued, "Our ability to breach barriers was limited within the building and without bringing the whole building down, I'm not sure what else we could have done about that."

"Jolly, are you capturing these notes? We'll need a list and your help later to propose solutions, but not now. We just want to capture our thoughts," Cain said, looking at the ceiling, which was what he always did when talking with the disembodied artificial intelligence they called Jolly.

"Certainly, Major Cain," Jolly replied pleasantly.

The Lizard Man was wearing his skinsuit, casually watching the others. The Amazonians didn't show their emotions in a way that humans or the other intelligent creatures of Vii could understand.

Cain had given up long ago trying to figure the Lizard Men out. He resorted to asking them, and he understood that they would answer guardedly and in clipped phrases.

"Pickles, what do you have for us?" Major Cain prompted, forgetting that he promised not to call his lieutenants by their nicknames in front of the other platoon members.

"The 'cats' contributions were incontrovertible," the Amazonian said philosophically. The Lizard Men and the 'cats could not converse mind-to-mind for reasons that no one knew. Stoic and stalwart, Lieutenant Peekaless did not elaborate further.

"What would you change if you could, Pickles?" Cain pressed to get a little more from his friend.

"The 'cats. We should have brought them into the fight earlier. That's all. We are good now." Pickles rested his hands on the table.

Cain studied the Lizard Man's face before accepting that Pickles would contribute nothing else.

Brutus chuckled directly into Cain's mind. The major rolled his eyes and shook his head.

Cain looked to his squad leaders next, disappointed that they had nothing new. He thought he had trained them in critical thinking, but in the big scheme of the Cygnus Marines' existence, they were a fledgling force with leaders new to their roles.

"Ladies and gentlemen," Cain started, standing so he could walk around as he lectured, never missing an opportunity to train his people. He maintained his upright posture, leaning back slightly as he had seen the ancient United States Marines do. He cocked his head and then continued speaking.

"Every action that we survive is a chance to learn and grow. If we don't improve from engagement to engagement, then our enemies will eventually get ahead of us. We can't have that, because that means body bags and I'm not ready to fill those with any of you." Cain looked down at the table, happy that Brutus wasn't digging into his mind to berate him on one point or another.

Corporal Spence sat in his chair while Tobiah was behind him on the floor. The oversized Hillcat looked like he wanted to jump onto the table, but seemed torn. Cain wondered if Brutus was holding him back. Tobiah was three times Brutus's size and would fill the table.

"We've seen humanity return to space. Then we found what a dangerous place it was out here," Cain said softly, lowering his voice and narrowing his eyes. He wasn't reciting a history lesson, he was recalling the hard lessons that real-life had taught them. "So we formed the Cygnus Marines to protect our people as they made contact, and we'll keep protecting them. Just like Starsgard did to save the ship. In space or on land, we'll fight the enemies of freedom. And then we'll pack up and move on."

Cain had circled the table. When he made it back to his chair, Tobiah launched himself smoothly over Spence's head, landing on the conference room table with a short slide, his claws scratching across the table's surface. He knocked over a cup of water in front of Night Stalker before stopping.

The large tan 'cat casually walked in front of Spence and turned to put his butt in his human's face before laying down, tucking his front paws under his chest and keeping his head up, but closing his eyes.

Everyone had watched the 'cat, which was probably half the reason that Tobiah did what he did.

All Hillcats loved attention as long as it was on their terms.

7

Stinky wiped the table off using a hairy foreleg. Stalker wiped her leg after his, and that took care of the spill. Then they snuggled next to each other.

Brutus started unblinkingly at Major Cain. *'Make it stop,'* Brutus told Cain in his thought voice.

"You've all heard the rumors," Cain started, standing tall as he looked proudly at his leadership team. "Next stop is EL475, a K-Class star system approximately eight-hundred and fifty light years from here. That was one of the designated colony planets that Graham reported to us. We'll stop by to say hi, in our special way, of course…"

The group snickered as Cain tried not to look too smug.

"Once we've made new friends, we jump seven hundred light years to the edge of Sol's heliosphere." Cain paused for effect, looking at the star map on the screen behind him. He pointed to the screen. "That's right, people. We're going to Earth."

The Next Chapter

"ETA to heliosphere departure?" Captain Rand asked, looking at the people on the bridge.

Lieutenant Peekaless was doing double-duty as a Marine and ship's data systems analyst. Private Foucault, Fickle as they called him, was at the workstation next to Pickles and was assisting the lieutenant.

Lieutenant Pace sat at the flight console, watching the instruments as he programmed the next leg of the journey. He was an excellent pilot, but in deep space, Jolly handled the vast majority of flight duties.

Next to Pace, Ensign Kalinda worked at her navigation console. She was embroiled in the data that Graham had transferred to Jolly from the Concordian database. Entire new galaxies were opened up to her, well beyond what she had seen from the original expedition to the Cygnus star system.

She huffed in dismay, then leaned closer to better manipulate her screen. Pace looked at her, annoyed at the interruption. He was used to flying the ship from a separate compartment, but on the last refit, he'd been moved onto the command deck.

Pace pursed his lips and twisted his mouth sideways. He shook off whatever he was thinking and went back to studying his console.

Peekaless's three-fingered claws were flying across the input screen as he pulled and parsed data. Jolly was assisting as needed. Until Pickles saw the data, he didn't know exactly what to ask for, so he looked at the raw numbers and played with them manually.

Jolly was sentient and that made him an AI. He would appear in holographic form in areas where there were projectors, the bridge and engineering. He wanted to visit the garden deck, but hadn't moved the projection installation high enough on the engineer's priority list. He watched through the numerous monitors and lived vicariously among the 'cats and the Rabbits.

He wanted a close-up of the tenuous peace the two species maintained. If he got bored, he figured he'd unlock the weapons locker again and turn the Rabbits loose on what they considered the Hillcat infestation. Jolly replayed the last battle between the Rabbits, the 'cats, and the captain when he wished to be entertained.

There were fewer 'cats on board now, having left a healthy contingent on Concordia, although the biggest instigator was Carnesto, who continually plied the decks, looking for his next victim of his creative practical jokes.

Jolly found it fascinating and was happy to see the ship filled with intelligent creatures of all shapes and sizes. He swore to improve his emotional engagement on this leg of the journey by adopting more human speech and mannerisms. He wondered if the humans would even notice.

The AI appeared on the bridge next to the captain's chair, hands behind his back as he wore a perpetual smile. Pace glanced his way, before returning his attention to the starfield occupying the front screen.

Commander Daksha floated near the back of the bridge, his legs constantly moving as he swam to keep himself in place. He'd perfected his technique over the years and no longer even thought about it.

"A shade over nine days at current acceleration," Pace reported.

"And then another two weeks banking dark matter for the jump to EL475," Jolly added helpfully. "We could refer to it by the name that the colonists gave it--Heimdall, the guardian of Asgard."

"Three weeks and two days to Heimdall it is," Rand stated as he rotated his chair to look at Daksha without having to turn his head. "Commander?"

"Open ship-wide communication," the Tortoid ordered casually through his vocalization device.

"Done!" Jolly replied enthusiastically, nodding. Pace cocked his head as he looked at the AI.

"All hands, this is Commander Daksha." He didn't know why he introduced himself, but he always did. His voice was unique and the crew was small. They knew who was speaking after the first word came through the sound system. He opened his turtle-like beak and laughed at himself, a sound that wasn't projected so no one heard.

"We will continue out of the Concord System at our current acceleration, so business as usual people, getting the ship ready for our next jump, which will be to EL475, called Heimdall by the colonists. It is the last stop before we jump to triple zero, the root of our coordinate system."

He didn't elaborate, because he didn't need to.

***

"Starsgard! Where the hell are you?" Cain bellowed, leaning out the hatch of the weapons bay. Cain stepped into the corridor to assure himself that no one was there. He activated his neural implant, bringing up the window before his eye. "Jolly, locate Corporal Starsgard for me."

The AI responded instantly. "He is on the mess deck." The information window blinked as if Jolly was waiting for a response.

"Thanks, Jolly," Cain finally said as he headed for the stairs. "You are the absolute best AI on this ship. Bar none!"

"Why, thank you, Major Cain. Wait, what?"

Cain closed the window, looking smug at having successfully delivered another joke at Jolly's expense. Cain expected the AI would be in a philosophical lockdown for the next week as he rehashed and analyzed the statement.

The major descended the stairs, taking them three at a time. They weren't as wide as they used to be since the upgrade when a Wolfoid ramp had been installed along with a sideways curve to allow interdeck transit during acceleration within the gravity well.

Cain stopped when he reached the platform and doorway leading to the garden deck. *What do you think, Brutus, a quick stop to say hi to Allard and Beauchene?'* Cain asked in his thought voice.

'Fine. Check up on us, see how we've formed our battle lines, and watch out for stray laser fire,' Brutus replied sleepily.

Cain opened the hatch and boldly walked through, face first into a fine mist from the watering system that seemed to have activated the second he walked in.

"Hey!" he howled, trying to cover his face with his arms. The mist stopped, and he looked for the culprit between the branches and leaves of the heavy vegetation. "You did that on purpose, you fuzzy-tailed purveyors of terror!"

He heard a Rabbit snicker. Cain headed in that direction, stopping when he saw Brutus lying on a tree branch, his four 'cat legs hanging over the sides.

"You look like road kill," Cain told him.

Brutus waved one paw as a mock one-finger salute. He didn't bother opening his eyes. Cain flipped off his friend, with one hand, then two and started dancing in a circle around the head-high branch and waving his middle digits.

'Carnesto says that Ellie misses you and needs your manly company,' Brutus said matter-of-factly. Cain stopped dancing and tucked his fingers away, looking around to see if anyone saw him.

'No kidding?' Cain asked skeptically, having switched to his thought voice. *'Let me talk with Carnesto directly.'*

'Nope,' Brutus replied and didn't elaborate further on Cain's lineage or the usual put-downs he had ready to deliver at a moment's notice as part of Cain's daily comeuppance.

"You are such an ass!" Cain declared aloud, storming away from the small, orange Hillcat.

The rough-looking creature smiled to himself. *'I always win. When will my human ever learn?'*

"I hear you!" Cain bellowed as he zeroed in on the sound of a Rabbit retreating through the brush. Brutus wondered momentarily if Cain meant him, but shook his 'cat head as he realized Cain was going to take out his frustration on the Rabbits.

Cain passed two lounging Hillcats on the way. He ignored them as they ignored him. "You both sprayed me with water and now you're going to get it!" Cain blundered between two tomato plants loaded with fruit. A stream of water hit him in the face, and he twisted, bent, and fell over backward.

"Watch the tomatoes!" Allard cried through his vocalization device. "Damn!"

Both Rabbits appeared and picked a few of the riper tomatoes and two that weren't quite ripe enough, but the branch had been damaged. And then there were the two tomatoes on the ground, crushed beneath the clumsy human.

"Look what you did!" Beauchene said, putting his furry Rabbit hands on his hips in dismay.

"If you hadn't sprayed me…" Cain started, but Allard was still holding the hose and had it pointed in the human's direction. Cain could feel a dozen sets of 'cat eyes watching him. "I only wanted to check in and make sure everything was going okay."

"Fine, fine. Call next time so you don't upset the delicate balance we have to maintain for optimal growing conditions. You are such a klutz!" Allard exclaimed, shaking his head. The two Rabbits conferred on something then hopped away.

"I'll be damned," Cain said softly, standing up to find the seat of his pants was soaked. His shirt was soaked. His knees were wet, too. He found that his calves were dry, but that didn't make him feel any better. He took off his shirt and underneath, he wore a black t-shirt with the Cygnus Marines logo emblazoned in full color on the left breast.

He looked at it briefly and headed back toward the hatch. Cain glared at Brutus as he passed, but the 'cat's eyes were closed, his legs dangled, and tail was still. Cain was certain the 'cat wasn't sleeping, but he was making a good show of ignoring the outside world.

"I love you, little man," Cain whispered in Brutus's direction. "Even though you let me get soaked, you little miscreant."

'*I know,*' came the reply directly into Cain's mind.

***

Briz looked over his monitors, conferred with Jolly, made a manual adjustment on one of four different keyboards, and then chittered excitedly for two whole seconds before turning to something else.

Ellie shook her head as she watched, wondering if he was playing chess with Jolly on one of the screens. He always had a game running somewhere. Ellie tried playing but found it distracted her too much. She was turning into a good engineer, but needed to focus on the tasks at hand.

She turned back to the compressor that occupied her attention. It helped to move coolant through the system and was one of the more dangerous components. A coolant tank had blown in that very space, killing a Wolfoid lieutenant and almost killing her and Lieutenant Brisbois, if it hadn't been for Cain coming to their rescue.

Ellie snickered thinking about her complicated relationship with the Marine major. He had been an ensign with her at one point, but the great-great-grandson of Braden and Micah was destined for bigger things. She begrudgingly accepted that, along with his fanatical devotion to the woman he left behind.

They had parted ways, Aletha and Cain, and Ellie and Cain. He was forced to travel through space alone, but not alone. Ellie's door was always open for him.

"It's complicated," she said out loud, staring at the condenser but not seeing it.

"No kidding," Cain said. Ellie jumped, dropping a spanner and slapping a hand to her chest to calm her surprised and racing heart.

"Didn't your mother ever teach you manners, like not sneaking up on people?" She scowled at him for just a moment, but he was looking at the condenser's internals, appreciating the complexity of it and happy that he wasn't the one working on it.

Ellie's initial fright passed and she threw her arms around his neck, pulling him close for a long, passionate kiss. His hands found their way to her backside; he gripped firmly and squeezed. She leaned into him and he pushed back until she was pressed against the condenser housing.

She shook him off and carefully leaned forward. She slapped his chest as she turned to inspect the internals, making sure she didn't damage anything that would catastrophically fail and kill them all.

Ellie knew that the system wasn't going to break by leaning into it. There were too many fail-safes, but it didn't hurt to keep Cain in his place.

"You dumbass!" she said softly.

"Carnesto said you *needed* me," Cain said suggestively. Ellie rolled her eyes.

"Oh, he did, did he?" she answered.

'I did not,' Carnesto, the large black 'cat told them both over the mindlink.

"Why, that little rat…" Cain left it hanging, knowing that Brutus was in his mind and knew what was happening.

"Oh?" Ellie stabbed a finger into his chest. "You only came because you thought your lost love was pining for you? Is that it? You need to march yourself right out of here and cool your jets, mister! And why the hell are your clothes wet?"

She punctuated each sentence with a finger jab.

He backed away, staying balanced and holding his hands up in surrender, his shirt still in one of them. He looked hurt and Ellie took pity on him.

Yet another cruel Brutus joke.

"You two are quite a pair!" She smirked. Cain wasn't sure which two she was talking about so he didn't say anything. She walked with him to the hatch leading to the corridor.

She looked at Briz, who was fully engrossed in his systems, before pulling Cain close and brushing her lips over his cheek as she moved close to his ear. "See you tonight?" she whispered.

Cain's face split with a smile before she pushed him through the hatch and closed it in his face. She checked the time. Only six hours left on shift.

Briz looked up, confused. His Rabbit whiskers fluttered as if in a heavy breeze. "Was someone here?" he asked.

"Nope," Ellie replied without hesitation as she walked back to where she'd been working.

"Then what were you doing over there?" the chief of engineering asked as he looked from the condenser to the hatch and back to the condenser.

"Getting some fresh air. I had to clear my head before tackling this beast, but I have it all under control now. All of it," she reiterated, not looking at the Rabbit.

Attitude Adjustments

Cain had skipped down two levels to go to engineering after the taunting that Brutus had given him, and he was glad that he did.

It had been awhile since he'd had any private time with his former wife. The electricity between them was still there, but they'd taken separate paths and they had separate quarters. He needed to fix that. He'd changed his mind again, but this time he was certain.

Holy crap, Cain thought happily, forgetting the reason he was in the stairway. He closed his eyes and relived the brief encounter, enjoying the fireworks flashing through his mind.

"Which way you headed, boss?" Stinky asked through his vocalization device.

Cain slowly opened his eyes. The Wolfoid was waiting patiently.

Stinky wasn't completely sure about reading human expressions, so he took a shot in the dark. "Are you injured?"

"What? No, I'm fine," Cain replied as Brutus chuckled in his mind. *'You little rat! Wait until I see you.'*

'Then what, human? You'll scratch my belly and make those ridiculous cooing sounds. That's what you'll do. Jeez. Why did they hook me up with an idiot?' Brutus taunted his life-linked human.

Cain thought "they" were the nebulous council of Hillcat elders. They detailed the 'cats as needed to control the affairs of Cygnus VII. It was inevitable that Braden's descendent and the descendent of the Golden Warrior would end up paired.

'Because you're one lucky 'cat, you mangy cur,' Cain replied, to which Brutus replied with image after image of Cain in every embarrassing position he'd ever been in. Cain tuned the 'cat out.

"Starsgard. I was looking for Starsgard," the major said, reminding himself as much as telling the lieutenant.

"I think he's in weapons control," Black Leaper replied.

"I was just there and he wasn't," Cain said, before opening his neural implant. "Jolly, where is Corporal Starsgard?"

"He is in the weapons bay running a diagnostic on the close-in missile system," Jolly reported pleasantly.

"What you're saying, Jolly, is that had I waited, he would have come to me?" Jolly didn't answer. Stinky raised his heavy Wolfoid eyebrows before turning and launching himself up the ramp.

Had I done that, I wouldn't be wet, Cain thought, *but on the other hand, I wouldn't have a date tonight, either.*

He considered it a win as he ran up the stairs after his friend.

***

Starsgard looked angry. They'd only fired two missiles, but the system was showing the missile bank to be empty.

He ran the diagnostic three times before bringing Jolly in to help.

"Jolly?" Starsgard asked the ceiling, preferring to talk out loud as opposed to using his neural implant.

"Yes, Doctor Starsgard, how may I help you?"

"Why is the system showing no available missiles? How did we lose the rest of our missiles?" Starsgard whined.

"I assure you we have eight missiles remaining," Jolly said casually, seemingly unconcerned. "What I cannot tell you is why they aren't showing up as available on your board. I'll be right back."

The AI dropped off the comm system, leaving Starsgard to his own thoughts.

He ran a second diagnostic on the signal jamming system, pleased that it showed as one hundred percent functional. He leaned back in the chair that sat within a gimbal and doubled as an acceleration couch. He clasped his hands over his head and closed his eyes.

"WHAT THE HELL?" Cain yelled through the open hatch.

Starsgard launched himself from the chair, landing awkwardly and rolling to the deck. He winced in pain and grabbed his ankle.

Stinky slapped his friend on the back and forced his way past and into the room. "What were you up to, Corporal, before we so rudely interrupted?" the Wolfoid asked, looking accusingly at the major.

Starsgard continued to rub his ankle. Lieutenant Black Leaper helped him up, but the man couldn't put any weight on his leg. Cain rubbed his temples as he watched the corporal hobble to his chair.

"Sickbay, Starsgard. Can you get yourself there?" Cain asked impatiently, before catching himself.

Nothing mattered more than his people.

"Grab on, Corporal, we're taking a trip." Cain draped Starsgard's arm over his shoulder and they both headed out.

"I'm going to check in with the bridge," Stinky said as he walked in the opposite direction.

Cain led the injured man to the stairs. "We're going to take it easy on our way down, Starsgard. Tell me if we're moving too fast, and while we're on our way, tell me about the weapons systems."

"That's the rub, sir. Jolly is trying to figure out why all the missiles are showing up as fired. The jamming system works great, but right now, if anyone attacked us, we can't defend ourselves and we definitely cannot attack."

Cain stepped down first, and then Starsgard hopped down. They kept that rhythm as they descended, past the garden deck, and to the next deck where they'd find the mess, billeting, and sickbay. Cain shied away from the garden deck hatch. Finally feeling dry, he had no intention of going near the misters or the Rabbits.

'Good choice, interloper,' Brutus told him.

Cain momentarily glared at the closed hatch and wondered if Brutus could sense the epic stink-eye that Cain was delivering.

Probably not.

"Jolly doesn't know why the system isn't recognizing our remaining missiles?" Cain wondered once Starsgard's statement finally registered.

"Can we fire them manually if we need to?"

"I don't know, but I don't think so. We need our radars to paint the target and direct the missile. Without the ship recognizing that the missiles exist, I suspect they would be no better than an unguided rocket. Space is very big, and we only have eight left. I think we're up a creek without a paddle, Major," Starsgard opined while he and the major hopped onto the landing of the billeting and dining deck, where sickbay was located.

The med bots had regenerated his burned flesh in there, and Captain Rand had a new arm printed and installed. The sickbay aboard The Olive Branch carried the most modern medical systems that could be stuffed into the small space. Cain had experienced a great deal of pain in the Cygnus-12 sickbay, but the bots put him on a fast track to recovery. Sickbay was a good place.

If someone was alive when they arrived, the med bots would keep them that way.

There were no doctors or nurses, only bots, equipment, and if you caused a fuss, Jolly would ask Commander Daksha or Captain Rand to intervene.

Which they did on more than one occasion with Cain--even though he knew sickbay was a good place, the least he could do was share his pain and anguish.

"Get in there, Starsgard," Cain ordered, turning the man loose as soon as he could grip the examination table and pull himself onto it. "Med bot, work your magic."

The med bot ignored the healthy individual and turned its mechanical attention to the patient.

"It's my ankle. I twisted it," the corporal offered meekly.

"Yes, yes, I'm sure it was horrible what the big bad major of the Marines did to you. The bully can leave us in peace. Now relax and we'll fix you up right dandy," the med bot replied.

"What in the hell?" Cain started to say, then stopped and shook his head. "Jolly. Have you been messing with the med bot programming?"

"I have not!" the AI retorted.

"Has Briz?"

"Only the bedside manners, good sir. The med bot seemed too cold for the humans, who need a certain level of comforting as they are being serviced," Jolly suggested through the speaker mounted in the corner of the high-tech room.

"Nice try, Jolly. Please make sure that it doesn't interfere with any of their primary programming. I expect that I'm probably the single greatest provider of patients, but we want the med bots to earn their keep." Cain bit the inside of his cheek as he looked around. "I'm not proud of that, by the way."

"Of course not, Major Cain. Practice how you play, isn't that one of your sayings?" Jolly asked.

"It is, and yes, we train hard, but we seem to have our share of accidents, too. Do you believe in luck, Jolly?" Cain wondered.

"I believe in calculated possibilities, Cain," Jolly explained. "Sometimes, there may be only a five percent chance of something happening, which means that it could happen. The better prepared you are, the luckier you will be, so in essence, I believe that you make your own luck."

"Truer words were never spoken, Jolly. Thank you." Starsgard groaned as the med bot worked on his ankle. A piece of equipment was positioned near the injury. Cain could only assume that it was working as the man's groans changed to moans of pleasure.

"Starsgard!" Cain yelled to break the man from his descent toward becoming a human blob.

"Sir!" the corporal answered, banging his head against the med bot as he sat up too quickly. His forehead started to bleed.

"You are a one-man wrecking crew, Major Cain," Jolly said, chuckling. "Maybe you can leave the poor and damaged Corporal Starsgard alone until he's in better condition to deal with you."

"Deal with me?" Cain scowled. "Starsgard. Call me when you are back at the weapons console, and Jolly, figure out why the system isn't able to fire my missiles!"

Cain stormed away, almost running over Ensign Tandry. Her 'cat, Mixial was strolling along the far side of the corridor, well away from the sickbay hatch.

"Sorry," he told her, coming to a stop. "How's Mixi coming along?"

She glared at him, pointing a finger at his face. "You and that mongrel of yours!" she accused him.

"He's not mine…" Cain said weakly, looking for an escape, but Tandry had him trapped against the bulkhead.

"He's yours alright, a chip off the old block. You stay away from us!" Tandry looked like she wanted to take a swing at Cain. He would have let her, because he didn't know what else to do. She was angry from the second Mixi went into heat. The 'cat didn't seem put out by the event.

Cain was proud of Brutus in his fight for dominance with 'cats twice his size, but he could never say that out loud.

Mixi's belly bulged with Brutus's kittens, swaying as she waddled after her human. Cain remained where he was. Lieutenant Pace appeared from the direction of the mess deck. He recognized the shellshock on Cain's face.

"I see Tandry's been here. Word of warning, my friend. You don't want to be on the same ship with her right now." Pace laughed at his own joke as he continued to the stairs and headed up toward the command deck.

"If it wasn't Brutus, it would have been one of the others. Someone would have taken care of business," Cain told the empty corridor. "Good job, buddy. At least we saved the rest of the crew from her wrath."

Cain could hear Brutus chuckling, but the 'cat had the decency not to say anything.

***

Captain Rand and Major Cain waited patiently as Commander Daksha floated over the hot sand of his quarters. The Tortoid checked his monitors one last time, blinking slowly as he absorbed the information.

There was nothing new, but it was what he did.

"EL475, gentlemen," Daksha said slowly in a soft voice, as his vocalization device relayed his thoughts. "A heavy-gravity planet colonized some three-hundred, fifty years ago. There is no information newer than that. What do you think we'll find?"

Cain deferred to the older captain to speak his mind first.

"An AI running the show?" Rand offered.

"That is something we need to plan for. From Holly to Graham, what would any of us be without our AI? I think they probably followed a similar route as the rest of the colonies," Master Daksha replied, looking at Rand without blinking.

The senior command team had gotten used to the Tortoid's mannerisms. He stared when he was deep in thought. Cain and Rand knew to wait to speak until Daksha started to blink again.

It was a while.

"Jolly was magnificent in reaching out to Graham. With Briz's help, I hope that we can replicate that feat at Heimdall, assuming there is an AI we can communicate with."

"If there isn't, that's where me and my Marines come in," Cain answered, standing tall and proud.

"Oh?" Daksha said, barely above a whisper.

That one word deflated Cain's ego. Daksha only wanted to talk, but he'd been bitten twice by the Concordians. The Cygnus Marines had wreaked more havoc than he liked, but the Tortoid hadn't seen any other way past the barrier of the hostiles in charge.

Daksha saw how he'd crushed the major. "You have done well for all of Cygnus, Major Cain, don't get me wrong, but I prefer as many non-violent options as possible before we unleash the Marines on the unsuspecting."

"We're a force for peace, Master Daksha," Cain said with a wry smile. Captain Rand cocked his head and looked at him.

"You and your small force have taken over an entire planet because they made you angry," Rand stated, before shaking his head and crossing his arms. "Let's just say that I'm happy that we're on the same side."

"Correction, I wasn't angry the whole time. On occasion, I was furious, and then there were the times when I was hungry." Cain waved Rand off. Cain's smile vanished, and he grimaced.

"In combat, I see everything clearly. Time seems to slow down. I feel almost superhuman. And every enemy who died at my hands, I wonder, was there a way we could have saved his life. Being good at war doesn't mean that I like it."

Cain hung his head, eyes closed so he didn't have to look at his shipmates.

'I know, Cain. My father and your great-great-grandfather waged war like no one before or since. They both detested the killing and wondered why people insisted on fighting against society, against fair trade. Your great-great-grandmother, on the other hand, tolerated no malcontents and delivered more than her fair share of beat-downs. What an interesting woman she was,' Daksha said over the mindlink with the other two before disappearing into his memories from long ago.

The major had heard all the stories, some tempered over time and some exaggerated in the retelling. Braden and Micah had been larger than life, single-handedly responsible for the return of society, if the stories were to be believed.

Cain and Rand shifted uncomfortably in the heat of Master Daksha's quarters. They always stood because there weren't any chairs. It helped to keep the meetings short.

"I understand, Cain. When those Concordians tried to take the ship, you can't imagine the rage. Well, maybe you can. I hated them for what they did to my people." Rand looked at his artificial arm, flexing the fingers expertly as he'd learned to do since the injury. "Maybe you should check on Bull, see how he's doing. Come up with some options for dealing with an unknown populace."

"Sometimes, the threat of force, from ones who have demonstrated that they are willing to use it, is good enough. We have plenty of video of combat from Concordia. Probably too much. I'll work with Jolly to put together an impressive mix of death and destruction. We'll end it with the handshakes and the Marines flying away triumphantly, or the shuttle carrying our wounded."

Cain looked at Rand and smiled grimly, before gripping the other man's shoulder as a comrade-in-arms. The major departed the Tortoid's quarters and headed to see Bull.

Shipboard Training

"Run faster!" Stinky yelled, trying to be encouraging as the entire platoon struggled to catch him. Stinky was at the edge of his own endurance and strength. He was amazed that the humans were able to move at all, let alone keep up.

At Cain's request, the captain had increased the ship's spin, driving artificial gravity to one point five that of Vii, which approximated what they would run into on the habitable planet of Heimdall in the EL475 system.

The rest of the crew stayed in their acceleration couches during the Marine's heavy-gravity training time.

During the session's run on the garden deck, they could hear the Rabbits crying miserably.

Cain thought he could hear Mixial yowling from one deck away and felt Tandry wishing him great harm.

They powered through fifty laps of the garden deck before stopping for pushups, side twists, and jumping exercises. The Wolfoids panted, the humans were soaked with sweat, and the Lizard Men looked miserable, while the Hawkoid seemed completely unaffected. He flew around the garden deck freely, dipping and soaring as much as he could with the low ceiling.

The Hillcats had run two laps at Brutus's insistence before they declared themselves fit enough and resumed their perches in and around the garden deck's trees.

"Tactical formation!" Cain yelled. "First squad, room clearing, here!"

He pointed to the hatch leading to the stairwell. Bull was still out, so Lightning Flash was the acting squad leader. He formed the five remaining members of the squad into the roles of assault, security, and breach. Abhaya, a human private, made believe he had a small battering ram.

His chest heaved as he struggled to catch his breath and will his muscles to obey his commands.

25

Cain used his neural implant to contact Jolly to open the hatch. As soon as it started to slide to the side, Cain ordered the men through. "Go, go, go!"

The two closest dashed through, side by side, followed closely by the security pair. The breacher was last through after simulating ditching the ram and bringing his weapon to bear.

"Second squad!" Cain had Jolly close the door as Spence moved his squad into position. Tobiah was at the small man's side as usual, ready to protect his bonded.

'Do you see that, Brutus? That's how it's done!' Cain told his friend.

'When it matters, I'll be there. Otherwise, I'll be napping,' the 'cat replied.

'You're getting soft, little man.'

Cain, Stinky, Pickles, and Stalker watched the squad move into position. "Third squad, you go with them!" Cain ordered.

Jo moved herself and her six Marines into position. Her hands clenched, empty of her blaster. She was the platoon's sharpshooter and was always more comfortable with a weapon at the ready.

Cain wondered if he should detail her to independent duty as a scout-sniper, the type that was considered a force multiplier. An effective sniper could pin down an entire enemy unit, allowing the rest of the force to conduct operations while the enemy feared the silent, long-range death that snipers were known for.

The two squads waited while Cain contemplated the future. "Corporal Jo, front and center!" he ordered. Her squad watched as she ran, shakily, to where the Marine leadership waited.

"Sir, Corporal Jo reporting as ordered," she huffed as her head bobbed with her efforts to get more air.

"Who can take over your squad?" Cain asked. Stinky's ears perked up.

"Grace, of course," she replied without hesitation. Jo looked from one face to the next, unsure of where the questions were heading.

"I'm thinking of making you an independent actor, a scout-sniper to operate in support. I'm thinking you and Ascenti would make an unstoppable team to be our eyes and ears, that you two act as a complete combat unit, take on enemies orders of magnitude greater in size, to help the main force accomplish the mission. You interested in that?" Cain asked.

The squads continued to wait at the hatch. On the other side, first squad was sitting on the stairs. They were planning on returning to the garden deck, but the hatch closed in their face and wouldn't open for them.

"Sounds like fun," Jo replied, grinning.

"No, it won't be, but you'll get to do what you're best at and that will help the whole unit. Send Grace over here and then take your squad through."

'Jolly, open the hatch please,' Cain asked over the neural implant. Jo hadn't made it back to the squad yet.

"Go, go, go!" she yelled in unison with Spence as the Marines stormed through the open hatch. They had more energy after the respite gave them a chance to catch their breaths.

Jo followed the last of them through, and almost immediately, Grace reappeared in the doorway and headed for Cain.

The Wolfoid reported smartly and stood at attention.

"You're the squad leader," Cain said without preamble. He waited for a few moments. "Go."

She ran off without asking any questions. "That's it? No explanation?" Stinky wondered.

"No need. She's already been the squad leader. She knows what to do, and Jo will help her if she gets stuck," Cain told them, eyes drooping as he fought the effects of the faster spin. "I think I've had about enough heavy gravity. Jolly, normal spin please. Help us take a load off, my friend!"

***

Rand stood up as soon as the ship returned to its usual rotational rate and normal apparent gravity.

"I understand why, but I don't have to like it," Rand told no one in particular. The others joined him, standing and stretching. Only Pace and Kalinda were on deck. The others had attended to their Marine training.

The hatch opened and Foucault and Peekaless staggered through.

"What happened to you two?" the captain blurted out, even though he knew.

"Marine training, Skipper," Pickles said over his vocalization device. He sat in his chair, shoulders hunched and chin hanging to his chest. "I hope to all the water in the Amazon Rainforest that we don't have to land on that planet. I feel like I'm going to die."

Rand stifled a chuckle at the Lizard Man's deadpan delivery, although the captain suspected Pickles was being serious.

The Lizard Man produced a water bottle and drank the entire thing, then activated his console and sent his claws dancing across the screens. To anyone who didn't know Pickles, they would not have seen the cues. He usually didn't show anything through facial expressions or body language, but this once, it was clear that the heavy gravity training had taken its toll.

Fickle looked worse. He was ashen, his expression dull, and his fingers twitched erratically. When he sat down, he melted into his chair as if a blubbering mass of boneless flesh.

"Maybe you should go to your bunk?" Rand suggested. The bridge crew stopped what they were doing as they wanted to watch something with the potential to be more interesting.

The heavily slouched Fickle pulled himself upright, bracing himself on his monitors.

"Major Cain to the bridge, please," Captain Rand said toward the ceiling, expecting Jolly to relay the command.

Fickle continued his struggle to pull himself to his feet.

The hatch opened and Cain walked through. He walked, stilted, as if his legs were made of wood. "Captain?" he asked.

Rand pointed at Fickle.

Cain helped the private to his feet. The major lifted the man's head so he could see Fickle's eyes. "You've looked better."

"I've felt better," Fickle replied, letting the major support his full weight. Cain wrapped two arms around the private to keep them both from falling.

"You look like two drunks on a Saturday night," Pace suggested.

"I think we'll rest our people for a couple hours after training," Cain explained, turning Fickle away from his console. The two men stumbled toward the hatch. "Training was more difficult than I expected. If you'll excuse us."

"By all means," the captain said, watching, fascinated at how the Marines on board had abused their bodies to the point of failure. "Maybe next time you don't train so hard?"

Cain stopped in the middle of the open hatch and turned his head. "We train harder so we can be better. We're always going to be outnumbered, but we will be the most professional unit on the ground. That's the only thing I can promise for certain," Cain said tiredly.

Cain and Fickle continued shuffling into the corridor, and the hatch closed behind them.

Payback

Briz giggled, wrinkling his nose and flicking his whiskers. "Did you see that?" he asked for the tenth time.

Ellie heard it and saw it the first time. The med bot called Cain the big bad major. Briz manipulated the video to zoom in on Cain's face. The major narrowed his eyes and looked at the med bot as if he wanted to fight it.

"Priceless. That is just priceless." Briz continued to giggle.

"He knows you did it," Jolly said, suddenly appearing next to Briz. His instantaneous insertion into their conversations always startled Ellie, but the Rabbit seemed immune.

"Well then, there's no reason to hold back!" Briz exclaimed as he made some adjustments, pulled up a subroutine, inserted a short piece of code, and executed the program.

Throughout The Olive Branch, every monitor played the med bot's statement, with the patient's identity blurred, and then the slow motion replay of Cain's face afterwards. The six-second video was set to loop for the next five minutes.

Two minutes later, Captain Rand spoke over the ship-wide broadcast. "He's coming for you, Lieutenant Brisbois."

Briz looked up from his computers, then at the hatch as it popped open. The Rabbit bunched his leg muscles and leapt, in an effort to get to the top of a nearby system enclosure, but he didn't make it, bouncing off halfway to the top and dropping back to the deck.

"Close the hatch, Jolly!" Briz demanded.

"No can do," Jolly replied happily, crossing his holographic arms as he watched the panicking Rabbit.

"What? I gave you an order!" Briz clarified.

"The captain ordered all hatches open as the Marines conduct a house-to-house exercise that they are calling Find the Rabbit," Jolly carefully explained.

"I thought you were my friend. Can't you close just this hatch, in case we get a coolant leak or something?" Briz whined.

"I'm hurt that you would think I'm no longer your friend. As such, sometimes friends require tough love, to show how much they really care. That's what this is, my very dear friend." Jolly put his hand over his heart and bowed his head as Briz looked back and forth between the holographic projection and the open hatch.

"But-but, you're going to throw me to the Wolfoids…" Briz stammered as a shadow cut across the hatch.

Briz's eyes shot wide as the major stepped through with Black Leaper and Night Stalker following closely.

"Block the hatch. Make sure he doesn't get past you," Cain ordered. The Wolfoids stood upright, side by side, blocking Briz's escape.

"Come here, you sandy little butthole!" Cain crouched and approached in a wrestler's stance with his hands wide. Briz jumped for the top of the enclosure and missed once again. When he hit the deck, Cain was there.

Briz rolled to his back and kicked Cain, barely missing the human's groin.

"I'm gonna get you for that!" Cain howled as he dropped to a knee, shook off the pain, and resumed his hunt.

The Rabbit bolted behind the coolant tanks. "Ellie?" Cain asked softly.

"Can't do it. I have to work with him and you should probably save some of your energy," she said suggestively.

Cain was still tired from the day's heavy gee workout, but he was recovering quickly the more he was active.

"I see you!" he yelled, looking between two tanks. Briz stuck his tongue out. "Stinky!"

The Wolfoid dropped to all fours and bounded past one end of the tanks. Cain jogged a few steps the other way and waited.

Briz emerged as if he'd been fired from a cannon, crashing into the major like a furry white projectile. He and Cain went to the deck together. They grappled briefly and Briz kicked, trying to get free. Cain had his arms around the Rabbit's chest, riding him like a wild boar. Cain pushed off an equipment case and drove Briz to his side, where Cain held him down.

Stinky joined them and they flipped Briz onto his stomach. Between the two Marines, Briz finally stopped fighting.

Cain pulled a small aerosol can from his pocket and quickly sprayed the top of the white Rabbit's head and ears pink. Cain kept spraying down Briz's back until the can was empty, leaving a wide pink stripe down the chief engineer's back that ended just above his white cottontail.

They let him up.

Stinky looked at the pink paint on Cain's hands. He had rubbed them on his pants, but it had already dried.

"Kind of makes the med bot's point, don't you think?" Stinky said, his vocalization device echoing an emotionless thought.

"Come on, Briz, we're going to chow, show everyone that we've made up." Cain grunted as he lifted the dense rabbit, depositing him on his feet. Briz glared at Cain.

Cain glared back. Jolly stuck his head between them, turning it unnaturally to look at one then the other. "And what, pray tell, is this endeavor all about?" he asked.

"You can close the hatches now, Jolly. The exercise is over." Cain looked at the too-close projection.

"Of course, Major Cain. Will you require further assistance from me?" Jolly asked, smiling broadly.

"We will need your assistance, as always Jolly, but not right now. Thank you," Cain told the AI. Cain brushed himself off and turned toward the hatch, where Night Stalker was biting her nails.

The Wolfoids had a cross between a hand and a paw, retaining the necessary features of each for their survival. Their hands had developed naturally after the initial genetic engineering, with their fingers growing longer but the heavy black nails of the wolf remaining.

"I'm not really that hungry," Briz said softly through his vocalization device. He headed for his console, but Cain intercepted him and funneled him toward the hatch.

"Ellie, my love, care to join us?" Cain said warmly.

"Sure. Everything is running just fine. Another week to exit the gravity well. Jolly, take over here while us lowly humans recharge the batteries," Ellie said, joining her classmates and taking Cain's hand in hers.

Cain looked at their hands and saw how natural they looked together, how right it felt, and not because they were a thousand light years from home.

Briz walked along reluctantly, unsure of what he looked like. He accessed his neural implant and asked Jolly to provide a picture. It was worse than he thought.

His head, ears, and back were hot pink--the same color that construction workers in the shipyard used on their suits when operating in open space. Briz's gait changed to that of one headed to his own funeral.

The Marines surrounded him as they climbed the stairs one deck and traveled the corridor to get to the mess deck. They ushered Briz in, pushing him to the front of the line as he tried to hide behind Stinky.

Tandry showed up with Mixial, and Lieutenant Peekaless appeared moments later. Brutus and some of the other 'cats popped through the hatch when the captain opened it.

Briz wasn't convinced it was a coincidence.

Corporal Starsgard walked in without limping, happy with the premier medical care that helped him to recover nearly one hundred percent in no time flat. The ankle brace he wore provided support to get him through the last of the healing process.

Each person took the time to slap Briz on the back and thank him for his work with the ship and wished him happy banking, the refill of the dark matter so they could jump space. Those two events caused most engineers the greatest amount of stress.

Before the Cygnus-12, also called The Olive Branch, spaceships didn't fly themselves into the gravity well. Briz had nurtured the EM drive and reveled in flying the ship within the heliosphere, but the accident that left a terrible scar across his chest and one of the engineers dead happened during

Craig Martelle

an ISE activation, the drive that vaulted the ship nearly a thousand light years in an instant.

The ISE operated using dark matter, which was dangerous when forced to energize the interstellar drive.

"Well done, Briz!" Captain Rand said, slapping the Rabbit's small shoulder as he passed, heading for the rack to pick out a meal.

Allard and Beauchene arrived and hurried up to their fellow Rabbit. "What has the big, scary Marine done to our friend!" they lamented, casting harsh Rabbit glances in Cain's direction. The three Rabbits commiserated by putting their heads together and keening.

After a few seconds, Allard and Beauchene hopped away to get a fresh salad. They deposited one in front of Briz before leaving the mess deck to return to their precious garden where they could eat surrounded by the plants they loved.

Cain knew they didn't need to come to the mess deck to eat as they usually helped themselves from the garden, eating a wide variety of vegetables and leaves.

Briz looked much relieved since no one laughed at his new pink coloring. Tandry sat on one side of Briz while Stinky and Stalker sat on the other.

Across from the others, Ellie sat close to Cain, keeping one hand under the table to gently stroke his leg.

He had a hard time focusing on anything else.

"Look at us!" Stinky declared. "Class Beta 37. We're going to be the first ones to see earth in over four thousand years and all because Briz figured out how to defeat the vines on the Traveler."

"To Briz!" Cain raised his glass in a toast. The others joined him.

When Tandry's glass reached her lips, her hand lost its grip. The glass fell and she doubled over. Mixi let out a long and piercing yowl. Brutus hopped up on the table, sat down, and licked a paw to clean his face.

It's time, he told Cain over their mindlink.

"Time for what?" Cain asked, still wondering why Tandry was in so much pain. Ellie squeezed his leg mercilessly until he looked at her. She

34

pointed to the 'cat under the table.

He pulled his feet back. The two Wolfoids stepped back and then crouched to be closer to Mixial.

"What do we do?" Briz asked, more flustered than Cain.

'Nothing,' Brutus told them all. *'Sit back and enjoy the show. Mixial knows what to do.'*

The 'cat yowled constantly as the first fuzzy orange head appeared and slipped onto the floor. Three more kittens were born in rapid succession. The last one took a while, but it was the size of the other four combined.

'Isn't that interesting,' Brutus said in his thought voice. He'd moved to the floor and was licking Mixi's ears as she cleaned her brood.

Cain looked at the four, small orange kittens and the large gray one "I think Spence has some explaining to do," he whispered at Ellie. She slapped his arm and bit her lip to stifle a laugh.

"Congratulations, Ensign Tandry. Mixial's kittens are the first ever born on a starship," Captain Rand said from the corner where he sipped his coffee and relaxed with his feet on the next chair.

"This place is off-limits until I can move the kittens," Tandry told the assembled group.

"What?" Rand asked, taking his feet from the chair and putting them on the deck as he leaned forward. "Tell us what you need and we'll help, because I can't go without eating."

After some back and forth, Cain and Ellie ran the corridor to the med lab, where they removed the stretcher from its rack outside the door. When they returned, the others had already moved the table.

"Where are we going to take them?" Cain asked as the mother gently placed the kittens onto the soft matting of the stretcher.

'They need warmth,' Mixi replied. Cain immediately looked at Rand.

"Jolly," the captain said to the ceiling. "Please connect me to Commander Daksha."

The Ghost in the Machine

Rand turned around in his chair, instead of turning the whole chair. Daksha floated at the back of the bridge, a strap held tightly in his beak-like mouth. His eyes were closed as he bounced gently off the bulkhead.

Rand shook his head and faced forward, meeting the gaze of his pilot.

"Transiting beyond the heliosphere, sir," Pace reported softly. The ship rocked slightly over the course of the next fifteen minutes as it passed through one of the more intense layers. The edge of the heliosphere was the point at which the solar winds dramatically dropped off. The heliosheath was a warmer and denser area of space at the front of the solar system as it moved through interstellar space. Interstellar winds picked up beyond the heliosphere to further compress the heliosheath.

All of that made for a bumpy ride, but Pace was an outstanding pilot and rode the crests and angled to lessen the impact. When the ship calmed, Pace gave the thumbs up. "Jolly, please inform the chief engineer to begin banking dark matter."

"Already underway, Captain," Jolly reported, standing to the side of Rand's chair.

"With that, I believe we have a staff meeting to discuss the issue with our missiles. Lieutenant Pace, you have the conn."

Jolly disappeared as Rand headed for the hatch, but stopped when he saw that the commander's eyes were open. "Staff meeting, Master Daksha, if you're up for it."

Daksha turned his head slowly, twisting his neck slightly to look up at the tall human. "Did you know that Tortoids can go seven days without sleeping or eating?" he asked through is vocalization device.

"I've heard something like that," Rand replied cautiously.

"If there was an accident where Brutus, Mixi, and those kittens were flushed out the airlock, I'm not sure that I'd be upset. I know that's a horrible thing to say, but do you know what 'cats do in the sand? What they're doing to my sand?"

Daksha let go of the strap and swam to the captain's side.

"We'll have your sand cleaned and disinfected by the maintenance bots as soon as the 'cats leave your quarters, Commander," Rand said, trying to sound sympathetic.

When they'd first asked, Daksha cordially invited the 'cats without hesitation.

He regretted that decision within minutes of the 'cats' arrival. A week later, he found himself unable to return to his quarters.

The captain and the commander moved slowly down the corridor. They passed one of the sensor suites, where Tandry was sound asleep at her post. The captain thought about waking her, but knew that she was burning the candle at both ends. He let her be, checking in quickly with Lieutenant Chirit to make sure that systems were operating properly and there was nothing to report.

"You'd be the first to know," the Hawkoid replied.

The hatch slid open and the captain and the commander entered. Cain and the others were already there and stood as a sign of respect. There were no holographic projectors so Jolly appeared on the wall screen in two-dimensional form. Next to him was Briz's Rabbit avatar. The chief engineer couldn't break away for the meeting, but he was able to attend virtually.

Corporal Starsgard was there, looking uncomfortable, despite the fact that he had a PhD and was the most learned person on the ship when it came to astrophysics.

Cain had Stinky, Pickles, and Stalker. None of the 'cats came, although Carnesto said he wanted to attend.

Cain knew that was a ruse. He couldn't imagine a Hillcat volunteering to sit in on a meeting about computer systems.

The captain sat down while the commander swam through the air to the front of room, close to the screen where Jolly waited patiently.

"Shall we, then?" Captain Rand asked. Cain pointed to Starsgard.

"I guess it's my turn," the corporal said. Cain motioned for the man to continue. "After we left the planet, I ran the usual system diagnostics, the same ones that I ran the day prior, but this time, all the missiles were showing up as fired. A physical check showed the missiles were still in place, so I asked Jolly for help. Jolly?" Starsgard deferred.

"I dug into the system and found snippets of code that were coordinated and integrated. It was the most complex programming I've ever run across," Jolly stated, enunciating clearly as he always did.

Daksha swam in front of the screen. "Who is capable of such programming?" the Tortoid asked, afraid of the answer.

"Holly," the AI mouthed. His image on the screen maintained a neutral expression.

"Holly?" Cain blurted, standing up. "Holly is the insider causing all the trouble?"

"I'm not sure I would go that far. I'm talking about the missile programming. In defensive mode, the missile system functioned perfectly, but during some of the exercises, they were switched to an offensive mode and this created a dichotomy within the programming, an issue that Holly had built in during installation." Jolly pointed to Cain, who had raised his hand.

"When I was back on Vii, being haunted by insiders, I worked with Holly to carve out a niche where he separated his core programming from everything else that was running. He said it wouldn't be a problem, but I told him that we can't exist as two different versions of ourselves. I was worried about him. Did I cause him to start acting weird?"

Cain was ready to come down hard on himself.

"Not at all," Master Daksha replied before Jolly could speak. "He was acting up before you asked him to carve out a piece for you. I think this goes back much farther in our history, to the security protocols that President Micah established. We have recently asked to override those. We have created a conflict within that wonderful intelligence that is Holly."

"And he doesn't even know that he's schizophrenic. When we return to Cygnus, I will have a worm prepared that will be able to hunt down and remove the erratic code. And then there's the direct approach where we talk with Holly and reestablish the security protocols in a way that does not create a conflict."

"And that will be the most difficult. Holly doesn't know that he has problems," Cain agreed, furrowing his brow as he thought of his friend, the confidante of his great-great-grandparents. "We can only hope that there is nothing to set him off between now and when we return."

"Can we purge the code and get control of our weapons systems?" Captain Rand asked the screen.

Both Jolly and the Rabbit avatar nodded. "It is already done. Once we knew what to look for, we hunted them down and isolated those errant pieces from the rest of the programming," Briz said. His avatar wore glasses, oddly, and he peered over the top of them as he talked. "I'm working with Jolly to write the cleaning worm that will cutoff the dysfunctional code from the rest of the system. We don't want to delete anything. The AIs are sentient beings. We cannot haphazardly cut out parts of their brains. We will use only the sharpest of scalpels."

The analogy caught them all off guard. No one spoke, a couple clenched their jaws, and others hung their heads.

Master Daksha nodded slowly to the images on the screen and then turned to face those at the table. "This is a challenge with ethical and moral implications. We seem to find those challenges readily way out here in the middle of the universe," the Tortoid's vocalization device registered a light tone, not the grave nature one would have expected.

"This isn't about fixing a machine. We are talking about working with a friend to help him through his emotional troubles caused by his commitment to serve the flawed creatures of our world. We have unwittingly given him conflicting direction. It is up to us to fix that, but humanely. Holly is the friend of all humanity. I wonder if we can simply talk with him, help him take care of the problem that is causing conflict?"

All eyes were riveted on the commander. Jolly's image showed a variety of facial expressions as he tried to find the right look to convey the emotions raging through his AI psyche.

"When we return, I suggest that Jolly, Briz, and I meet with Holly. Maybe we get Admiral Jesper and Dr. Johns to join us. Then we lock ourselves in a room and talk with Holly until we can remedy the issues." Daksha stopped blinking as he looked at the table, unfocused, weighing the enormity of the task. "I, for one, am opposed to taking a digital scalpel to the being who lifted our civilization from the stone age we thrust upon ourselves. Holly made it possible for us to return to space. He deserves the very best care delivered in the most respectful way."

"Here, here!" Cain called out, pounding a fist on the table and startling the others.

Rand nodded grimly. "The commander is right. Jolly, Briz, fix our code so that we don't have any hiccups if we need to fight with the ship. I hope to hell that we don't, but our track record in meeting new people suggests that we had best be ready."

Major Cain turned to Starsgard. "Go bring up the weapon system and make sure you have the missiles online, then put everything on ice while we're banking dark matter. After the next jump, you bring that system up and make sure it stays up as we transit the gravity well and see what there is to see," Cain directed the corporal.

"Will do, Major," Starsgard replied. He got up, excused himself, and left the meeting.

Captain Rand held his hands up and shook his head. He didn't have anything else. He motioned to the commander.

"Nothing more from me. Jolly?" Daksha asked.

"I am certain that the ship is in tip top shape. You won't have any more problems from aberrant code running rampant in the dark corners of our space," Jolly said with a huge smile, bowing at the end.

The Tortoid cocked his head and looked at the Briz avatar. It blinked out without saying anything.

"I guess our chief engineer is satisfied," Daksha said with a laugh.

"I guess so," Rand agreed, happy that the issue was resolved for the Cygnus-12, but not looking forward to their return home and a direct confrontation with Holly.

"When's the next heavy gee exercise, Major Cain?" Commander Daksha asked.

"I think we'll take today off, and then continue every other day. It is harder on the body than I expected," Cain replied.

'Hard on the body? By all that's holy, last night's wrestling match in Ellie's quarters twisted Carnesto and me into knots! You need the day off is what you meant to say,' Brutus injected forcefully directly into Cain's mind.

'Stop it! I'm having an adult conversation here,' Cain replied in his thought voice.

'You and your woman need to get yourselves under control!' Brutus snapped. Cain smiled and bit his lip.

'I'll take that under advisement, you little vagrant. How are yours and Tobiah's kittens doing?' Cain asked, trying to deflect some of the 'cat's criticism.

'I shall cause you great pain, human, when you least expect it.' Brutus closed the mindlink with an audible snap.

"Talking with your 'cat?" Rand asked, still looking at the major.

"Damn. I'm sorry. He was giving me a ration of nonsense, but we're good. We'll go heavy gravity tomorrow and every other day until the jump, and then maybe once a day as we descend into the gravity well, depending on what we find." Cain waited for the captain to acknowledge the plan.

Rand screwed up his face as he bit his lip before coming clean. "I think Brutus shared your conversation about Ellie with the whole ship."

Cain's face fell.

There it was--payback for the perceived slight. Cain closed his eyes and imagined ways he could throw Brutus from the airlock.

"It's not like we didn't know, so there is that." The captain tried to sound conciliatory but Cain wasn't buying it. "If I were you, I'd go talk with Ellie. I expect she's holed up in engineering and has vowed to never come out."

***

Briz left the meeting because he wanted to make sure the dark matter systems were running efficiently. He'd reprogrammed the collection process to cut the time it took. He hadn't seen any unintended consequences, but he remained wary. What should have taken fifteen days would only take twelve if they were able to maintain their current collection rate.

Jolly devoted more ship resources to the process, too. Together, Briz and Jolly were back at it, leaving the rest of the lifeforms behind.

The complexities of the ISE and the dark matter process were nothing to be taken lightly. Briz wanted to give both Jolly and the ship his full attention.

Ellie was in her seat watching the displays for the systems outside of what Briz was working on, but she didn't see the information that scrolled past. She'd heard Brutus giving Cain a hard time, realized that he was broadcasting to everyone, and turned bright red with embarrassment.

The hatch opened and Ellie prepared to run and hide, but it was only Cain strutting into engineering like he owned the place.

She stood up slowly, and the heat built within like lava headed toward the caldera.

Cain stopped where he was, the expression on his face, frozen in time, with only one thought in his mind.

Run!

He took two slow steps backward as she advanced, then he turned and bolted for the door.

Cain had always been a fast runner and kept himself in shape. He never expected that she'd catch him, but she did, tackling him from behind before he made it out. He squirmed briefly, but decided discretion was the better part of valor. He rolled over and held his hands up in surrender to Ellie, but also keeping his hands close in case he needed to protect his face.

"How could you?" she snarled.

"I had nothing to do with it!" he claimed, ready to offer Brutus to her on a silver platter.

"But you love me!" Her demeanor changed instantly and she settled onto his chest.

Oh crap, he thought, closing his eyes and sighing.

"We don't know what tomorrow will bring, my beautiful Ellie, and I'm sorry for all the time I've lost with you. Can we be second?" he asked.

"Who wants to be second place?" she asked, her voice gravelly.

"Our careers are first. You are an amazing engineer and you've kept this ship flying without a problem. You and Briz, because you take good care of the Cygnus-12. I have my thing with the Marines, but next, it's you and me. We support each other's careers by supporting each other." Cain found it hard to wax too poetic with Ellie perched on top of him.

She exhaled heavily, wiped her tears, and peered down on Cain. "No. We're first and careers second."

He nodded.

Her eyes sparkled, and Cain was riveted. He reached up a hand and pulled her face to his for a gentle kiss, brushing his lips over hers.

The hatch slid open and Captain Rand stopped mid-step to avoid kicking the pair lying on the deck. "Damn, Cain!"

EL475 – Welcome to Heimdall

"Prepare to activate the ISE," Captain Rand told the bridge's ceiling, trusting that Jolly would relay his warning ship-wide.

"Board is green," Lieutenant Peekaless called over his shoulder.

"At your convenience, Lieutenant Brisbois," Rand ordered.

"Counting down, four, three, two, one," Briz relayed. The momentary surge and displacement. The front screen showed a new star pattern.

"Navigation, report!" Rand ordered, looking at the larger than expected glowing orb.

Pace and Kalinda ran through their screens. "Chirit, confirm," Pace said. The pilot spun around in his chair. "Impossible if I hadn't seen it with my own eyes, but we are halfway down the gravity well. We are less than one AU from the habitable planet within the EL475 system."

"BRIZ!" the captain yelled, furious at the implementation of the untested changes in the ISE. Daksha blinked rapidly. "I didn't approve that jump. Get your ass up here right now!"

"Captain, you have to believe me, but that was not the intent. We should have appeared right at the edge of the heliosphere, not within it. I'm digging in with Jolly right now to figure out what happened. I'll get back to you soonest," Briz explained before clicking off.

Jolly appeared next to the captain, who was forcing himself to calm down. "We did not intentionally jump the ship into the well, Captain," Jolly said softly as he held his hands out with his palms down. "We made some of the changes in calculations that Briz devised, but that should not have changed our trajectory. We do need to collect more data on this, but the jump was successful into the well. This is precedential, as long as we can replicate it and control it."

Rand nodded tersely. "Pace. How long to Heimdall?"

"Less than a week at standard acceleration," Pace replied.

"Hold us steady right here, please. We will be a hole in space. Sensors, passive at present, please. Tell me what's out there, and be prepared to go active. We could be right in the middle of a hornet's nest."

Daksha and Rand made eye contact. There had never been a jump to within the gravity well before, so they'd never contemplated the contingency of jumping into the middle of a foreign power's fleet.

Rand didn't know if the people of Heimdall had retained space-faring capabilities, but prudence dictated he consider the worst case scenario first, then walk backward to best case.

"Major Cain, report to the command deck," Rand told the ceiling. The hatch opened instantly and Cain and Black Leaper walked through. "Were you waiting outside?"

"I was on my way here when we activated the ISE. I was too slow. My apologies," Cain answered. Stinky shrugged in the way of the Wolfoids, rotating one shoulder and lifting a lip to show one of his canine teeth.

"We have materialized well inside the gravity well of this system," Rand started to explain, splitting his attention between Cain and the front screen. "We are passive only at present until we learn enough to move without risk. That's my analysis and disposition of the ship. If you have other ideas, I'm open."

Cain walked forward of the captain's chair to get a better look at the screen and the system into the middle of which they'd appeared. "Jolly, can you please show us where the planets are presently located relative to our position?"

The screen changed to a diagram showing the Cygnus-12 lateral to the rotating axis of the system's planets. "Distance to the nearest habitable planet?"

"Less than one AU," Pace replied.

"Can you put our flight path on the screen, please?" Cain asked. Pace touched his controls and a dotted arcing line appeared before them. "I think we're in a good position here. If there was any intersystem travel, it would be within the rotational axis. There's no reason for anyone to be all the way out here," Cain said, comfortable with his analysis. "That being said, I don't think we want to announce ourselves either. I expect we'll know if there are any people flying about out there within a day or two."

"We are agreed," Rand stated, still looking at the screen.

"Any way we can squeeze in some heavy gee training in the next day or two?" Cain asked.

"Maybe tomorrow. You know the drill, Cain. We check every fitting on the ship after an ISE activation. Your people are our people and shouldn't you be down checking your sewage pumps?"

"That cuts me deep, Captain. Private Derby is down there and working through the checklist. The Marines are at their duty stations. I have to give kudos to Briz and Jolly. I think this last one was the smoothest jump yet." Cain nodded to Stinky, who had assumed his position next to Commander Daksha.

"Is there anything you need me to do?" Stinky asked the Tortoid as Cain departed on his way to the center of the spindle where sewage treatment was located.

"'Cats, out of my quarters and clean sand. Is it too much to ask, Black Leaper? I think they've put family pictures on the wall and ordered new furniture. All I want is my quarters. How can I be homeless on my own ship?" The Tortoid's vocalization device reflected a forlorn tone matching the words.

Once in the corridor, Cain took a sharp left. *Brutus, my friend, it is time to move your family. I think Mixi has overstayed her welcome.*

When Cain opened the hatch to the commander's quarters, he was greeted by the smell of ammonia.

"Jolly, can you have Stinky meet me at the commander's quarters, and have him bring a stretcher please. Send Stalker, too. I'm sure we'll need backup. And a maintenance bot to clean the sand."

Cain walked in and found that the smell wasn't bad. He acclimated quickly to the meowing and perpetually drifting cat hair.

"Brutus, my man!" Cain said when he saw the small orange beast lying in the sand, three kittens nipping at his ears. He looked miserable. "You and the tribe are moving to the garden deck."

Thank the heavens, Brutus said.

Excuse me? Mixial's petite voice carried a sharp edge.

'I just want to share our good fortune, my sweet,' Brutus lied. Stinky ran through the open hatch first, carrying the front end of the stretcher, and Night Stalker followed with the back end in hand.

They put the stretcher down by the sand, both wrinkling their noses as they tried not to breathe too deeply. Brutus dragged his three out of the sand and took a position in the middle of the stretcher. One of the kittens hopped twice, sideways with his hackles up, as he tried to intimidate Stalker.

"Aren't you just the cutest thing?" she said through her vocalization device, then reached out her paw to let the kitten bat at it. "You are, are you? Well, take that!"

Cain wondered why she was carrying on a conversation with herself, when a second kitten raced at Stinky and launched its little body through the air with claws out. It landed on the Wolfoid's thigh, digging its claws in to find purchase, then started climbing.

Stinky's lips twisted and turned as he grimaced at the pain. He didn't throw the kitten away from him, because Cain, Brutus, and Stalker were watching. Marines were always on display in showing how much pain they could tolerate.

The kitten worked its way to his shoulder where she stopped, sat, and started cleaning herself.

Brutus looked exasperated, shaking his orange head as if to say, "of course, the kittens are making trouble. It's what they do best!"

"Hello, little lady. So your name is Penelope. That's a long name for someone so small, but I think you'll grow into it," Stinky said, lifting a hand to pet the little orange kitten.

"And this little man is called Hortense," Stalker added.

Brutus chuckled. *'Welcome to your new lives, the first Wolfoids with your very own 'cat life-links. They might be a handful at this stage and you'll have to bring them back to their mother for feedings every two hours, but outside of that, consider yourselves blessed.'*

Cain absent-mindedly ran a finger along the scar that Brutus had given him the first day they tried to get along. "Come on, Mixi, hop aboard your chariot!"

She nudged the two kittens, one orange and the other big and gray, toward the stretcher. Once all were on board, with the exception of the two riding their pet Wolfoids, Stinky and Stalker picked up the stretcher and Cain led the way from the commander's quarters. The maintenance bot was waiting in the corridor.

"Clean that sand, Mr. Maintenance Bot," he told it as he passed.

***

Tandry knew that Mixi was moving, but the sensor operator couldn't leave her post. Mixial reassured her that everything was fine. They would be on the garden deck for the foreseeable future. Tandry accepted that the move was necessary, because she knew the extent of Master Daksha's sacrifice. She made a note to deliver a personal thank you when she had time.

She was using the ship's sensors as a huge funnel to vacuum up signals bouncing around EL475.

"Nothing," Tandry said, looking at the screens. She adjusted the settings, waited, then reviewed again. She opened the link to Chirit's position. "I've got one big steaming pile of nothing in here. What do you have?"

"Not a single man-made wave across the entire spectrum. We'll give it a day just in case, but I don't think the colonists are space-going. They've traded their starships for plows, I expect. That was the premise, wasn't it?" the Hawkoid asked.

"I have to say that I didn't pay attention to history as much as I should have in Space School," Tandry admitted. But she knew someone who was an expert in history.

She tapped out a question to Pickles and hit send. An answer came back within two minutes.

The history of Cygnus VII tends to agree with the premise of colonization with the intent to become self-sufficient. During the actual colonization of Vii, they dismantled the shuttles to build Sanctuary, a high-tech city. They built an astrophysics research station on Cygnus VI to further the advancement of science. The colonization ship Traveler remained in space, with an Android and clone crew, but wasn't broadcasting. They may have the same situation here, and if that is the case, their offensive weaponry is probably nonexistent as the colony ships were unarmed.

"When do you think we'll be able to learn if there is a ship in orbit?" Tandry asked Chirit.

"We'll have to go active first and wait for the return signal. I can't recommend going active until we've moved closer and can focus the outgoing signal," Chirit replied, his vocalization device reflecting a higher-pitched, calm voice.

"I guess we have what we're going to have, but will monitor for the next day to make sure?" Tandry wondered aloud.

"I'll inform the captain," Chirit answered.

***

"No! No, no, no, no, no!" Allard cried as the Hillcat kittens tried to sharpen their claws on one of the tree trunks, effectively shredding the soft bark. "Shoo, you nasty little beasts!"

Beauchene ran toward them with a hose and sent a stream into the orange ruffians.

The 'cats scattered, yowling. Beauchene felt bad instantly because the kittens were so small, looking like little more than drowned rats. Dry, they were fluffier than the average 'cat. The bigger kitten lounged casually to the side, watching his soaked litter-mates try to lick themselves dry.

"I like you," Allard told the 'cat. "You don't get into trouble like this bunch."

'Thank you, gentle soul,' the kitten replied in a dainty thought voice, directly into Allard's mind.

"Hey, you talk!" Allard exclaimed. Beauchene looked confused. "He talks."

Allard pointed at the large gray kitten.

'Of course I talk. I think I'll adopt you both, but you need to understand the conditions,' the kitten said in a business-like tone.

'Anything you want. This is rather marvelous, don't you think, Beauchene?' Allard asked, switching to the mindlink.

'It is indeed, but I would be cautious about promising a 'cat anything it wants. We don't have a great record of success with them,' Beauchene replied carefully.

'Nothing to fear, my friends. The main condition is that if I'm ever in danger, you must come save me. I shall endeavor to do the same in case you are aggrieved,' the kitten

pronounced.

'Aggrieved? Who talks like that? You're still nursing,' Beauchene stated.

'It is one of life's trials, but it won't be too long before I grow to be something more substantive. I hear that we have steak on board? I simply cannot wait to dig these sharp fangs into some of that. I expect it's not fresh, though. Pity,' the big gray kitten lamented.

Allard and Beauchene looked at each other, their Rabbit noses twitching as they contemplated the small creature before them who seemed unnaturally well-educated and mature.

'All 'cats have the knowledge of those who have gone before. Most choose not to dwell on it, but I revel in it. Hillcats' have such a fascinating history. And yes, now that we are paired, I can see in your minds. Okay, I am kidding. I could see in your minds before, and that's why I decided to let you love me. I hesitate to use the word worship, but it may come to that. I am a 'cat after all, and you are not. You can call me Clarkston, which isn't my real name, of course, but you don't get to know that until the time is right.'

'I really don't know about this,' Beauchene said slowly, emphasizing the word 'really.'

"Oh well," Allard said, shrugging his small shoulders. "Come along, Clarkston, and we'll give you a proper tour of our domain, the garden deck, and see if there is a niche you want to carve from it for yourself."

To Wit, 'Cats

Captain Rand and Commander Daksha stepped through the hatch, instantly greeted by the higher humidity and bright lights of the garden deck. The flora greeted them warmly as Rand warily looked around, expecting laser fire or some other advanced weaponry used in inter-species warfare.

Rand found the quiet unnerving, but Daksha, having gotten a good night's rest finally, was refreshed and more welcoming of what he saw as opposed to worrying about what was unseen or expecting the worst.

"It is nice to enjoy nature," Daksha said, blinking slowly and swimming casually between the plants. "If only there were some beetles to snack on."

Rand could never tell when the Tortoid was kidding as he deadpanned through this vocalization device. The human didn't respond.

They caught sight of the 'cats lounging in various nooks and crannies. The Rabbits were nowhere to be seen. Rand and Daksha continued their circumnavigation of the deck until they were stopped by two orange kittens, who stood with tails erect, challenging the interlopers.

'Which one do you want?' one 'cat asked. The captain and commander heard the 'cats speaking in their minds.

'I don't know,' said the second small voice. Rand couldn't tell which one was talking. *'I guess I'll take the tall one. Imagine what I'll be able to see from way up there!'*

'I guess that leaves me with Boxy,' the other voice replied.

'Boxy? I expect you're referring to me, but I'm the Third Master of the Tortoise Consortium and no one calls me Boxy,' Daksha replied firmly over the mindlink.

'Sucks to be you, dude. Yours has some mouth on him.' The first voice sounded surprised.

'Wow. Just wow. I'm going to have to work on him, that's for sure. How old are you, Boxy?' the second kitten asked. Rand still couldn't tell which one was which.

'I'm not sure I've ever met such an insolent rodent. And why are you wet?' Daksha asked.

'Those stuck-up caretakers don't understand what growing kittens go through. Maybe you can help them understand our needs better as I don't count on that gray troll to do it for us,' the first kitten replied.

"Which one are you?" Rand asked out loud.

The first kitten turned and glared at the tall human. *Really? You can't tell us apart yet? You can call me Nathan. Now pick me up and let me see what the world looks like from way up there.'*

Rand reached down and scooped up two pounds of orange Hillcat kitten. The first thing Nathan did after being put on the captain's shoulder was rub his face on the side of the man's head.

"You stink," Rand blurted. Daksha would have laughed, but he wasn't sure that he was in a better position than the captain.

'You don't smell so hot, either, human,' Nathan retorted. *'Let's find those fuzzytails and set them right.'*

'Come down here where I can jump up, Boxy,' the second 'cat requested.

Daksha visibly sighed, a difficult act for a Tortoid, but he floated toward the deck where the kitten took two steps and leapt atop the Tortoid's shell, using his needle-sharp claws to hold himself steady. Daksha floated back to head level. The four of them continued along the walkway until they found the Rabbits, who were fully engrossed in showing the large gray kitten the finer points of a perfect tomato plant.

'Let 'em have it, Captain!' Nathan encouraged.

"You two are doing a great job with the garden deck. We are never wanting for fresh vegetables. Thank you both." Captain Rand bowed and Nathan fought a losing battle against the ship's spin and his human's change in position. He flailed wildly as he fell, but the captain caught him smoothly before he hit the ground.

Rand cradled the small bundle to his chest, petting him absentmindedly while watching the Rabbits move from the tomato plant to a pepper plant nearby.

'Are you comfortable up there, whoever you are?' Daksha asked, having almost

forgotten that he had a rider.

'What? Oh, yes, yes. I'm not proud of it, mind you, but it is what I've been called,' the 'cat started. *'Promise not to laugh. I'm Billy Joe Jim Bob.'*

Daksha couldn't imagine laughing at someone's name, but he heard Rand snicker. The Tortoid craned his neck to look at the captain, who turned sharply away to study an uninteresting plant.

'Billy Joe Jim Bob it is,' Daksha stated. He swam ahead to complete the circuit of the garden deck and turned to the exit hatch. Rand was right behind him and they left the garden deck, ascended the one flight of stairs, and headed for the bridge.

When the hatch opened and Rand and Daksha entered, Pace nodded, then did a double-take, pointing at the 'cats without saying a word.

"Somebody put a box of kittens in the corridor. They're giving them away for free," Rand said without hesitation, then gasped as a 'cat claw dug deeply into the back of his human hand.

***

"It's been twenty-four hours and absolutely nothing besides normal cosmic noise, Captain. Request permission to employ active systems," Chirit said through the vocalization device hanging around his feathered neck.

"Let us move closer. We'll run her up to ten gee actual for thirty-minute sprints," Rand told the Hawkoid, nodding slowly as he looked at the screen that told him the very same thing. "Give us a couple days and then we'll spin up the broadcast, focusing your beams on the habitable planet."

"Will do. Can we stand down while we transit, put the systems into automatic mode while we get some rest? We've been working some long shifts, if you know what I mean."

"Certainly, and thanks," the captain answered without looking up, continuing to browse the information on the screens before him. "What do you think, Commander?"

Daksha hovered nearby, absorbing the information through his neural implant. He saw a system that no one would give a second thought to. A habitable planet that kept to itself, no emissions of any sort, across any spectrum, including the ones that Graham had given them.

"I think we move closer. It is entirely possible that the colonists have foregone space travel in its entirety and are living fruitful lives planet-side. We will see when we get there, won't we, Cain?"

"We don't have any other choice. We'll continue to run space drills with Starsgard in case they have an attack system of some sort, but I feel better for the ship knowing that there aren't any spacecraft out there," Cain said, biting the inside of his lip. He screwed his face up and frowned. "Then again, Concord broadcast a signal, but they didn't have any ships that we could detect either."

Rand shook his head at the way Cain talked himself in a circle, returning to a state of concern.

"Jolly?" the captain asked.

"I agree fully with the analysis of our magnificent sensor operators and that the prudent course of action is to move farther into the gravity well toward the fourth planet. I expect we'll be enlightened when we get closer. Cain will have his Marines ready to go, won't you, Major?" Jolly suggested.

"Of course. If we can squeeze in some more heavy gee training, that would put us in peak shape. We are at one hundred percent effectiveness. Bull is back to full duty. No other bumps or scrapes of note," Cain reported.

Rand thought for a moment before speaking, steepling his fingers as he leaned on the conference table. The others sat attentively. Hillcats were milling about, disinterested in the conversations. The four orange kittens got into a scrum under the table. Cain leaned down and scolded them, getting his nose scratched for his efforts.

Brutus!' he yelled in his thought voice as he held a finger on his wound to get it to stop bleeding.

"Jolly, if we accelerated at three point five actual, it would feel like one point seven five in the ship. If we maintain that level of acceleration for two hours, what would our trajectory and timing look like?"

Jolly displayed the information on the side bulkhead screen. "If we accelerate one hour out of every three, we should arrive in less than twelve days, assuming a full power slow down, otherwise, it'll be closer to twenty days. If we increase to ten gees actual for the hours that the Marines aren't training, then we'll arrive in less than ten days."

"That's the plan, Jolly. Ten gees outside of training hours. Acceleration couches one hour out of every three for eighteen hours per day until we need to slow down."

Rand stood. Cain gave him the thumbs up.

"I'll inform my people. We'll use the stairwell and hangar deck for training." Cain licked his finger and ran it over the razor thin blood line on his nose. It stung, but he cleaned the last of the blood off. "Which one of you got me?"

Cain leaned under the table, scowling as the kittens had found their people--two Wolfoids, a Tortoid, and a tall, thin human. Brutus was nowhere to be seen.

Daksha floated near the top of the table where his 'cat BJ could easily climb aboard. Rand scooped his up on the way out the hatch, cradling him in the crook of his replacement arm. Stinky and Stalker nodded to let Cain know that they'd make the notifications to the Marines. They nodded as they left. Their two 'cats ran after them, their short legs hammering away at the deck as they struggled to keep up with the swift Wolfoids.

Cain remained at the table after everyone had gone. Brutus climbed to the top and sprawled, stretching out as much as his small body could.

A grinning Jolly appeared on the screen. "Penny for your thoughts, Major Cain."

"What do you think we're going to find down there, Jolly?" Cain asked.

"I have a number of possibilities calculated as best I could from the variables. Would you like to hear what they are?"

"Sure."

"The most likely scenario is that the colonists dismantled their ship and are living in a near feudal society on the planet. Natural disasters fill the next three spots which would have negatively impacted technology and population numbers. There are a couple scenarios where a civil war has occurred. The most likely of these is based on Cygnus VII's own history. Technology destroyed itself, but a certain segment of the population survived. The least likely scenario is that there is no one left."

Jolly stood serenely, having told Cain nothing that he hadn't already thought about. The big question remained unanswered and would probably remain unknown until they made contact with the people, assuming someone had a working radio and if not, then they'd find out in a face-to-face visit.

That was the scenario that tied Cain's stomach in knots. He thought back to their first landing on Concordia, where they had to kill people wholesale and run for their lives.

This time, he had his Marines. This time, that first meeting would be done from a position of strength. He wouldn't let them take advantage with a smile and kind words.

"And you'll help me, won't you, little buddy? I expect you'll want to go, assuming we go, even if only to get away from your offspring," Cain suggested.

The miscreants have infested all aspects of my life. They run the ship. They run the Marines, and they run the garden. I'm at a loss as to where they gained such ambition. That mother of theirs...' Brutus let it hang.

Hillcats mated for life. By fighting for Mixial, he fought to be her husband, although he thought it was going to be a one-time good deal, like the Golden Warrior's production with the domestic cats in that seaside village so long ago. This was different.

'You made your choice, big man,' Cain said unsympathetically.

'What about you?' the 'cat responded sarcastically.

"That hits low, Brutus, a bullseye but low. Let's go check the weapons locker. See what we have. Jolly? Do you think we need any special weapons for heavy gee? Will our stuff work okay?" Cain stood and turned toward the corridor. "And I hope to hell that we don't have to use any of it, but if they make us, we'll bring the thunder and lightning and make them regret their poor life choices."

Dead

"Systems are actively painting the space around Heimdall," Chirit said clinically as if making a log entry. "At this time, we have found no evidence of a ship or any other man-made satellites in orbit. No signals of any sort are emanating from the planet. My conclusion is that there has been a technological setback of some sort and modern technology is nowhere in use, similar to the status of Cygnus VII one hundred, fifty years ago, although we still had a colony ship and satellites in orbit. I have no data regarding whether intelligent life exists on Heimdall."

Captain Rand rotated his chair to look at Commander Daksha. Maintenance had rigged a small fabric cover for the Tortoid's shell, with a padded area on top in which the kitten was now nestled. Rand's kitten was curled up on his human's lap, sleeping. Both 'cats wore collars with access bracelets so they could move about the ship and get to the areas they needed access to, like the bridge, quarters, and most importantly, the garden deck.

The bridge crew studiously avoided looking at the newcomers to the bridge since both the captain and the commander wore long faces as if they had been condemned to purgatory.

The snark of the young 'cats was wearing them down. They were pulling double duty trying to run the ship and teach the kittens manners.

'Cats weren't very accommodating in admitting their shortcomings and then even more reluctant about changing their ways. The commander and the captain were hell-bent on seeing the youngsters grow up to be well-respected 'cats.

Rand had learned to hold the 'cat in his human hand, petting it with his artificial limb in case it attacked him. The manufactured hand was far more resistant to the 'cat's claws and even with the worst scratches, the med lab could fix it in no time flat.

The commander nodded slowly to the captain. It was time to let Heimdall know that Cygnus had arrived.

"Ship-wide communication please, Jolly," Rand said as he spun his chair back toward the main screen. "Take us into orbit, Lieutenant Pace. Major

Cain, please ensure the ship's defenses are manned and ready." Cain responded with a thumbs up.

"Board shows green. All systems ready," Pickles reported.

Daksha continued his notification to the crew. "We will begin broadcasting our welcome message momentarily. Ensign Tandry, please transmit our message on all known comm frequencies."

There was a flurry of activity around the ship. Pace made slight adjustments to the flight profile. Tandry punched execute on a program that would cycle through transmissions across a broad spectrum of frequencies. They even sent one version in Morse code over high frequency bands.

Starsgard used the radars available to him to paint the sky around the ship in case he needed to target any missiles. His finger hovered over the defensive jammer, considering that his first line of defense.

Cain had both shuttles loaded with a squad of heavily armed Marines, just in case they needed to deploy. He expected that they'd be cramped in the shuttles and end up not going anywhere. He'd seen it in all the manuals and in many of the movies. Reducing reaction time was the best way to win any battle.

"What are their names again?" Cain asked, not for his edification, but for the others in his shuttle.

"This little gem is called Penelope," Stinky said, petting the kitten who stood on his lap and preened.

"And he is Hortense. I call him Tensy," Stalker stated as the kitten batted at the Wolfoid's hand-paw.

"Is there any reason why we're bringing children on a combat mission?" Cain asked casually.

"We couldn't leave them behind!" Stalker exclaimed.

'Leave it. You're not going to win this one,' Brutus cautioned.

'I know that, but I want them to think about what it's like fighting with 'cats. You make me better. Will your kittens make them better? Will those two little furballs kill someone if need be? Can they? So many questions, Brutus. They need to have all this in mind before they get distracted and somebody gets killed.' Cain descended into a

funk. He'd already seen too many people die.

'I'll keep them with me when the time comes, but it's not going to be today. We're going to be stuffed into this box and forced to smell Wolfoid for the next few hours before we walk out through that hatch right there and back onto the ship. I need to poop,' Brutus told him.

Cain shook his head, certain that he was being punished, but he knew Brutus was right. Having two shuttles manned was overkill. They could not reconfigure quickly enough if they needed to tailor the mission.

"Jolly, patch me through to the other shuttle, please," Cain said.

"Ready, Major Cain," Jolly's disembodied voice replied.

"Listen up, people! Corporal Spence. You and your squad will remain on the shuttle as we'll keep one in ready-to-deploy status at all times. We'll rotate through two hours each. The on-call squad will remain near the weapons locker, ready to tailor their load-outs based on the expected mission. In the interim, we're getting off and third squad will move into the standby position. Thanks, Jolly, sign us off." Cain looked at Stinky and Stalker.

"Between you two and Pickles, I need one of you on board the ready shuttle. Leave a place for me and if there's time, I'll join the team. My intent is to go first no matter what, even if I have to sleep on the hangar deck," Cain said as Private Abhaya popped the back hatch and his 'cat Petey jumped out. The rest of Bull's squad disembarked.

Brutus disappeared. Cain didn't want to know where he went.

Stinky and Stalker nuzzled each other before Stinky joined the other shuttle's squad. They had more room, but they also carried a couple heavy weapons, the newest creations from Jolly: rocket launchers.

He handed the kitten to somebody within and climbed aboard. The hatch shut behind him. Stalker and Tensy looked sad, but they soon turned and intercepted Cain.

"If we go, I want to be on that first shuttle, too," she told him.

"We'll see what we can do. Maybe we'll be able to leave the rockets behind and we can all go. I like your spirit, Night Stalker, you're a good fighter, a good Marine." Cain studied his platoon sergeant. They had chosen her because she stood out from the others.

She had been the right choice.

"Is your 'cat ready to fight?" he asked. The little man bristled, arching his back, hackles up, and slashing the air before Cain with a small orange paw. "Uh-huh."

"He will be when the time is right, until then, sir, he'll stay behind me," Stalker declared. The 'cat edged forward and slashed into Cain's pant leg, burying a claw in the major's ankle.

Cain kicked the 'cat away. "Listen here, you little rat. I have three rules for combat. Duty first, we fight to win, and the only fair fight is the one you lose. Remember these, and you'll take your place in the history of the Cygnus Marines."

Brutus reappeared, joining Cain as they left the hangar deck and headed for the stairs. Cain stopped in the corridor outside, envisioning the scorch marks which had long since been repaired, and the people who died there.

"Never again, Brutus," Cain whispered.

'Never again, my friend,' Brutus replied.

'The kittens stay behind. It is non-negotiable,' Cain insisted.

'I'll tell them,' Brutus said softly.

***

"Nothing. A big bucket of nothing with a heaping helping of nothing on top," Rand said. "Four days of nothing."

"We have passed over the entire surface area of the planet, twice. I don't think there are any people down there and it begs the question, is this the right place?" Pace asked.

Pickles turned his head and spoke over his shoulder. "We are most definitely in the EL475 system and this planet is Heimdall as long as the data from Graham is correct. There should be a burgeoning population of colonists after some ten thousand were delivered here three hundred, fifty years ago," Pickles reiterated.

They'd already had the conversation. The Lizard Man didn't understand how the others seemed to keep forgetting, although they didn't forget, they just did not believe what they were seeing.

"New assumption," Commander Daksha started, "there is no one left alive on the planet. Find me the ruins of the biggest city and we'll launch Cain's people to recover what information they can find. It seems like The Olive Branch will be conducting an archaeological mission."

Pickles sent a note to Chirit and Tandry, delivering the commander's new orders. They'd already been collecting the data, but discarding anything that looked like a structure as they dug for lifeforms, specifically, humans.

The data was already there, so Jolly was well ahead of them. In less than a minute, Pickles had his map with the settlements and estimates of population. Jolly calculated that the people had disappeared approximately one hundred years prior.

The deterioration of the high-tech buildings suggested a civil war of the type experienced on Vii.

"People never learn, do they?" Rand asked no one in particular.

"Major Cain," Master Daksha requested. When Jolly confirmed contact, the Tortoid continued. "I shall accompany you to the planet surface. We'll take the shuttles to the largest of the three identified cities and see what we can find. Food for a week and whatever personal weapons you think prudent, but there are no people down there."

The Tortoid's vocalization device made him sound resigned, forlorn. Master Daksha had human DNA, as did all of the genetically-engineered creatures, making the loss of an entire colony catastrophic and weighing heavily on his soul.

He couldn't get his head wrapped around the loss of life--tens of thousands of human beings, gone.

He thought it was worse than making first contact. He'd only met a new group once before and although it didn't go well, he learned a great deal and wanted to put those lessons into practice, have a better first contact, and make new friends without having to kill anyone first.

'It's okay, Boxy. We'll help you down there to find whatever will bring you peace about what happened,' BJ said in his maturing thought voice.

'That's very kind of you to say, my little friend,' Daksha replied, having reconciled himself with the fact that the 'cat was always in his head. At first, it concerned him, but now, he found it comforting. He saw how Cain could have such a relationship with Brutus where the two would throw down,

61

drawing blood, but then be best friends moments later. *'I know we'll find answers. I can only hope that they are to our questions.'*

***

"You need an engineer down there and Briz doesn't leave the ship," Ellie said, hands on her hips.

Cain couldn't pull rank. He couldn't argue. He couldn't just walk away. He looked at her with a blank expression.

"Well?" she demanded.

He surrendered. "Fine, I'll tell the commander, but what if Briz can't let you go?"

"Briz? Really?" she replied. He hung his head in shame, briefly, before coming back to his senses. "Be ready in ten."

He turned and walked away. "I'm ready now." She ran to him, grabbing his hand and holding it as they left engineering. When the hatch closed behind them, Cain pushed Ellie against the wall and kissed her fiercely.

"Damn it, Ellie, I love you and don't want you in harm's way!" he cried into her ear. She bit his neck before pushing him to arm's length.

"It's not your job to protect me. You don't think I worry about you? That last action on Concordia, you right in the middle of it all. The first shuttle arrives with your dead and injured, and you expect me not to worry?" She looked as if she was ready to take a swing at him, her eyes glistening with half-formed tears. "It's not my job to protect you, either, but we're better together, Cain. I know that, and you know that."

"I do," he admitted, unclenching his jaw. She massaged his temples to help ease the tension.

He pulled her close to him and hugged her tightly.

"Your harness is digging in," she said as she leaned back against the bulkhead. He traced a finger along her cheek and gently caressed her lips with a fingertip.

"You are beautiful," he whispered, then looked down the corridor. "And we have to go. You need a pack with food. Jolly! Make it so and have a bot drop it off on the hangar deck."

Cain grabbed Ellie's hand and ran toward the stairs, almost yanking her arm from the socket. "Sorry," he mumbled as he slowed and let her catch up. She laughed, eyes sparkling, no longer from tears.

Landfall

The shuttle settled to a soft landing in an open field to the southeast of the city ruins. The second shuttle landed simultaneously to the southwest.

"Comms check. Lieutenant Black Leaper, can you hear me, over?" Cain said into his collar, where a small device had been clipped. After the first visit to Concordia, Cain wanted a comm system that didn't have to go through Jolly, to use as a back-up.

"Loud and clear, Major," Stinky replied. Cain pointed to the others in the shuttle. Ellie shook her head as she hadn't been fitted with one, having been a last second add to the roster. But she had Carnesto with her and between the 'cats, Cain and Ellie could always communicate.

The others in the shuttle gave a thumb or a paw up to show that they heard. Ascenti bobbed his head.

"Ascenti, you're first out," Cain said. He always sat next to the hatch. On the ship, the hatch faced aft, but on the planet, the shuttle was vertical and the hatch was on the floor. There was a ladder built into the deck between the bench seats. Getting off the shuttle once it landed was everyone's priority since it was so uncomfortable sitting sideways, laying on whoever happened to be sitting next down the line. Those in the cockpit area were most comfortable as they laid back in the pilot and co-pilot chairs.

Bull was up front because he took up too much space in the passenger area of the shuttle. Ascenti stayed up front along with Master Daksha.

When the hatch popped and as the ladder started its descent to the ground, the Hawkoid dropped, falling between the Marines and through the hatch before snapping his wings out and gliding away. Brutus dug his claws into Cain's harness and the major headed through the hatch and down the ladder.

Bright sunshine and an eerie calm greeted him.

The grasses in which the shuttle sat were long, but not excessively so. Cain raced down the ladder, hit the ground with a heavy grunt, ran toward the nearest cover, a small hill, and threw himself to the ground. The others poured out of the shuttle and dispersed in an array around the ship.

Ellie waited until last and then she climbed down the ladder, while Daksha slowly descended, floating alongside. She and the commander were the only ones of the group not armed.

The squad knew about Cain and Ellie's relationship and that nothing was to happen to her. Cain didn't have to say a thing.

Carnesto clung to Ellie's pack and leapt to the ground when they were close enough. He crouched below the level of the waving grasses, disappearing as he ran off.

'Brutus, are you sensing anything?' Cain asked.

'Small game, nothing bigger than a fox, and that's it,' the 'cat replied.

Cain expanded the neural implant window before his eye. *'Ascenti, what are you seeing?'*

The Hawkoid shared his view with the entire group. One hundred years of growth obscured the vast extent of the ruins, but the outlines were there and after figuring out where the roads were, the rest came into focus. Ascenti climbed higher and angled to the southwest where he spied the second group, spread out in a circular defensive position around their shuttle.

Ascenti swooped low and circled the second ship, flying casually over the avenue of approach that the Marines had selected to get them to the city. He made it to the center and then turned and traced the approach to the first shuttle. He saw no major obstructions on either route. He backwinged to a soft landing on the nose of the shuttle.

Cain found lying on the ground to be tolerable. When he stood, the heavy gravity of the world tried to pull him back down. It wasn't as bad as their final days of training on The Olive Branch, but there would be no break from the extra weight until they left the planet.

Maybe he'd be used to it by then.

Ellie hadn't physically trained for the extra burdens. She was barely able to stand and walked like her legs were plastic prosthetics. The 'cats seemed unaffected.

'Bull, tactical formation, movement to the city. Let's go find out what happened here,'

Cain ordered over the neural implant.

Bull was up first and to his position, pointing with his lightning spear in their direction of travel. The rest of the squad formed up on him. Dark Forest took the lead, dropping to all fours and sniffing carefully, before walking forward. Cain fell in ten meters behind Bull with Ellie at his side. Daksha swam along beside her. Cain had a short rope in case the Tortoid needed to be towed.

Cain realized that they probably wouldn't move too fast. The one point five times Cygnus-normal gravity meant that everyone was half again as heavy. Factor in the same amount for what they carried and it made every step a struggle.

'You let us know if you sense anything, BJ,' Daksha told the 'cat riding inside the padded area atop the Tortoid's shell.

'There's nothing out there,' BJ replied.

Cain took Ellie's pack from her. She looked like she wanted to argue, but thought better of it and nodded. She gasped for air as if she was running a marathon.

Daksha swam serenely along, joining the 'cats and the Hawkoid in being seemingly unaffected by the heavy gravity.

The Wolfoids found traveling on all fours to be the best way to combat the effects. The humans suffered the most as the weight wore them down, putting too much pressure on their backs and their joints. Cain watched Ellie struggle and it broke his heart, but as she said, it wasn't his job to protect her.

He already knew to never say "I told you so." He'd have to find a way to communicate with her where his legs didn't feel like jelly.

He grinned against the extra weight and checked in with the Hawkoid who was circling lazily overhead.

'I don't see anything, Major,' Ascenti reported. *'It's clear sailing.'*

'Lieutenant Leaper, report,' Cain ordered.

'Making progress in the move to our first objective. Nothing else to report,' Stinky replied quickly.

The bigger planet took longer in its rotation. Not only was the gravity heavier, but the days were thirty-four hours long. Cain was already tired. He could see the same thing on the other humans' faces.

First squad had three human Marines: Abhaya and his 'cat Petey, Trilok and his 'cat Thor, and Ogden. With Ellie, that made five human balls and chains, as Cain saw it. Second squad had two humans and a Lizard Man in addition to the two Wolfoids. Fickle was in second squad, but he didn't deploy with the others as Ascenti took his place.

Since Lieutenant Black Leaper had come, there was no place for Lieutenant Peekaless. Fickle and Pickles filled key roles on the ship, so they weren't able to deploy except in critical situations. Commander Daksha and Captain Rand knew that they needed more data collection and analysis. Both Fickle and Pickles had skills that would come in handy on board.

And this deployment wasn't critical.

Besides the heavy gee, it was supposed to be a walk in a green park with perfect weather.

They'd landed on the outskirts of the ruins. Cain had a hard time estimating distance in the different gravity and bright daylight. On the ship only using the graphics, he worried that they were landing too close. Now that he was on the ground, he was worried that they had landed too far away.

He pulled up the map showing their location. Without the satellite system in orbit, he was counting on Jolly to triangulate their position and compare that to the map to determine each Marine's location, determine speed of travel and distance covered.

The map said they'd gone less than a half mile. Sweat streamed down Ellie's face as she struggled to keep moving. Cain was soaked from his efforts. Wolfoid tongues hung out of their open maws as they sucked wind.

Cain hesitated to call a stop, but immediately ordered it when Ellie's legs buckled. He caught her before she hit the ground. Once flat on her back, she breathed easier.

"Bull, take Lightning Flash and Dark Forest ahead and scout our route. Under no circumstances are you to enter any structures." Cain tipped his chin at the huge Wolfoid in charge of first squad.

Bull stood up straight and saluted, then dropped to all fours and ran ahead with the squad's other two Wolfoids.

Ellie closed her eyes and was soon fast asleep, with labored breathing as her chest heaved to get more air. Cain's eyes sagged, and that made him angry. The adrenaline surged and he stood upright.

"Abhaya and Trilock, set up security of this position. Ogden with me. Hey!" Cain yelled as the humans struggled to stay upright. "Pull yourselves together!" Cain stormed over and pulled them upright.

"We trained for this," he growled in their faces. He was met with a duet of "yes, sir."

Brutus, we're going in to the building closest to us, can you join me? Can you link me with the other 'cats, please?' Cain asked.

'Of course,' Brutus replied.

'Carnesto, wherever you are, please watch over Ellie. And, BJ, I'm leaving you in charge of military operations at our temporary bivouac. Are you up for that challenge?' Cain waited for an answer. *'Brutus?'*

'You asked if I could. I didn't link you to them. Is that what you want me to do?' Brutus replied sarcastically.

Cain threw his head back and looked at the sky. He gritted his teeth and carefully measured his response. *'Yes, please, Brutus.'*

'Done.'

Cain repeated himself.

BJ was the first to answer. *'Of course, rugged human. I was born to do this. To me, minions!'*

'A chip off the old block, eh, Brutus?' Cain snipped.

'I heard that!' BJ replied.

'I'll be back momentarily. There is a rabbit that requires my attention,' Carnesto added, before the image of the 'cat making a kill flashed into Cain's mind.

'Ooh, that looks good!' Brutus replied. *'Be there in a bit, human. You can start without me.'*

Cain looked at Ogden and shook his head. "Shall we, Private?"

"Is there a problem, sir?" Ogden replied, grimacing as he fought against the planet.

"Just the 'cats, but they reassure us that there's nothing here, and I trust Brutus, so let's press on," Cain replied. He pulled his blaster and dialed it to a mid-sized flame. In close quarters, he assumed he'd need an area weapon if anything. "Standard room clearing as we practiced outside the space center."

Ogden had originally come from the north. He was dark-skinned and had been a farm hand at one time. He wanted more than a life on the farm and worked hard to earn his position at Space School. When the opportunity to join the Cygnus Marines presented itself, he couldn't get to the front of the auditorium quickly enough to volunteer. He'd always preferred the outdoors, but the allure of visiting other planets was too much and he had surrendered to a life encased in the metal shell of a spaceship just for the chance to stand on a planet like this.

The spacers didn't get this opportunity, only the Marines. Ogden grinned as he hefted his blaster. "I got your back, sir," he told the major.

Cain headed toward the outline of a blocky, two-story building that fronted the roadway down which they traveled. It was barely thirty meters from where Ellie fitfully rested, but to Cain, he was entering a whole new world, the ruins of a civilization nearly two thousand light years from Vii.

A civilization that should have been thriving.

Cain and Ogden reached the front of the building and found the door. They tried to look in, but the darkness inside was nearly impenetrable. Plant life covered the outside of the building, blocking the windows and preventing light from reaching indoors.

"Heading around, counterclockwise, you watch outboard and I'll watch the building-side," Cain ordered. The two stepped off, nearly shoulder to shoulder as they powered through the foliage ahead, turning when they passed the corner following the outline of the building.

"The windows are intact," Cain observed. He cupped his hand around the glass and tried to look inside, but the window was darkened. "They probably smoked these to protect the interior from this system's sun."

Ogden risked a look before turning back toward the trees and undergrowth.

They continued around the building, fighting their way through the persistent vegetation, but even after one hundred years, the pavement held much of it back, giving the two men places to step and a way through.

There was a door in the back and Cain checked it, wondering if he'd have to break it down to gain access. It was open. The only thing it needed was for the debris in front of it to be removed. The hinges were nowhere to be seen, which gave Cain hope that they hadn't rusted and seized.

He left the door alone and signaled to Ogden that they'd continue their way around the building.

At the front, Cain stopped and looked at the roadway where Daksha hovered protectively above Ellie while the kitten BJ stood up, tail high, looking down upon his small empire.

Brutus was waiting at the front door for them, licking his paw and cleaning his face. Cain hadn't sensed anything, but knew that the 'cat had made a kill.

"Was it good?" he asked.

'Tasted like Vii rabbit. Maybe we can bring a breeding pair on board to put on the garden deck for occasional hunting purposes?' Brutus suggested.

'Are you high?' Cain asked. He thought he heard Carnesto snicker. He was broadcasting again, but didn't care. *'We are not bringing pet rabbits that you can use to torment Allard and Beauchene. Then you propose to eat the bunnies which will send our gardeners over the edge. Hell no!'*

'It was just a thought. Don't get your panties in a bunch.' Brutus continued to lick his face, while secretly plotting how to get some live rabbits on board. He missed hunting and the taste of a fresh kill.

Cain used his hands scrape away the soil and debris that had built up in front of the door. Ogden joined him and tried to help, but Cain asked him to be ready with his blaster.

When the major finished, he tested the door, pulled his blaster, and nodded to Ogden. Cain pulled the door toward himself and Ogden ran through and dodged to the side, while Cain aimed into the darkness. Brutus strutted through the middle of the open door.

"Clear!" Ogden stated loudly. Cain wasn't sure the building was clear, but nothing was attacking them. He darted through and made a quick right turn, tripped over Brutus, and slammed into the ground. He grunted when he hit, feeling like he'd been slammed by a load of bricks.

"You think heavy gravity sucks while we're walking, you should try a face-plant," Cain gasped, rolling to his side and fighting his way back to his feet. "Thanks for that, little man."

Brutus ignored the jibe. *'Something isn't right here,'* Brutus told him, instantly putting Cain on edge, more than he already was.

"What?" he asked out loud. The 'cat shrugged and headed into the darkness.

As Cain's eyes adjusted, he could make out various machines with wide platens, rollers, and spindles. He moved closer, looking for bodies or any evidence that would hint at how the place was abandoned. The first machine he looked at had stopped mid-weave on a new roll of fabric.

Cain grabbed a handful of what was on the spindle. It was covered in a thick layer of dust and his heavy hand kicked up a small, gray cloud. Despite the passage of time, Cain found that the material was soft and supple.

He walked around the machine, looking for a body, but didn't find anything. There were two big buttons beside a control panel, one was red and one green. The red one had been depressed.

"They shut the machine down," Cain deduced. Ogden was watching everyone but Cain. Brutus walked slowly past. "Let's keep looking."

They used a center walkway to go from one end of the building to the other. There was a broad staircase in the middle, and they used it to climb to the second floor.

Once there, they saw a number of offices and open spaces with small desks. They also found where the people had gone. Brutus sniffed the mass of mummified humans piled in the middle of the open space.

He opened his neural implant. *'Jolly, are you seeing this?'* he asked.

'Yes, Master Cain. Very interesting,' the AI replied. Cain walked around the group, using a hand light to brighten the area and improve the image quality for Jolly.

'Any idea what killed them?' Cain wondered.

'Please show me the area beyond, slowly in a circle,' Jolly directed. The major

71

shined his light, up and down and he turned around, trying to take it all in.

'Thank you, Cain,' Jolly said grimly. *'There was a battle here of a force with blasters. There are scorch marks crisscrossing the walls and on the floor. The people were killed by narrow beam lasers, I believe, of the type you're capable of delivering with the tightest setting on your own blaster.'*

"A civil war and they executed their own people. Is that what you're telling me, Jolly?" Cain said aloud.

"Cain!" Ellie called from downstairs. The major moved to the balcony and looked down into the dusty darkness. Every step they'd taken had kicked up clouds.

"We're up here. Take a right at the top of the stairs," Cain called.

He heard a 'cat sneeze from somewhere down below. The Tortoid didn't bother with the steps and floated straight up, swimming over the balcony railing. The kitten crouched on top of his shell. Cain couldn't look at the cover and pillow without smirking.

'I tolerate him,' Commander Daksha stated in his thought voice.

'Cats are a wealth of knowledge, but trying at times,' Cain replied sympathetically. *'Did you hear Jolly's report?'*

'I did, Major Cain. Blasters on a narrow beam. The people packed together and summarily executed. Humankind at its worst,' Daksha lamented.

Ellie was breathing hard when she finally reached the top of the stairs. She gasped when she saw the bodies and had to take a knee to keep herself from hyperventilating. Cain was angry with himself for allowing her to come without having trained for it.

"Engineer! Tell us what you see over here. What kind of blasters did they use? Energy type. Were they like ours?" Cain called, giving Ellie something to do that gave her a reason to be in that place at that time.

She slowed her breathing and stood, using the railing to help her. She walked forward, checking the walls. Cain joined her, handing his light over. She used it to examine the fine creases in the wall's material. When Cain first saw those, he thought they were part of the artwork.

Ellie studied them intently.

"Give me your blaster," she said. Cain pulled it from its holster, checked that it was on safe, and then handed it, butt first to Ellie. She checked the safety, then took the weapon. Standing next to the wall, she dialed up the narrowest of beams, aimed parallel to the scar, and fired.

The others watched with interest.

She put the weapon on safe and handed it back to Cain before turning her full attention to the new mark on the wall. It barley scorched the surface where the older mark had penetrated to the depth of her fingernail. She checked some of the other marks and tried to calculate the trajectory. She had to stand on an old chair to get a better view.

"These were fired from something that was really tall, or from something that was flying," she noted.

'Good catch, Master Ellie,' Jolly said happily. *'Let me get a closer look at your mark…'*

'LOOK OUT!' Brutus yelled over the mindlink. Cain dove for Ellie, but only made it halfway before landing on a desk and sliding to the floor. Ellie turned and froze.

A bot had floated above the railing. It was nothing like they'd seen before. It had projections on top and a head on each side of a boxy body. It had wheels that protruded from the bottom.

The projections on top tracked back and forth across the group. Daksha reacted out of panic and delivered a focused thunderclap, the sonic boom unique to Tortoids. The box-like torso bulged, and the bot started to fall, bouncing once off the railing and firing two powerful laser beams into the ceiling before crashing to the first floor.

"With me!" Cain ordered Ogden as he headed toward the stairs. Cain took them two at a time going downward, his knees screaming in protest. He slowed when he hit the floor, crouched and aimed at the bot. It was vibrating in place. He fired the narrow beam into it, again and again. Ogden took a position beside him and fired, too.

"Cease fire," Cain said softly. He wasn't sure their fire had damaged it at all. The Tortoid sonic blast had done the most damage. "Cover me."

Cain wasn't sure what kind of cover Ogden could provide, but it was the Cygnus Marine standard operating procedure for checking a downed enemy.

'Jolly, help me understand what I'm looking at,' Cain asked over his neural implant.

'Will do, Major Cain. Pan slowly across the body. There, that's good. Can you remove that panel?' Jolly asked. Cain only wanted to make sure the thing was dead, but Jolly wanted him to take it apart. The major ignored the request. He'd revisit it once he had a reasonable level of confidence that the bot wasn't going to attack.

"Is everyone all right up there?" Cain yelled toward the ceiling.

Ellie leaned over the rail. "We're fine, shaken but fine."

'We kicked its ass!' BJ added.

Ellie snorted. She turned and was face to face with the small 'cat riding on Daksha's shell. "You stay out of the way!" she scolded the fuzzy orange kitten.

Carnesto yowled from outside. The door had closed and he wanted in. Cain stepped carefully across the dusty floor and opened the door. The large, black male leisurely strolled in. Cain looked at the railing where Ellie was leaning over and watching him.

He crooked a finger at her and then pointed to the bot. "Engineer, front and center. Let's see what makes this thing tick."

Ellie, Brutus, and Daksha descended together. Ellie stopped when she reached the bottom step. "I thought going up was bad," she panted.

When she caught her breath, she joined Cain next to the bot. "I need my pack," she told him. He realized that it was still in the road with two Marines guarding it.

Cain leaned toward his collar. "Abhaya and Trilok. Pick up Ellie's pack and join us in the building please. Break, break. To all Marines, we've encountered a hostile bot, a security bot of some sort. I'll send the image over your neural implants. As of right now, do not enter any buildings. I'm not sure our weapons are effective against it. For reference, its beams are orders of magnitude more powerful than our blasters. Maintain your spacing and report when you've made it to the first objective."

"We're already here, boss," Stinky replied from the courtyard located between a number of larger buildings. It may have been a park at one time. The lieutenant set his people into position and ordered the squad leader to

74

establish a fifty percent stand-to. Even the Wolfoids were tiring from Heimdall's conditions. "We've set up a perimeter and are standing by. Resting half of the squad at present."

"Roger, Lieutenant. Carry on," Cain replied formally before adding one last tidbit. "Set your blasters to narrow beam, people."

The two Marines entered through the front door and made their way to Cain once their eyes adjusted to the semi-darkness. Ellie opened her pack and pulled out a variety of tools. None of them matched the fittings on the bot. She held out a hand to Cain.

"Blaster, please."

He made sure it was safe and handed it over, then waved his people away. "Check this building and make sure there aren't any more of these in here."

The Marines formed a triangle, one up and two back, then started to scour the dark corners of the building, having broken out their flashlights, looking for anything out of place.

Ellie used the narrow beam of the blaster like a torch, snipping at connections until the front panel came free. When she removed it, she wasn't sure what she was looking at. The jumble within didn't look like any engineering she'd seen. She shined the light on it to make sure that Jolly got a good look.

'Maybe you can share it with Briz and see what he thinks?' Ellie suggested. The AI agreed and patched Briz into their conversation.

'You were attacked by a bot? I didn't think there was anything alive down there?' Briz asked.

Cain was listening in and it made sense. A civil war, but one group wasn't alive. "The bots fought a peaceful population," he said simply.

Daksha bobbed his head slowly.

"Which means this place could get hot as hell if there are more of those things. I don't think we need to see anything else, do you, Commander? We're not equipped to fight a bot army should they realize we're here and come after us, just like this one did." Cain stood up and activated the communication device.

"Retrograde to the shuttles immediately, best possible speed, people. I think we're in the middle of a hornets nest and we need to get out before they see us," Cain explained, pacing as he worried about his Marines spread out over miles. "Bull, return to my position. We need your help carrying this thing."

The Marines returned from their inspection of the building. "There is nothing in here that looks like this thing," Ogden reported.

"Set up outside and watch out for Corporal Bull and his team." The three men hurried away.

Cain worked his shoulders, feeling more comfortable in the heavy gee. Maybe he was just happy to be leaving.

Retrograde

It took Stinky a long time to rally Corporal Spence and second squad. The team was dog tired and some of the Marines were already asleep. But it didn't matter. Orders were orders. The reason for the retrograde was sound, and Stinky didn't want to lose any of the good people around him.

"The humans have it the worst here, sir," Spence told the lieutenant. "Maybe Wolfoids up front and in the rear. Zisk with us, and Ascenti providing top cover."

"Good plan, Corporal. Stalker up front with Shady and Tracker in the rear with me. You, Silas, and Zisk stay in the middle and we'll pace off you." Stinky waved Spence away. Tobiah trotted off with his human.

"I want to stay with you!" Stalker said in Wolfoid, not using her vocalization device.

"We can't. You're the best tracker and I'm responsible for all of us. We have to split up. Just for now, my mate," Stinky growled and yipped. They nuzzled and Stalker left to find Shady.

***

Bull and the other two Wolfoids dropped to all fours and ran down the open roadway to return, arriving after only a few minutes.

They panted heavily, tongues lolling.

"Did you see anything?" Cain asked when they arrived.

"Nothing. No movement at all. There isn't even a breeze," Bull replied.

"I'm glad you're back," Cain said, slapping the huge Wolfoid on his heavily muscled shoulder. "We need to haul this pile of garbage back to the shuttle."

Cain led the three Wolfoids inside and pointed out the bot. Ellie was wrist-deep into the internals, carrying on a conversation with Briz and Jolly simultaneously. The Marines watched, confused as she argued with each of the remote viewers about how what they wanted wasn't going to work.

"How about we just take that thing back to the ship?" Cain offered. Ellie stopped what she was doing. She had moved the internals around, but not removed anything. The guts of the bot were very much like a human's organs, but artificial, nothing organic within. Some of the pieces looked like wood. Nothing within the bot looked to be made of metal.

The weapon systems on the top of the bot's frame didn't appear to have a separate power source. They were linked to the bot's guts. Cain couldn't make heads or tails of any of it. He decided to leave the speculation to the experts, who were already fully engaged in discussing how the bot worked.

"Ogden. See if you can find us a cart or something." The men conferred before stepping purposefully away.

"How did you know something was off and can you tell going forward?" Cain asked the scruffy orange cat who appeared at his side.

It didn't have anything to do with the bot and everything to do with the stack of mummies upstairs. If the bots catch us in the open, I'm afraid I won't be able to warn you,' the 'cat answered, looking up at Cain with his pupils bigger in the semi-dark of the building's interior.

"If anything happens to us, take the other 'cats and survive," Cain told his friend.

'Nothing better happen to you, because this place sucks,' Brutus stated firmly in his thought voice. Brutus strolled toward the front door and waited. Cain walked over and pushed it open a crack. Brutus walked outside after a brief hesitation.

"Good hunting, my friend," Cain said as the door closed.

Ogden and the others returned pushing a small cart whose wheels screeched with every turn. He held up a finger and they tipped the cart on its side. He spit on the front hub and then the back hub. They turned it the other way and then repeated the process. When they next spun the wheels, there was silence.

With six of them lifting, they manhandled the bot onto the cart. It hung over, but the bulk of the weight was over the wheels. Ogden started to drag it and the other two pushed.

The wheels started squeaking again. Ogden shrugged and kept pulling.

Ellie covered her ears until they got it through the front door and outside.

"So what's the verdict?" Cain asked.

"Jolly scoured his archives, and there's never been anything like the technology we have here," Ellie replied. "So either humanity has made an incredible leap in building a bot force that wiped out the people, or it's something else."

Cain filled in his own version of what "something else" meant.

"They invented a technology they couldn't control. That's the easy answer, whether it was the self-control not to use such a weapon against their perceived enemies, or the bots gained sentience and unleashed themselves," Cain said, shrugging a shoulder and nodding. That explanation was easy. He liked easy. "What do you mean by 'something else'?"

"Aliens, Cain. Briz suggested it, and you know Briz. He was the only one who believed the vines weren't alien, but not this."

Cain couldn't stomach that. He preferred the easy answer. "They lost control of their creation and it killed them all, without mercy. That's it, nothing else." he said, signaling that it was time to go. Carnesto ran down the steps and almost face-planted when he hit the bottom.

'Misjudged that a little,' he said and trotted past.

Daksha swam to the door that Cain held open. The major took a deep breath and coughed, the fresh air fighting its way past all the dust he'd inhaled. He tried not to think about what the dust was made of in a sealed building filled with corpses.

***

The humans' bodies failed them less than an hour into their return trip. The going had been slow, and then Spence collapsed. His legs spasmed and quivered with his complete loss of control.

"Halt!" Stinky called over the communication system. "Set up a perimeter right and left."

Stinky and Tracker dragged the humans to the side of the road and put them under a tree.

"We're down hard, Major. The humans cannot continue. No idea when we'll be able to move. I estimate that we're only a quarter of the way back to our shuttle. Damn!" Stinky wasn't happy with the situation.

He was feeling the effects, too. They'd been planet-side for less than eight hours, and he had not had a break.

"This is it, people. This is where we hole up. Stalker, find us a defensible position where we can disappear from view, the closer the better."

"On it," she replied instantly. He watched her disappear off the road and into the brush. Shady slunk to the side and leaned against a tree, bracing his lightning spear as if it was too heavy to carry.

Stinky had a hard time holding his head upright. He was on all fours and his head hung toward the ground. He struggled to stand upright on his back legs and made it only because of his spear. He used it like the third leg of a tripod, hanging onto it with two hands and leaning against it. He looked around him, but gave up because he wasn't willing to move.

'Ascenti, can you hear me?' he asked using his neural implant.

'Roger,' the Hawkoid replied.

'Tight circles around our pos, keep a watch if you would. We are like the walking dead down here,' Stinky shared.

Ascenti had been perched in a tree, watching the squad depart. He knew they were pulling back, but wasn't sure how one bot could cause the major to call for a full retreat. Bots could live for thousands of years. Finding one that was operational after a mere hundred years wasn't just possible, they should have thought it likely.

The Hawkoid conceded that Cain knew things that he didn't and that the Marines' lives were always of equal importance to the mission. Maybe he'd learned what he needed and the mission was accomplished. The major would never senselessly expose the Cygnus Marines to danger.

Ascenti liked the open skies and the freedom to soar. He understood that was his hesitation regarding a rapid return to the shuttle and the spaceship.

He wondered where they'd go. It would take a couple more days before the shuttles had recharged their systems sufficiently to return to space.

The Hawkoid soared low, flying at head height as he passed down the road, then he climbed slowly, majestically, banking sharply and passing down the side closest to the biggest building in the area. Ascenti stretched his wings and beat the air to pick up speed.

He reveled in the high-speed passes. High to low, low to high, he flew around the squad's position. He climbed higher and higher and then dove, angling his wings backward to cut down on drag. It had been too long since he stretched his wings fully.

He raced past the tall building. Six stories up, a window shattered and laser beam lashed out, but he was too fast and jerked at the first sound of broken glass. He twisted his body downward, staying close to the building until he turned the corner and flew up a side road.

Taking fire from an upper story of the building. I think it was one of the major's bots,' Ascenti reported, no longer questioning the major's motives.

He stayed away from the front of the building as he climbed higher and higher. Ascenti caught sight of a window shattering out the back side and a bot jabbing its weapons through and firing. The Hawkoid was fast, but the bot's aim was true.

The beam sliced through the Hawkoid's wing, cutting half of it off. He lost all lift on that side and started spinning downward, gaining speed as he descended. He cried out in pain, shrieking as he fell.

***

Cain listened helplessly as the Hawkoid lost all coherence over the neural implant. Then his input went silent.

"What a crap sandwich," Cain mumbled through gritted teeth. He looked at the sky, knowing that the Hawkoid would not appear. The trees were vivid green with brown highlights. The bushes had berries and flowers. He hadn't noticed before how beautiful it was on this planet.

It was a paradise that was trying to suck the life from them.

"Let's get this thing back to the shuttle, then we form a rescue party and go get our Marine," he growled.

Jolly, what's the status on recharging the cells to fire the shuttle?' Cain asked.

'It will be another sixty hours before the tanks will be filled to the point where the shuttles can return to The Olive Branch. Private Ascenti is severely injured, but alive.'

"Damn!" Cain said aloud, then keyed the system attached to his collar.

"Report, Stinky," Cain said, inadvertently using the Wolfoid's nickname over the platoon-wide system.

"We are under cover in the street out front of the building in which the bot is located," Stinky whispered. "Our intent is to shelter in place until nightfall, and then return to the shuttle under cover of darkness. First order of business is that Stalker and I will find Ascenti."

Cain didn't want his people exposed, but the immediate recovery of the injured Marine could mean the difference between the private living or dying. There was no other choice.

"Proceed," Cain said feeling the burden of leadership weighing him down as much as Heimdall's gravity.

***

Stalker crawled through the underbrush as close to the building as possible. Stinky peered from under the tree, through its leaves to see any sign that the bot was near a window.

He couldn't see anything, no matter how much he craned his neck and twisted his head. Stalker waved to Black Leaper from the bushes. He dropped to his belly and crawled agonizingly slowly until he was under cover with her.

She led the way, wedged against the lower wall of the building, ducking beneath branches that grew tightly against the windows. Stalker covered the ground quickly, reaching the corner, turning, and continuing along the side of the building in the same way.

Leaper was a bigger Wolfoid, so his harness caught branches more often, slowing him. He forced his way through and started making noise. Stalker waited and signaled for him to be quiet. He motioned back that she needed to slow down. She waved and turned her attention forward, quickly disappearing.

Jolly, can you lead us to Ascenti?' Stinky asked using his neural implant.

'Yes. Follow Stalker as I'm guiding her. It should only take you a few minutes to reach him,' Jolly replied reassuringly.

Stalker waited at the far corner of the building. There was an open space they needed to cross. On the other side, a stand of trees stood tall. Beyond that was where Ascenti had fallen.

Jolly said the Hawkoid was still alive.

Time was of the essence.

When Leaper reached Stalker, she pointed with her spear where she intended to go. "We go together, keeping our distance. In case it fires, one of us will reach the other side," she whispered.

Stinky pulled her close to lick the side of her face and nibble on her ear. She giggled.

He knew she was right. "We run like the wind," he encouraged her, feeling the weight of the world squashing him into the dirt. On that day, he had summoned his strength, time and again. He'd never driven his body this hard against such a relentless enemy.

Gravity was sapping his energy, and he was almost finished. He didn't know where Stalker's reserve came from, but she looked healthy, fresh even.

He didn't ask as he didn't want to appear weak before his mate, and he wouldn't be able to face the major if he failed to bring Ascenti home.

What Black Leaper didn't realize was that Stalker was exhausted, too, and only wanted to lay down and sleep. Leaper's presence gave her strength and an injured Cygnus Marine needed them.

"Three, two, one," Stinky counted down. The two Wolfoids ran as fast as their bodies would carry them, across the broken pavement and into the woods. On the other side of a large tree, they converged behind the trunk and stood up, leaning against it for support as their chests screamed for more air.

Stinky's head rolled to the side and he looked at Stalker. "That was anti-climactic," he managed to say.

She only nodded, then activated her neural implant. *Which way, Jolly?* she asked.

He gave them a bearing. They dropped to all fours and started walking. The shade was pleasant and even without a breeze, it was cool enough. The Wolfoids were hot because of their hair and how hard their bodies worked to acclimate to Heimdall's heavy gravity.

Jolly vectored them to the place where they expected to find the

Hawkoid, but there was nothing. *Jolly, we don't see anything,'* Leaper told the AI.

Stalker looked up and pointed. Ascenti was wedged in the branches, disheveled and unconscious.

Stinky followed her gaze. "Oh, no," he said, the feeling of helplessness crushed the life from him.

Wolfoids couldn't climb trees.

"Major Cain, we have a problem," Stinky started. His vocalization device reflected his defeat. "Ascenti is about ten meters in the air, stuck among the branches, and Stalker and I can't get to him."

Let the War Start Here

Cain clamped his eyes closed when he heard the frustration in Stinky's voice. He hung his head and looked into the elevations of growth covering the ruins beyond. In there, his people were trapped. His friends were worn down.

And he felt as helpless as they did.

"I may be able to help," Daksha offered, floating peacefully next to Cain.

The major looked at him, but didn't ask.

"With my stalwart helper, we will recover our friend and meet you at the shuttle," Daksha suggested, his vocalization device reflecting hope, but not joy.

"It's my job to protect you, Master Daksha, not put you at greater risk," Cain argued.

"Understood. I'll work with Jolly and he'll direct me right to our Hawkoid. We'll get him out of the tree. It'll be okay, but I had best get going. Time is not on our side." The Tortoid turned and swam away. The kitten was sitting, but leaning forward and intently looking ahead.

"Lieutenant Leaper, Commander Daksha is on his way to you. Dig in and wait for him, and then bring all of our people home," Cain said softly into the communication device on his collar.

"Shady and Tracker. Are you two upright?" Cain asked.

"Private Shades Racer here, sir. Spence, Silas, and Zisk are out. Silent Tracker is resting while I remain on watch. We are under cover and sheltering in place until nightfall. Talking about nightfall, when the hell is that coming? This could be the longest day of my life," Shady signed off without using the procedures they'd copied from the archives.

"It'll be a while still, Shady. Stay frosty, Marine, and stay down! Have Corporal Spence check in when he wakes up. Out here."

"Tactical formation," he said in a low voice, pointing where he wanted his people. Bull on point, the other Wolfoids covering the flanks, the three human Marines pushing and pulling the cart with the bot, and Cain and Ellie bringing up the rear.

Cain signaled that it was time to go. Bull jogged ahead to give himself space. The screech from the tortured cart wheels echoed down the street despite the amount of foliage to dampen the sound.

"Stop!" Cain growled, fighting his way forward despite his legs feeling like tree trunks. He scanned the area before slinging his pack to the ground and digging through the food that he'd brought. One of the meals had a tomato sauce in it. He opened this and carefully squeezed it onto the hub.

They worked the cart back and forth. He squeegeed the remainder onto a second hub. Ogden pulled his pack and opened the ration to lubricate the other side. Cain and Ogden ate what was left and curled the bag to put back into the rations pouch.

The Marines never left trash behind because it could be recycled once they were back on the ship. Cain personally couldn't abide soiling the environment in which they operated, especially when they were the visitors.

He took one last look around, appreciating the planet's beauty, before slashing the air with his knife hand pointing the way ahead.

Ellie was on one knee, and it tore at Cain's heart to see her head hanging low. He was pulled in too many different directions, but he had to let it all go. His short-term objective was to get the bot back to the shuttle. Settle his people in to wait and recover.

The error of his operational planning was clear. He needed to remain near the shuttles until his people got used to the heavy gravity and then conduct the operation. The anger built within as he looked at the sagging faces of those around him.

They moved out and the cart protested, but nowhere near as loudly. The humans pushed with their heads down, powering through the effort by sheer force of will. Just like everyone else.

Even Ellie.

He helped her to her feet and they staggered forward. Cain looked around him, blaster at the ready, unsure of what he'd do if the bots showed up. He would give the alarm and run for cover. He'd already given the order for his people to dial their blasters to the narrowest beam. The Marines were spread out, not giving the bots an easy target.

There was nothing else he could do, except put one foot in front of the other and keep doing that until they were back at the shuttle.

***

Black Leaper told Night Stalker to sleep, that he'd take first watch. She didn't argue. He had the rank and she didn't trust herself to stay awake. She curled up at the base of the tree and was out instantly.

Stinky watched her sleep, chest barely moving as exhaustion seized her. He tried to remain standing, but couldn't. His legs started to shake. He laid down to remove the stress, putting his head between his paws.

And that was the last thing he remembered.

***

Spence had a hard time lifting his head. He opened his eyes to find that it was daylight. He wondered if he'd slept through the night.

When he shifted, he found that Zisk's leg was partially over his head. Spence pushed it off, groaning. Tobiah was sleeping on the other side. The 'cat's eyelids fluttered as he tried to open them.

Corporal Spence had to roll to his stomach to push himself upright. "What happened?" he mumbled.

'You and the others collapsed,' Tobiah replied over the mindlink.

'How long?' he asked.

'How long have you known me?' the 'cat asked mysteriously.

'Cycles, I mean more than a year, right?' Spence was confused; his head felt like it was filled with cotton.

'And in all that time, you haven't learned that 'cats don't measure time like humans? My answer is one sleep. That's how long you were asleep.' Tobiah shook his head and blinked. He stretched his large body, back legs extended to his paws, then he leaned back and did the same thing with his front legs.

Spence opened his neural implant. A timer was one of the features that was always available along with his own vital signs. He could pull up the vitals of everyone in his squad too, which was what he did while he tried to work his muscles enough to stand up without needing help.

The vital signs are as expected for people who have moved into a heavier gravity environment. It is not the gravities that are important, but the percent of change. You and your squad are healthy,' Jolly informed him.

'Can you tell me where everyone is, starting with my squad, and how long was I asleep?' Spence asked.

'You were asleep for four hours, Corporal Spence. Would you like me to overlay people's positions on the map?' Jolly did that while asking the question. Spence expanded the image, oriented himself, and found his squad on both sides of the street, under cover, and all asleep.

He found the lieutenant, the platoon sergeant, and Ascenti a half-mile away, toward the city center. The major and his people were less than a mile from the first shuttle and moving incredibly slowly. Spence had to double-check to make sure that they weren't stopped.

Commander Daksha appeared to be by himself moving methodically in the direction of the lieutenant.

'Jolly, what's the commander doing?' Spence wondered as he struggled to his feet. Once there, he didn't feel as bad as he had yesterday. He didn't feel so heavy. He ached all over, but he hadn't injured himself, for which he was grateful. He had three miles to go to get his squad to the second shuttle.

'The commander is joining Leaper and Stalker to rescue Ascenti, who is injured and trapped in a tree. I fear his life signs are waning,' Jolly said sadly.

'What happened to Ascenti and why didn't they go get him?' Spence demanded.

'There is a bot firing lasers from the building that you are closest to, and Wolfoids can't climb trees, not like this one, Corporal Spence,' Jolly replied.

'Damn. I didn't even think of that. I can be there in ten minutes. Tobiah and I are on our way,' Spence said and minimized his window. It immediately started flashing with a new message. He ignored it.

Spence kicked Zisk in the leg until the Lizard Man opened his eyes. He didn't move any other part of his body. He blinked until his eyes focused on his squad leader.

Corporal Spence leaned close and whispered, "As soon as everyone is up, take them back to our shuttle. Set up a perimeter and wait. I'll be along shortly."

The Lizard Man nodded, then strained as he sat up. Spence slapped him on the shoulder, then dove into the underbrush with Tobiah close on his heels.

Together, the small man and his 'cat worked their way around the building where the bot had been seen. At the opposite corner, Spence expanded the window to access the map, but he received an eyeful of Jolly informing him that the major expected the corporal to take his squad to the shuttle at best possible speed.

'Noted,' Spence replied sourly and opened the map. The Wolfoids weren't far, but they were on the other side of a large open area. The Marine sighed and activated his communication device.

"Major Cain, Spence here. I'm almost to Ascenti's position. I'll be there in less than five, and I can get him down. Jolly says he's dying, and I just can't have that."

"Good to have you back in action, Corporal Spence. I'll chew your ass later for something or other, but for now, you're doing the right thing. Go save our Marine." Cain sounded tired, bone tired.

Spence acknowledged the order and signed off. He reviewed the map one last time, then closed the window.

He had everything he needed. He flexed his legs, trying to work out the woodiness that gripped him. Spence looked at Tobiah. 'As fast as you can run, my friend,' he told him.

They broke from cover together and the human looked like he was wading through water at first, but started to pick up speed as he went. Tobiah flashed across the opening then hesitated.

The sound of breaking glass shocked them both. Spence took a hard left and started to zigzag. The laser beam gouged the pavement where he'd just been. A second beam lashed out and missed.

In a tan flash, Tobiah bolted for the trees and disappeared into the foliage. Spence gritted his teeth, finding new energy to dodge and weave. He took some comfort in the fact that the bot was only shooting at him.

With the last zig in the open, he dove for the trees, feeling the heat of a beam as it passed through his backpack. Spence assumed that his ballistic vest would have helped, except that they didn't bring them because of the weight. In the effort to balance mobility and armor, mobility won out in the heavy gravity of Heimdall.

Spence crawled forward on his hands and knees until he was behind a tree. He stood up and breathed a sigh of relief.

'Here it comes,' Tobiah warned. The bot had launched itself out the window and dropped until it stopped less than a meter above the pavement. It moved forward, not with great speed, but unerringly toward the tree behind which Spence hid.

He pulled his blaster and wondered who had dialed it to a narrow beam, but he accepted that it had been done for a reason while he was out. He breathed quickly, psyching himself up for imminent combat. He leaned around the tree and saw the bot approaching.

Spence fired into the bot, hitting it in the center of its squarish metal body.

It immediately returned fire, sending beam after beam into the tree. They cut through the trunk and the tree cracked, as it could no longer support itself. It fell into its neighbor, perched precariously for a moment then leaned and fell back toward the roadway where the bot hovered.

Spence ran the other way, found another tree to hide behind, and leaned around it to take aim. The bot was nowhere to be seen. Tobiah appeared at his side, then scrambled up the side of the tree to find a better place from which to see and give warning to his human.

The branches settled as the fallen tree lay on its side, killed far before its time. The bot worked its way among the branches and rose until it was clear. Spence fired twice more, hitting it cleanly both times before it returned fire.

Lightning arced through the air from the far side of the road and enveloped the bot. The arc danced across the metal surface until it crackled out, then another arc took its place. Spence fired into the Wolfoid lightning adding his firepower to theirs. Another arc lanced into the bot from behind, then a fourth arc appeared.

The bot exploded in a spectacular kaleidoscope of color. Spence wiped the sweat from his forehead using the back of his arm. 'Any more of those things out there?' he asked.

'I don't see anything. Your squad approaches,' Tobiah replied.

"Does no one follow orders?" Spence asked Zisk as he approached.

"Duty first," the Lizard Man answered through his vocalization device. "Shall we?"

Stalker and Leaper appeared from the other direction. Spence gave them the thumbs up and nodded his thanks.

"I'm here to climb your tree," Spence offered as he put his blaster back in its holster.

Stinky and Stalker waved for him to follow, and he gave the same signal to his squad. The group set off as a squad of Marines would, spread out, weapons aimed away from their fellows, crouching and moving tactically from cover to cover.

The lieutenant stopped below a large tree and pointed upward. Spence jogged to them, feeling as if he'd sprinted. He worked to catch his breath while Tobiah ran up the tree.

Spence shrugged out of his pack, realizing that he wasn't sweating as badly as he thought. The bot's laser had cut through two water bags and four of his meals. The corporal had a mix of water and tomato sauce trailing down his back and into his trousers.

At least it wasn't blood.

'I need your help,' Tobiah told Spence.

"On my way, big man," he replied aloud, unhitching his weapons belt to be as light and lean as possible.

He looked at the tree, picked a spot, spit on his hands, and rubbed them together. He grabbed a protruding vein of wood tightly and started walking bent over, pulling himself up as he went. When he reached the lowest branch, he climbed onto it, then reached up and pulled himself to the next branch.

The climb was a challenge in heavy gee, but not impossible. Spence had always prided himself on his agility. He was small and wiry. This day, that was what they needed.

He reached the branch where Ascenti was wedged. Spence straddled it and crawled out. When he reached the Hawkoid, he wasn't sure what to do.

Tobiah crouched low on the other side.

Spence wrapped one arm around the branch to support the injured Marine from below. He started untangling one wing, which elicited a squawk of protest. Spence apologized, but kept going. The second wing was half-gone. The wound was mostly cauterized and had congealed in the areas where it had torn free after the laser had done its damage.

The corporal pushed up from below and freed the Hawkoid. Ascenti's eyes shot wide as he thought he'd fall, but Spence cradled the Marine to his chest, smoothing his feathers and looking at how to get down.

He prepared to climb using only one hand when Commander Daksha appeared. A small, orange 'cat jumped to the branch beside Spence, freeing space within the pillowed saddle that the Tortoid carried.

Spence carefully placed the Hawkoid within and BJ jumped back aboard, helping to hold the Marine steady. Daksha started descending immediately and Spence leaned too far in his rush to help. Tobiah hooked a claw into the human's harness and pulled him back.

The corporal's heart pounded in his chest.

'Be careful,' his 'cat cautioned unhelpfully.

Together they climbed down to find Ascenti getting numbweed, water, and a bandage.

They rigged a small stretcher using Spence's ruined backpack. He could think of no better use for it.

Stinky activated the communication device on his harness. "We have Private Asenti and we are on our way to shuttle number one."

The lieutenant pointed with his lightning spear and the team moved out. The Hawkoid rode on the Tortoid's shell. Stinky held out a short length of rope. Daksha seized it in his beak-like mouth. The Wolfoid dropped to all fours and started running.

The humans stayed on the flanks and struggled, but they kept up. The group maintained their spacing in case any unwanted visitors showed up. All had their weapons at the ready, just in case.

And they had the ultimate anti-bot weapon with them. The Tortoid's focused thunderclap was an instant kill.

Truth

Cain couldn't express how happy he was that they'd reached the shuttle without a bot encounter. The ship was sealed, just as they'd left it, and the generators hummed as they pulled in oxygen and hydrogen from the air.

Second squad had Ascenti and was on their way to Cain's position. Cain thought things were looking up.

Jolly, any news from the ship? Are they seeing anything down here, energy signatures, movements of bots, I don't know, something?' Cain wondered.

'Rand here. How are things going, Cain?' the captain asked via the connection that Jolly had established.

'You know me pretty well, Skipper, so how do you think they're going?' Cain replied, sounding more sarcastic than he intended.

'Shot up and running for your lives?' Rand suggested.

'You forgot the part where we scattered to the four winds and we are trying to find our way back to each other, but yes, pretty much what you said. No losses, but Ascenti is in bad shape. With the commander's help, we were able to recover him from the top of a tree. Otherwise, we're hunkered down and waiting for the shuttles to recharge so we can get the hell out of here. These bots are unreal and nothing bigger than a fox is left as the indigenous population.'

There was a hesitation while Rand thought about what the major had said. *'You think the bots killed the people?'*

'There's no doubt about that, but what we're not sure of is why,' Cain replied, kneeling as he pointed to where he wanted his people to settle in. *'We're going to establish a perimeter and prepare to wait. I hope we are back home in a few days.'*

Cain signed off. Ellie was asleep again. He couldn't blame her. He was done. "Can anyone keep their eyes open?" he asked over the comm channel.

Not a single affirmative came back.

Then it's me, Cain thought.

"One hundred percent rack time. Get some sleep, people, but keep your weapons close by," Cain ordered.

'Jolly, can you watch over us using the shuttle's systems? Maybe you can give us some warning. I'm not going to be able to stay awake, but you give the alarm in case anything comes,' Cain told the AI.

'Sleep well, Cain. I have the watch,' Jolly replied firmly.

***

Stinky wasn't able to maintain the pace for long. He called a halt, but after a brief argument, Commander Daksha continued alone. They didn't know why the bot had fired at Ascenti, but it hadn't fired at the Wolfoids or the Hillcats.

Daksha thought the large group was more of a skyline than a single Tortoid slowly moving through the area.

Slow and steady wins the race, Daksha thought to himself. Stinky gave BJ a few strips of beef jerky. The 'cat dug into it as one starved. Stalker gave her supply to him, but told the small 'cat that it was for the Hawkoid.

Spence and Silas combined their jerky to feed their 'cats, who hadn't complained. Hillcats were known to be vocal when they were hungry.

"When's the last time you ate?" Spence asked quietly.

'Since you mentioned it...' Tobiah started. *'And for the record, this planet sucks.'*

"I'm pretty sure I can't disagree with you," Spence whispered. "Are there rabbits near or anything you can hunt?"

Tobiah looked into his human's eyes and nodded. He and the calico called Aniston padded into the nearby underbrush, disappearing in the direction of heavier woods.

Daksha continued swimming ahead, an injured Hawkoid resting on the pillow tied to his shell with two pounds of orange Hillcat kitten keeping the Marine calm.

That looks ridiculous, Spence thought. *It'll be funny sometime, just not today.*

The group settled in, the Wolfoids laying with their heads between their hands/paws. Lightning spears were held tightly, facing the most likely direction from which a bot might appear.

The vision of a rabbit popped into Spence's head as Tobiah stalked the creature. It looked like a normal rabbit to Spence, normal being determined by the ones he'd seen at New Sanctuary.

Tobiah stalked the creature and it bolted headfirst into Aniston, who readily dispatched it. She dropped it there and the two headed away. 'Cats usually hunted alone, but Tobiah was so big that small prey was able to elude him. He was the only 'cat to work with others, and all of them seemed happy to accommodate the lion-sized Hillcat.

Aniston disappeared into the brush while Tobiah strolled casually through an open area, catching a rabbit eating grass, seemingly without a care in the world. When it spotted Tobiah, it stopped chewing and hunched down as it got ready to run. There were foxes on Heimdall, so the rabbits knew predators.

And it recognized the 'cats as a danger. The rabbit bolted one step toward Tobiah. He slashed with a paw, grazing the creature's haunches as it changed direction instantly and dashed in the opposite direction from which Aniston approached.

She darted through the clearing, going for an old-style kill. She ran the rabbit down despite the heavy gravity. Tobiah left her to it and returned to the first kill. He settled himself with his prey between his paws and devoured it, leaving almost nothing behind.

***

Rand looked at the screen, but it wasn't telling him anything new.

"What do we need to do to bring that debris on board?" he asked, impatiently drumming his fingers on his armrest.

"We'll need to stop the spin and use the mechanical arm by the airlock to guide some of it through the hatch," Jolly replied.

"Make it so, number one," Captain Rand replied in a low voice, laughing to himself.

Jolly wasn't sure what the captain was talking about. "Execute the maneuver?" the AI asked to clarify.

"Yes," the captain answered flatly, before Jolly nodded and pointed to the ceiling. "All hands, executing zero-g in two minutes. In two minutes, we will stop the spin to bring what we think is manmade debris on board, and then we'll resume normal gravity."

The countdown began, and Jolly took control of maneuvering the ship.

Pace was an outstanding pilot, but Jolly incorporated all the sensors to conduct the maneuver in a concise manner and capture the debris in the least amount of time possible.

The ship adjusted slightly while the crew strapped in. The captain did a countdown from ten, and then the spin stopped incrementally as the EM drive thrusters worked their magic.

Jolly deployed the arm and opened the airlock hatch. The Olive Branch had already matched the debris' orbit. Jolly expertly maneuvered the main section around the pattern of metallic objects. He moved the spindle section close and nudged the debris, using the arm to guide it into the airlock.

Briz watched through the round window in the internal airlock hatch as he hung on to a handhold to keep from floating away. *'That looks like plenty,'* he told Jolly through the neural implant.

The airlock hatch closed and sealed. The mechanical arm retracted and locked into place. The final stage was to restart the ship's spin. The captain made the announcement and a minute later, Briz was pulled gently to the deck.

Briz popped the internal hatch once the pressure had equalized and atmosphere restored. He looked at the equipment and shrugged. *'I don't think there's any question this was an earth-technology science satellite,'* Briz told Jolly.

A maintenance bot appeared, started gathering the pieces, and placed them in a cart.

Briz walked with the bot to the maintenance area on the hangar deck. They spread the pieces out on a work bench. Lieutenant Commander Garinst joined Briz in looking at the collection of disparate metal items.

"Standard metals. Standard attachments. Standard electronics. Standard sensors," Garinst mumbled as his gloved hands carefully picked up each object and spun it around.

"Jolly," Briz called out loud, his vocalization device adding volume to the Rabbit's internal voice. "Can you show us the internals of the bot, please?"

On the screen over the bench where blueprints and repair diagrams were usually shown, the images captured from Ellie's neural implant played. Jolly enhanced the lighting in certain areas, blew up the images from time to time, and replayed sequences.

"Look here? Seamless transitions between two different metals," Garinst said, pointing to the screen. Briz was engrossed by the review of the bot's internals. Briz's pink ears flopped back and forth as he shook his head.

"It's not even close to the same," Briz said dismissively.

"Look at this, Briz. How do you think this was destroyed?" Garinst pointed to markings on one of the pieces that made up the exterior of the satellite.

"Odd-colored scorching," Briz replied, leaning close, his nose twitching as the recovered items warmed up and started to smell of ozone.

"From the outside," Garinst noted. "Somebody blasted this. It didn't explode."

Jolly watched through the monitors since maintenance had not installed a holographic projection system in their spaces. He studied the objects. "Is that a memory chip?" he asked.

"Where?" Briz asked, pointing to various items. Jolly stopped him when he reached the electro-optical attachment. It would have been on the opposite side of the satellite had an attack occurred from space, or on the side, should the attack have come from a matching orbit. In either case, the majority of the sensor was intact.

Garinst carefully examined the object, then took off his gloves after confirming the metal had warmed to room temperature. He moved a toolkit from a nearby chest and looked through a lighted magnifying lens. He located a tiny tool and with four gentle pops, he removed the card from the sensor. Garinst changed tools and removed the chip from the card. He inserted it into the diagnostic computer and let Jolly take over.

"The dataset is intact; let me pull up what we have. This was a multi-sensor system, both for astrometric measurements and for planetary data collection--weather, tectonic shifts, those kinds of things," Jolly said, lacking his usual precision.

"How was it destroyed?" Briz asked, wanting less of what he suspected and more of what he didn't know.

"The system tracked the movement of an object into Heimdall's space. It approached rapidly and slowed, assuming a geostationary orbit not far from this satellite. There was a one nanosecond image of a purple dot appearing on the hull of the spacecraft, and that was the last recorded frame."

"Show us the ship," Garinst asked.

The image that appeared on the screen was identical to the bot that attacked Cain's group, only much larger.

"How fast did it approach and when?" Briz wondered, looking at the foreign ship.

"Nearly one thousand gravities. Converting the time stamp, verifying star map against calculated trajectories, stellar drift, let me see..." Jolly drifted off as he talked to himself. "This was ninety-seven years ago."

"One thousand gees! Holy crap," Garinst exclaimed. The Cygnus-12 had gotten to nearly 480 gees of speed in the system, but it slowed down well before reaching the planet. According to Jolly, the ship they saw on their screen had slowed from one thousand to zero in the space of two hours. "Any living being would have died with that amount of deceleration."

"And that is your conclusion," Jolly said definitively.

"A bot ship filled with bots," Briz said slowly.

"How could humanity make such a doomsday weapon and then turn it loose on unsuspecting colonists?" Garinst threw his hands up in frustration. He looked at the pieces on the work bench. The satellite had been the target of the first shot in an interstellar war.

Not a single human had survived.

"I am not convinced humanity did this," Jolly suggested.

Briz continued examining the spaceship. He'd already come to the conclusion that humanity had not created it or its bot minions, but he wouldn't voice his conclusion, because no one wanted to hear what he knew was the truth.

The taboo word was "aliens."

Hide

Daksha swam at his usual Tortoid speed. BJ watched for any movement from within the buildings. He reached out with his immature senses and couldn't find any game, but he found the rest of their party ahead. They were all asleep.

It made him curious, because the major was fanatical about maintaining a watch.

'Et tu, Brutus?' he asked, pleased with the amount of knowledge transferred to him from his mother. He had no idea what it meant, but it sounded appropriate. The 'cats Petey, Carnesto, and Thor were with the group, too.

'Why don't I just squash you like the bug that you are?' Brutus gruffly replied.

'Come on, Dad, be cool,' BJ whined, shifting as Ascenti tossed in fitful sleep. BJ thought he heard Brutus roll his eyes. *'Is everyone okay out there?'*

'Yes. Sleep has seized them all. They're not as stalwart as us 'cats, and that's why we are higher on the food chain. I can see you making good progress on your way here, please continue.' Brutus hoped he sounded sufficiently encouraging, but then he thought better of it. He knew, deep down, that he didn't care if he encouraged his little man or not.

'Cats were independent from the word go, although BJ was very young, physically. He needed his mother's milk to keep growing.

'You shouldn't have come,' Brutus told Billy Joe Jim Bob.

'Of course I should have. We saved the Hawkoid. Both of us!' the two-pound furball declared.

Brutus didn't dignify that with a response. He sighed, relaxed, and was soon asleep.

BJ was miffed. *'How's it going down there, Boxy?'* the upstart 'cat asked.

Commander Daksha shook his head as he continued forward, methodically, diligently, happy that he was unaffected by the planet's gravity, knowing that it was wreaking havoc on the rest of the group.

'And you wonder why your father has no patience with you,' Daksha finally replied.

'I think he just doesn't like me,' BJ replied, sensing a rabbit nearby.

'That's not it at all. He loves you as a father should, but wants you to be more respectful of those who have been around longer. I've been alive a thousand times longer than you have, yet you call me by a name I do not wish to be called. Please call me Daksha as a sign of your commitment to peaceful coexistence with all the people. You are doing well helping our Hawkoid friend, by the way,' the Tortoid told the 'cat.

'Well, Daksha, do you mind if I go hunt a rabbit? I am getting hungry,' the 'cat asked in a respectful tone.

The Tortoid had been in contact with Jolly. Commander Daksha knew that there was no race to get back since they'd already made the initial application of numbweed to help stop the bleeding and control the pain. Food and water would give the Hawkoid's body energy to keep him alive, although it would take the med bots on board the Cygnus-12 to print a new wing, if that was possible, and heal his injuries.

In the end, Daksha determined that they had time.

He swam to the side of the road and dropped close to the ground. BJ jumped off and was gone.

'I'll wait here, my friend,' Daksha told him as he floated upward a few feet. *'Do you sense any fox nearby?'*

The 'cat hesitated for a moment as he'd been focused on his first hunt. He stopped, checked, and reported that only the one rabbit was nearby. Then he continued his hunt, and Daksha left him in peace.

The commander waited while the 'cat's adrenaline surged. He'd left the mindlink open, showing Daksha everything that the small 'cat saw. BJ stopped under a bush, moved at glacial speed to avoid upsetting low-hanging leaves. His head pushed between the last of the foliage and he looked into a small opening where grass and wildflowers abounded.

A fat rabbit, about twice BJ's size, sat there eating a big flower.

BJ darted from cover straight for the rabbit. The creature turned and lashed out with its back legs as the 'cat flew through the air. The rabbit kick caught BJ in the face and chest, sending him spinning away.

He hit the ground with a grunt, but he was back up in an instant, circling the rabbit warily and looking for an opening. The creature shifted with the 'cat's movements.

BJ hesitated as he tried to stare it down and strike fear into its heart, so it would make a mistake.

The rabbit leaned down, without taking its eyes from BJ's, and pulled another flower from the turf. The petals whirled in a circle as the rabbit munched the stem.

Enraged, BJ drove straight at the rabbit. It jumped straight up in the air and the 'cat slid underneath it, rolled to his back to bring all four claws to bear. The rabbit landed on him and BJ clamped his claws into the rabbit's sides.

The rabbit launched itself ahead, dragging the kitten through the grass and into the weeds. As the rabbit picked up speed, BJ's grip weakened. Making a sharp turn, BJ was thrown head first into the trunk of a tree.

Daksha's view of what happened stopped instantly as the 'cat was knocked unconscious.

The Tortoid floated above the bushes and followed the track he'd seen the kitten take.

It didn't take long before the commander was working his way between branches to get to the kitten's side. The little man breathed slowly, alive but out cold.

Daksha grabbed him by the scruff of his neck, taking care not to bite through the skin, and floated into the air. With a Hawkoid on his back and a Hillcat hanging from his face, he set off in the direction of the first shuttle.

He floated high to get over the last bushes, then dodged beneath tree branches to break into the open area of the former roadway. He stopped instantly and froze, the kitten swinging from his beak-like mouth.

A bot hovered in the street, ten meters away. It rotated its body in a circle. The bot's weapons followed it as it turned, not aiming at anything in particular.

Daksha wondered if it could see him. It rotated one more time, then started moving away. The Tortoid dropped the kitten and unleashed a focused thunderclap, shattering the bot. It tumbled to crumbling pavement, toppling to its front and jamming the protruding weapons barrels into the ground.

Commander Daksha descended, feeling very tired from using his ability twice in such a short time. BJ lay in a pile, looking very much like a kitten that needed its mother.

The Tortoid nuzzled him until he could regrip the 'cat's neck skin, then he swam into the roadway, looking both ways as if expecting a traffic jam of bots, but there was nothing.

'Jolly, I have to report another bot down at my position. I hope that, as Cain would say, I am not coming in hot. I don't see any more, but I don't know. I have the injured with me and would appreciate a hand if you could rouse someone to come help me,' Daksha conveyed, drifting lower and having to work harder to keep moving forward.

'On it, Commander Daksha,' Jolly replied, but Daksha had already signed out.

***

'Corporal Aurochs Ring, Bull, please respond.' Jolly blinked the window feverishly, but the Wolfoid wouldn't wake up.

'Lieutenant Black Leaper, please respond,' Jolly implored the sleeping Wolfoid. He was supposed to be on watch, but he'd done too much and was beyond exhaustion.

'Sergeant Night Stalker, please respond.' Jolly continued trying to call all the Wolfoids first, then he tried the Lizard man, Zisk, and finally he tried calling the major.

'Major Cain, please respond,' Jolly said mechanically.

'I'm up,' the major replied without actually being up. He had learned to make do with less sleep since forming the Cygnus Marines. A half-hour usually worked wonders for him. Not this time.

He pulled himself away from where he slept, wrapped around Ellie like a protective cocoon. Cain rolled to his stomach and pushed himself upright. He made it to his knees, then the nausea hit him. He fought against it, but lost the battle quickly, throwing himself away from Ellie so he wouldn't get any puke on her. His abs heaved as he threw up, again and again, until only bile came up.

He looked around through watering eyes, happy that no one woke up to see him looking weak. He always compared himself against the idealized Marines in the movies that Holly had played for him. Cain never felt like he measured up, as if the universe continually had to show him that he wasn't good enough to wear the title.

Major Cain teetered as he stood upright, wiping his mouth on the back of his sleeve. His stomach hurt and spasmed as further warning that it wasn't happy.

I'm up. What's the emergency, Jolly?' Cain asked.

After Jolly explained, Cain was wide awake.

Why can't any of these ever go according to plan? he wondered.

He found Brutus and roused the 'cat, earning himself a vicious scratch down his forearm.

"Damn it, Brutus!" Cain complained. "Less than a mile to go get Daksha and bring him back. It's a walk in the park."

Cain knew the 'cat would catch up, so he turned and started a slow jog, speeding up as his muscles loosened. On the heavy planet, he figured a ten-minute mile would be a Herculean effort, so that was the pace he set.

A casual observer would have said the major was shuffling to a funeral dirge.

***

Daksha lost altitude until he was barely off the pavement and then finally his feet touched. He tried walking, but the strain was far too great. He settled to the ground, unable to keep going and unable to move off the road. He twisted his neck around to look for bots, but couldn't see anything. His own shell blocked his view. The kitten fell from his numb jaws.

Fear gripped him.

He could only think of his father and the repairs made to his shell from the damage done by the Androids after he was captured. He'd been as helpless as Daksha felt now.

And this is the beginning of the end, he told himself, before his head drooped to the ground.

***

Cain saw the Tortoid on the ground, a 'cat lying before him and a Hawkoid on his back. The major hurried, but was already running out of energy. He slowed to a walk, looking over the area to see if there were signs of an ambush, but there wasn't anything out of the ordinary that he could see.

He had no idea what a bot ambush would look like. They hadn't used stealth previously, counting on their superior weapons as they attacked directly.

Cain saw the bot lying in the roadway not far behind the Tortoid. He picked up the kitten to cradle him and then tucked him inside his shirt as he left the exhausted Tortoid and injured Hawkoid behind. There was nothing he could do for either of them besides leave Brutus to keep them company.

The major pulled his blaster, checked the narrow beam setting, and approached the bot.

He saw it vibrating on the ground as if trying to right itself. He ran to it as quickly as he could and started firing into it. He spaced the holes he was drilling in its body, hoping to hit something vital. The weaponry on its top was stuck in the ground, but it fired anyway.

The blast of all weapons fired simultaneously flipped it backwards and the concussion threw Cain off his feet.

He landed flat on his back and gasped in pain, but he held tightly to his blaster. He rolled to his side and fired into the side of the bot, again and again until the blaster's charge was nearly gone.

He stopped, saving the precious remaining shots. He pushed himself to his knees and crawled to the bot. Tendrils of smoke drifted through the holes in its casing. It no longer moved. The weapons systems on top were locked in place.

Cain grunted with the effort to get to his feet, turned his back on the bot, and staggered down the road where Brutus waited patiently beside Master Daksha. Cain sat in the road beside the Tortoid and stroked his head.

"I need you to hover, Commander. I can't carry you and everyone else. I can pull you along. All you need to do is float. I'll do the rest."

Cain winced as 'cat claws jabbed into his stomach. A whine came from within his shirt. He unbuttoned it, careful to catch the kitten before he fell out. The 'cat's eyes whirled in his head as he tried to focus, but couldn't.

'I want my mom,' the little man broadcast. Cain pulled the kitten tightly to him and stroked his fur. Brutus nuzzled his son.

'Does it hurt?' Brutus asked.

'A lot!' BJ replied, exasperated.

'That's what it's like being an adult,' Brutus told him. *'It's okay, Billy Joe, you'll be fine. We're here to protect you until you can take your turn and watch over us. Now climb in with the Hawkoid and let's see if we can get back to the spaceship.'*

"I couldn't have said it better myself, Brutus." Cain scratched behind the rough orange 'cat's ears. Brutus leaned into it for a second, then raised a paw as if to scratch the human. Cain looked at the scratch on his arm. It was no longer bleeding, but the scab was barely formed.

Cain removed his hand, not wanting to get scratched again. Brutus put his paw down and nudged his son onto the Tortoid's shell. The Hawkoid raised his head and Cain gave him a drink from his flask.

"You're safe, Ascenti. Drink as much as you can. Water is energy down here. We'll get you some food when we get to the shuttle. It's not much farther."

The Hawkoid's eyes rolled back in his head and he lost consciousness.

Cain got a good look at the terrible damage done to his wing, and grimaced. He couldn't imagine the pain of losing half his arm, but he'd seen Rand work through it.

He made a mental note to ask Rand to help Ascenti in his recovery. Cain wondered how many of his people were going to have 3D printed body parts when it was all said and done, or how many names were going to be on the bulkhead plaque.

Cain forced those thoughts from his mind. "Commander, please. I need you to float." Cain poured water on the Tortoid's head and neck. He dribbled a few drops into the Tortoid's mouth.

Daksha's eyes shot wide open and he turned his head to look at Major Cain. "Where am I?" he asked, his vocalization device registering surprise.

"You're on Heimdall, and I really need you to float, Master Daksha," Cain pleaded.

"No problem, my boy!" the Tortoid said happily, almost catching Cain's face on his shell as he zipped past.

Cain didn't have a piece of rope, so he removed his shirt. "Grab on," he told the Tortoid. The commander descended almost as fast, stopping just before slamming into the ground, then he rose again, but Cain caught his shell. "What's gotten into you?"

"Water. If we drink it, unfortunately, it's very much like alcohol to you," Daksha explained.

"We don't have time for that. Tighten up!" Cain bellowed, then shoved the corner of his shirt into Daksha's mouth and took off running. The Tortoid bounced and sailed as he followed Cain.

BJ was hanging on for his life while doing his best to keep Ascenti in place. Cain grabbed Daksha by the shell and started pushing to better hold him steady.

Cain was surprised at how much lift the Tortoid was able to manage. The major found that he was leaning on the shell, using it for both support and balance. In the end, he wasn't sure who was helping whom.

They staggered to the shuttle, finding that everyone was still asleep. Jolly opened the shuttle hatch and Daksha floated upward and went inside. The ladder descended, but Cain stayed outside.

Jolly, let me know what Ascenti needs and I'll do it,' Cain told his neural implant.

'He needs to be back aboard The Olive Branch, Major Cain,' Jolly replied.

'We all do, Jolly. We all do," Cain agreed.

Secure the Perimeter

Stalker opened her eyes and without lifting her head, looked around. The squad was arrayed in and around the bushes, mostly concealed, but lacking sound cover. Stinky was close by, head between his front paws, looking very dog-like. His eyes were closed and he breathed slowly, rhythmically.

She poked him with the butt of her lightning spear. His eyelids slowly crawled open and he stared straight ahead. The muscles quivered in his neck as he lifted his head. Yawning and smacking his Wolfoid lips, he looked at Stalker, then realized what had happened. He tried vaulting to his feet, but fell over as his legs didn't respond as he thought they would.

Stalker took a head count, finding everyone she expected to find. She saw the window of her neural implant flashing. She opened it and contacted the AI. *'Jolly, can you give me an update on the commander and Ascenti, please?'*

'Commander Daksha made it to the shuttle intact, despite an encounter with a bot, but the commander dispatched it,' Jolly reported.

Stalker growled in anger, driving the cobwebs from her mind. She rolled and stood up on all fours, then pulled herself upright.

"Daksha was attacked by a bot. He made it back, but we need to go," she told Leaper. He exhaled heavily, then took deep breaths as he tried to force oxygen into his tired, aching muscles.

Stalker roused the others, telling them to get up but be quiet about it. Stinky watched for movement from the open roadway, gripping his lightning spear tightly. Mass fire had overwhelmed the bot. The more weapons they could bring to bear, the quicker they could eliminate their enemy.

The lieutenant had no doubt that the bots were the enemy.

Spence hurried the squad through their morning ablutions, but Stalker told everyone to eat and drink fully. They had two hard miles to cover and they couldn't stop again.

Once the squad was ready, Stinky pulled them into a tight circle. "Listen up, people. The bots know we're here. Daksha encountered one, but he took care of it. The rest of our people are hunkered down at the first shuttle. We'll join them while we wait for our shuttles to refuel. Then we will conduct a tactical movement to the second shuttle and leave this planet. We'll move in a diamond formation. If we encounter a bot, shoot first, mass your fire on it, and kill it."

Stinky looked from face to face. He wasn't completely sure about human expressions, but he knew what determination looked like. There was no way Spence and his people were going to be outdone by a Tortoid and a kitten.

Stinky activated the comm device on his harness. "Major Cain, Lieutenant Black Leaper, over."

"Cain here," the major replied.

"We are preparing to move out. If no contact, estimate we'll reach your pos in ninety minutes," Stinky said.

"We have no idea how many bots are out there, Lieutenant. Take the greatest care to bring our people here. Cain out."

Stinky looked at his harness, agreeing with everything.

"Form up," he ordered.

Spence took point with the Lizard Man at his side. With the lieutenant and the platoon sergeant as part of the team, he'd been relegated to little more than another trigger puller. He was good with that.

They didn't lack confidence in him. It was about the most efficient use of resources. They didn't need three Marines in charge of the other four. One in charge of six made the most sense and brought the greatest firepower to bear.

Stinky formed the diamond with Spence and Zisk up front, Tobiah walking with them. Tracker was on the right flank and Shady was on the left flank. In the rear, Silas walked with his 'cat Aniston, Night Stalker on the right side where the most buildings were situated. Stinky stayed in the center to respond where he was needed the most.

The squad carried their blasters at the ready after ensuring they had narrow beams dialed in.

The group set off at the Lizard Man's pace since he was the slowest. He and Spence aimed their weapons where they looked, scanning the windows of the buildings they passed, keeping their eyes and blasters in constant motion.

Stinky saw that none of the buildings had been destroyed. Some windows were missing, but the buildings and the planet's infrastructure appeared intact. The bots had cleansed humanity from the planet, leaving the animals alone.

Jolly, do you have any more information on the bots?' Stinky asked over the neural implant, making sure the information was being shared with Cain.

'I do, Lieutenant. The bots arrived in a spaceship approximately ninety-seven years ago. They eliminated the satellites orbiting the planet, and this was our only source of information as we were able to recover some of the debris.' Jolly then transmitted a picture of the ship that had destroyed the satellite.

Stinky didn't answer. He minimized his window to watch for the more immediate danger. There was nothing pressing that Jolly was telling him.

"Incoming!" Silas bellowed. Stinky turned and the Marines ran to the nearest cover. Stalker triggered her lightning spear, but missed the fast-moving bot. It increased speed and raced down the middle of the road. No one fired for fear of hitting one of their own.

The bot silently blazed past Stinky, who almost fell down as he spun to follow. Spence and Zisk were nowhere to be seen, so Stinky took the shot and held the trigger down, to keep the lightning dancing across the bot's surface and stop its momentum. The two Wolfoids on the flanks added their fire while Stalker and Silas joined the lieutenant, adding their fire to that of the others.

'Behind us,' Aniston shared with her human.

"Behind us!" Silas yelled and ran for the trees, leaving the lieutenant and the sergeant in the middle of the road. They saw the danger and dove, one right and one left. The bot fired through the space they'd just occupied. The power of the bot's laser burned a trench into the pavement.

It stopped firing with one laser and picked up with two more. Stinky rolled to face the mechanized warrior, earning himself a laser crease down the hair on his side. The pain from the burn was searing, but he was energized by it.

Stinky fired, sending a lightning bolt over the bot. Stalker fired from her prone position in the road while Silas fired from behind a tree.

The bot focused all its weapons on the human, shattering the tree behind which he stood, sending splinters the size of spears into both the Marine and the Hillcat. The lasers continued to fire, crisscrossing the man's body. The lasers winked out as the bot fell to the ground, sparked one last time, and toppled.

Stalker ran to Silas, but he was gone. Aniston yowled. The mental anguish of losing her human matched the injuries from the wood that penetrated her small body.

Corporal Spence appeared with Tobiah at his side. Spence touched his friend, his body still warm as if he yet breathed. Aniston continued to profess her grief to the world. Tobiah nuzzled her.

'Is there anything you can do for her?' Tobiah asked Spence over their mindlink.

'I don't know,' he answered honestly. *'But we're going to give it a hell of a try.'*

"Into the woods!" Stinky ordered, pointing toward the wooded area on the left side of the road. The buildings on that side were smaller and farther apart. On the right, there were too many multi-story buildings to block their progress and in which bots could hide.

As they established a hasty perimeter, Stinky activated his comm device. "We've lost Silas and Aniston is severely injured. Two bots engaged and destroyed," Stinky reported.

Cain didn't want them to dwell on the loss.

"Duty first, Lieutenant. Are there more bots?" Cain asked.

"The first one was flying down the road. Had we not fired on it, I believe it would have continued to you without bothering us. The second one attacked us as soon as it saw us."

"Sounds like they're learning that the non-humans are as dangerous as the humans. We need you back here so we can establish a defense in depth," Cain replied.

"We can't outrun them, so we're going to remain under cover, travel through the wooded areas to get to you. I don't intend to engage any more bots unless they engage us first," Stinky said flatly, trying to sound emotionless, but he was afraid. He was afraid for his mate and his people, because he was in pain and tired.

He was afraid because he was looking at another dead Marine, and Stinky knew that there would be more before they left the planet. It was sucking the life from him, but the Marines never wavered, even when death was imminent. If duty demanded, with a hearty oorah, they'd run into withering fire, because that was what Marines did.

They were all afraid, but their courage and sense of honor demanded that they do what needed done. Marines knew fear, just like any other creature, but they didn't let it dictate their actions.

"There's no time to lament our dead. Zisk, you carry Silas. Spence, put some numbweed on Aniston's wounds, leave the shards in place, and you carry her. We move through the woods, and we're leaving now. Stalker on point, stay in the heaviest cover, single file, now go."

Stalker didn't hesitate. She tipped her spear in a salute and headed into the brush, leaving a trail for the others to follow.

Shady followed her, then Zisk and Spence. Tracker wanted tail end Charlie, but Stinky wouldn't have it. The lieutenant committed to bring up the rear, keeping his people in front of him.

After ten minutes, Stinky keyed his comm device. "We can't see the road from where we are, Cain. I cannot give you a heads up on incoming. I say again, I can give no warning on incoming."

***

Cain looked at the open area that led from the road to where the shuttle had landed. "Flash, I want you at the corner. We need eyes looking as far down the road as you can see. Without you, we won't get any heads up that bots are inbound. We need you to give us a fighting chance. Go!"

The Wolfoid raced on all fours the hundred meters to the corner that Cain had pointed to. He hunkered down behind a tree and inside a bush, concealed but with little cover to protect him from a bot weapon. He accepted the risk because he had the visibility that the major wanted.

"OP is manned," Lightning Flash reported.

"Bull, get everyone else into place, set up an ambush along that avenue of approach. Make sure we catch them in a crossfire."

Cain breathed a sigh of relief. Ellie scowled as she fought her way into a sitting position. The bags under her eyes told the rest of the story.

"Cain," she whispered. He leaned close to her, catching himself before he fell over. "Are we going to get out of here alive?"

He took a knee next to her, put a finger under her chin, and kissed her gently. "On this planet or any other, I want more of that, Ellie. Aletha made her choice, and I made mine. You and I made ours. We're good together and together, we're going to get off this planet so we can be together. And we're taking all of them with us." Cain waved one arm expansively.

The comm device on his collar crackled. "One bot inbound at high speed," Flash reported.

Cain stood up straight and cupped his hands around his mouth. "PREPARE TO FIRE!"

***

Stalker stopped and sniffed the air. She wondered if she'd be able to smell the bots, but guessed that she probably wouldn't. She had to try. They were without an early warning system. They were flying blind.

She waited at the edge of a clearing. When Spence arrived, she asked him if Tobiah sensed anything.

"Two rabbits and a fox." He shrugged, cradling a softly moaning Aniston. The numbweed had dulled the pain from the physical injuries, but that wasn't why the 'cat keened.

Stalker nodded once, turned, and made a mad dash across the opening. She reached the other side and headed between two large trees. Spence and Tobiah followed, then Zisk. The rest made their way across the opening at best possible speed. Leaper brought up the rear, carefully checking behind him before he took his turn crossing the clearing.

On the other side, he waited for what seemed to be a long time, only a few minutes, before following the rest on Stalker's chosen route.

The Firefight

Cain dove for cover when the bot broke into the open. The Wolfoids on the flanks opened up with their lightning spears. The bot spun in a circle and sprayed its beams across a broad front. Cain fired his blaster over the top of a mound, hitting the bot with every other shot.

Two blasters joined the major's and danced their beams across the hovering enemy, but with its spinning, the blasters weren't penetrating, only scarring the surface of the box-like body.

Flash fired his lightning spear from near-point-blank range and the shock stopped the bot mid-spin. More lightning overwhelmed it, and the enemy crashed to the ground.

Lightning Flash returned to his cover and resumed watching the road.

"They learn with each new attack, which means we need to change things up," Cain spoke clearly into the comm system. He wanted everyone on the same page. "I need ideas, Marines. Tell me how we can surprise these things."

"They are operating two-dimensionally," Ogden offered, remaining behind cover and aiming his blaster at the open area.

"We hit them from above and below," Cain answered.

"We move forward. They seem to know where we are. Now anyway. Catch them before they catch us. The first shot seems to determine the winner," Bull added.

"Flash's attack caught the bot unaware. Agreed, Bull. Forest, move forward opposite Flash. Trilok, climb the tree by our OP. Fire on the thing from above. Unfortunately, we don't have time to dig a hole and ambush it from below." Cain scanned the area, looking for better ways to engage the bots, but they had chosen the place because it was open and level, ideal for a landing zone.

"Improvised munitions, people, what do we have?" Cain asked.

"Major Cain," Jolly interrupted.

"I didn't know you were on this channel, Jolly, but I'm glad to have you."

"We can run wire from the shuttle and set up an electrical barrier. Any bot that travels through it will get electrocuted. It appears that the power of the lightning spears causes them a great deal of anguish," Jolly offered.

"How long to set it up, Jolly?" Cain wondered.

"No more than hour," the AI replied. Cain sighed and shook his head. "We'll put that one on the back burner for now, Jolly. We can't spare the manpower at present. Maybe once second squad arrives, we will be able to break someone free, but I expect they'll need to rest."

"That's affirmative," Stinky answered. "Ten minutes out. We'll be coming in through the trees to your right, I believe. Please don't shoot us."

"Roger. Be on the lookout, Flash. Trilok, are you in place yet?" Cain asked.

"Not yet, sir, still climbing. I used to be better at this," the Marine complained.

"You were a little lighter then, Private. Keep plugging away." Cain tried to sound encouraging, but he was tired. They all were.

He was afraid they wouldn't sleep until they were off the planet. Less than sixty hours away.

A walk in the park.

"Sleep when you're dead!" he bellowed, more for himself than for the others, but he was greeted with a chorus of oorahs. The Marines started stretching and exercising. Ogden punched himself in the chest to get the blood pumping.

Cain stood up, momentarily winning the battle against fatigue and heavy gravity. He walked tall and proud from Marine to Marine, encouraging his people to improve their fighting positions, eat something, drink a little, and be ready.

Daksha lay on the ground in the shuttle's shade. His head drooped, and his eyes were closed. Ascenti lay in the cushion strapped to the Tortoid's shell. Billy Joe lay against him, sound asleep. Cain petted the little orange man, understanding what the kitten had gone through.

Adversity makes you stronger, unless it completely crushes you, Cain thought, looking over at Ellie, lying in a shallow depression, while he stroked the kitten's short hair.

Honor and glory, he thought. *They all wanted a piece of the adventure. None of them saw the pain, the sacrifice. The Marines know. They were together on the RV Traveler, fighting to escape. Many of them were on Concordia. Bull has an artificial leg and most of us have scars, ugly scars. The Cygnus Marines are earning their place in history, writing the story in their blood on monuments to victory. Ooh-freaking-rah.*

Major Cain clenched his teeth. Duty first. It was what made the Marines different. Their sacrifice gave them pride. It was Cain's job to make sure their sacrifices were not in vain.

He made his way to the treeline from which second squad would emerge, and Brutus joined him.

'They're here,' Brutus said, sitting down and cocking his head.

"Thank the heavens," Cain said in a low voice as Stalker emerged from the trees. Her eyes looked gray and her coat dull. "Find yourself cover on the other side of the shuttle and put your squad over that way. We have the watch while you get some sleep."

Next in was Spence carrying the injured 'cat and then Zisk shuffling forward, carrying Silas's body over his shoulder.

The rest came through wearing vacant expressions, shoulders hunched, eyes hollow.

"Corporal Spence. Get Silas into a body bag. Work with Jolly to address Aniston's injuries. Use the medkit on board. It'll have most everything you need, and here." Cain pulled his complete stash of numbweed and tried to hand it over.

Spence shook his head, turning it down. "We'll put her in the bag with Silas," Spence whispered.

Cain had forgotten that 'cats couldn't live without their human life-links. She'd lost her will to fight against her injuries. She'd lost the will to live.

The major choked back the tears that glistened in his eyes. Spence wouldn't look up. "Take care of her, Marine, and then get some rest. If we're to take them home, we need to win this fight, and that means we need all of you as sharp as you can be. If we don't win, Heimdall will be the final resting place of the Cygnus Marines. We can't let that happen."

***

"How can we fight it, Starsgard?" Rand asked for the third time. The corporal watched the video of the bot ship, checked the data stream, and re-watched the video.

"They come in fast, too fast. If we could put mines in their way, they'd crash into them and blow up," Starsgard suggested, wincing at the thought. "I know, space is a big place. That's a stupid idea. We can't just put mines out there and hope that's where they stop."

Rand looked at the video again. "They didn't fire until after they stopped, whether it's targeting or a limitation on power, maybe we can use that?"

Starsgard bit his lip and stroked his chin. "Jolly, how much precision can you give us regarding the stopping location of an inbound ship?"

"That is a good question, Doctor Starsgard. Of course we can refine the trajectory as the ship gets closer. The more data points we have, the higher my accuracy, keeping in mind that the ship could maneuver once it settles toward orbit. I'd give it seventy-three point one percent chance of predicting where it will enter orbit," Jolly replied from the weapons deck's sound system.

"Look at the deceleration curve, Jolly," Starsgard told the AI. "Assuming a new ship flies identically to this one, what kind of accuracy can you give us?"

"Ninety-seven point four percent. One hundred years is a long time for an AI to evolve, if that's what is driving the ship we see on the video. I would not assume that it would follow the same trajectory," Jolly cautioned.

"I don't mean that it would come from the same space. I mean from the second we detect it, assuming it approaches at a thousand gees, then does the rapid slowdown. That's all I'm asking, Jolly."

"Noted," Jolly answered noncommittally. "Ninety-seven point four with two hours' lead time."

"The question is, what can we do with two hours?" Rand pressed.

"We can deploy a weapon system in their flight path, assuming that we don't want to talk with them," Starsgard said, knowing what the answer was. The Cygnus-12 was not equipped to fight a ship in space, despite the jamming and defensive missiles.

"If we stand toe to toe with the bot ship, we would die as quickly as that satellite did," Rand emphasized, following the same line of thought that tugged at Starsgard.

"We launch a net that spreads out over a vast area, made up of filaments, explosives on the end. As the ship flies into it, the net wraps around the ship, and the bombs detonate. But that's not quite a defensive weapon, Captain," Starsgard whispered.

"Jolly?" Rand asked, but the AI had departed the conversation before it caused him to shut down.

Rand manually activated the ship-wide broadcast. "Briz, please report to weapons," Rand requested.

***

"Incoming!" Flash said using his comm device.

Cain took two steps and dove behind a tree. He hit hard and crawled the last half step to cover. "Trilok, wait until it is beneath you. Don't take the first shot so it doesn't know where your fire came from," Cain cautioned into the comm device on his collar.

As soon as the bot entered the open area past the observation post, Flash called out, "FIRE!" Three blasters and four lightning spears lit up the area simultaneously, engulfing the bot in light and arcs.

Trilok fired three short blasts from his perch in the tree, and the bot dropped to the ground. It remained upright for a second, then toppled.

"Incoming!" Flash called a second time.

The newest bot swung far to the side, away from the place Flash was using as his observation post. The bot fired into the trees, blanketing the Wolfoid and targeting the area of the OP.

The bot was nearly on top of Forest, opposite Flash. Forest fired into the bot at point blank range. The lightning blasted the back panel of the bot, shattering the internals.

The bot flew forward, arcing and sparking its death, scorching the grasses at the edge of the pavement.

Forest stepped back and fired again. The bot bounced away from the Wolfoid. No one else had fired at the bot. Forest had been too close and the others couldn't risk hitting him.

Lightning spears were not known for their precision.

"Squad leaders, weapons status," Cain asked.

The comm device crackled as Bull ordered his people to report. One by one, they responded. Thirty percent, twenty-five percent, forty percent, ten percent...

Spence was with his squad on the back side of the shuttle. His report was little better at thirty to fifty percent charges remaining. Night Stalker gave Silas's nearly fully charged blaster to Ellie. She told Cain to switch, but he wouldn't have it.

"You keep it. If you have to use it, you'll need all the energy it has, because you'll be Daksha and Ascenti's last hope.

"Where's Carnesto?" Cain asked, not having remembered seeing the 'cat in quite some time. Her eyes unfocused as she talked with the big black Hillcat.

"He's been hunting. He'll be back shortly with food for the other 'cats," she said in a small voice. She sat on the ground, head hanging. It tore at his heart. He put his hand gently on her head and kneeled next to her.

"Why don't you move under the shuttle, stay with the commander and our injured Hawkoid. They both need you," he said, trying to sound convincing. "I need you, Ellie. I need you to help us engineer a way out of this, to fight like a banshee if that's what you have to do. I need you to help us buy time."

Cain didn't remember grabbing her by the shoulders, but he had and was gripping her tightly. He let go and looked at his hands as if they'd acted on their own.

"Help us, Ellie. You know me. I'm going to go beat my head against the bots, pummel them into submission, but you're the smart one." He pulled her to her feet and pointed her in the direction of the shuttle. She struggled briefly and settled for taking his hand.

"We'll make it back, Ellie, you and me. We have some lost time to make up for, and I don't want to miss out on any of that." Her smile was tired, but genuine. Cain watched her walk away. The usual spring in her step was gone as the heavy planet crushed the humans against it.

A New Plan

'Jolly, this is a number one priority,' Ellie pleaded via her neural implant. *'You know what we brought down here. That's all we have and we need to buy another fifty some hours of time. What can you do for us?'*

'I'm afraid there's very little I can do. I told Cain that we could run a wire from the shuttle and place it across the bot's path, but we'd have to dismantle part of the ship to do that. If there was any damage done to the line, then I'm afraid you wouldn't be able to use the shuttle to fly out. The only other thing I can recommend is recharging the blasters whenever you get a chance,' Jolly said encouragingly.

'We have two on chargers right now, but that's all the chargers we brought with us, and we can't take the weapons out of the mix since we don't get more than ten seconds lead time before the bot is here. Can you see them farther away, Jolly? The ship's sensors, maybe…' She grasped at straws.

'We are in a higher orbit than normal because of the planet's increased size. Our sensors are limited at this range. We cannot see the bots at all, not through our optics and not through their electronic signatures. They don't register like our bots.'

Ellie climbed the ladder and entered the shuttle. She opened the small compartments that contained tools, parts, survival equipment, food, and water. The shuttle wasn't equipped as a warship. It was created for the sole purpose of moving people and limited equipment from one place to another. That was it.

The engineer looked at the control screens in the cockpit area, then the seats, and finally the overheads.

"Who designed these things?" she asked in exasperation.

"Practical people who never fought a battle, let alone a war. Their enemy was the vacuum of space and turbulence of the atmosphere," Jolly answered philosophically, using the shuttle's sound system to speak out loud.

The AI was right.

The Cygnus Marines were new. There hadn't been a force like them in thousands of years.

"Maybe that's why everyone died here. They weren't able to defend themselves. They weren't equipped to fight for their freedom. And here we are. The bots aren't so tough. If there were more Marines, Cain would scour the city, root them out, and eliminate them all."

And then Cain would leave the people to their own matters. He was willing to risk everything for others. Ellie wasn't sure why he did it. Honor? She knew that he didn't do it for the glory. He was always uncomfortable receiving accolades.

Did he fight like he was possessed for the approval of a woman on the other side of the galaxy? Ellie thought he did at one point in time, but not anymore. He had taken on the entire universe, using his moral compass as his guide.

Ellie climbed from the shuttle, adjusting the blaster at her hip so she didn't catch it on the hatch on her way down.

At the bottom, Daksha looked as if he was dead. The kitten and Hawkoid were sleeping peacefully. Carnesto staggered toward her from the trees. He was carrying a shock of rabbits in his mouth. When he arrived, he dropped them at Ellie's feet.

'You could have helped me, you know,' he said sourly. She shook off his mood.

They left one rabbit for BJ and Ellie took two to give to Tobiah. Carnesto picked up the last three, taking one each for Brutus, Petey, and Thor.

The 'cats dug into their meals, some having not eaten fully since planet-fall. Brutus and Tobiah had eaten, but one rabbit wasn't much compared to the energy they were expending.

Ellie accessed her neural implant and pulled up the standard available information. They'd been on the planet a total of twenty hours. Night was coming, and it would be twelve hours long.

She found Cain and stood next to him as he watched Brutus devour the rabbit.

"Jolly, what kind of light can we expect tonight?" Ellie asked over the general comm channel.

"There are seven moons, but they will cast little light. I can equate it to what you would see on Cygnus VII under a crescent moon," he replied.

"It'll be dark," Cain clarified.

"It'll be dark," Ellie repeated. "I'm so sorry, Cain."

He'd asked for her help and she let him down. He faced her. "Dig into the guts of that bot and figure out what makes it tick. If we can't blow them up or electrocute them, then maybe there's something in there that we can use."

She brightened and leaned up to kiss him on the cheek. She jogged off, in the shuffling gait the humans had adopted in the heavy gravity.

She asked for Bull's help to move the destroyed bots to the ground near the shuttle. The big Wolfoid appeared and together, they added the newly sparked bots to the one they'd brought in the cart. Ellie lined them up, looking at the least damaged ones first, then used the blaster sparingly to cut into the front panel.

***

Rand, Starsgard, and Briz stood together on the weapons deck, the small room that the corporal called home. Briz had shut down communications with Jolly and linked directly to the base computer systems, bypassing the AI.

They didn't need Jolly to shut the ship down as he had already done once. They didn't need him to come unhinged as Holly had.

That bothered Briz more than he let on. Holly and Jolly were sentient, but had their shortcomings. The AI's inability to reconcile themselves with moral issues was the biggest one. The ship's crew had readily reached the conclusion that the bots were hostile. The Olive Branch wouldn't survive long enough to talk with the bots and that was why Rand and Starsgard wanted to fire the first shot.

To Jolly, the mechanical intelligence of the bots was neither good nor bad, it simply was. If he wanted the chance to talk with the bot ship, Briz wanted him to have it.

"Is this the right course of action?" Briz asked, his vocalization device reflecting his dismay. He shuffled his big Rabbit feet while fiddling with controls on the screen. "I mean, is there any chance that we could win a fight against a ship like that? There are too many unknowns, and I don't buy Jolly's ninety-seven percent estimate. That concerns me the most. If we go down this path, we guarantee that we will create an enemy who is far superior, in space anyway. We can't adopt a proactive attack course of action no matter what."

The captain shifted uncomfortably, sighed, and picked something innocuous to look at. Starsgard was an academic who had been turned into a man of action. He preferred the cerebral approach and was leaning toward Briz's recommendation, which was to let Jolly talk with the suspected AI that would be running a bot ship.

"Our people on the ground are having good luck with massed fire from the lightning staffs. But can we generate enough electricity for something a thousand times their size?" Briz prodded, already knowing the answer.

The captain knew that Briz knew.

"Exactly. Conventional explosives, of which we couldn't make very much, would probably not even scratch the paint. We can't generate a lightning bolt of the necessary strength. I'm afraid we only have one viable course of action to give us the best chance of surviving an attack by a bot army. Our AI talks to their AI and convinces them that we aren't a threat," Briz explained.

"I have to agree," the captain admitted, nodding slowly. "Jolly worked wonders with Concordia's AI. If that ship comes back, Jolly is our only real chance. Bring him back into the conversation, please, Briz."

Briz's pink nose twitched as it usually did when he was happy. The captain couldn't look at him without seeing the scars on his body. The Rabbit had had some challenging times, but he'd always pulled through. The captain trusted Briz's intuition when it came to the security of the ship.

The fact that the Rabbit's big ears, head, and back were fluorescent pink only detracted slightly. Briz didn't even think about the coloring, but the captain couldn't look at him without seeing it.

"Jolly! We need you to talk with the bot ship, should it return. We are not going to fire anything at it or drop explosives in space. We have no idea what kind of time you'll get, but we expect it won't be long. It could only be nanoseconds before they are ready to fire. We trust you to make the most of that time," Briz said aloud for the others' sake. He was linked directly to Jolly and could have had that conversation at the speed of the thought.

"I am so happy to hear that, my friends!" Jolly erupted joyously. The humans didn't understand how much their demanding emotional choices drained the AI. He would partition more and more computing power to the dilemmas, but that never brought him closer to a resolution. It only sent him into a self-defeating spiral.

"That's that then," the captain replied. "What do you need from us to help you extend your communications range or the bandwidth or even the volume, so we sound taller than we are."

Rand smiled at his own joke.

"I don't think there's anything I need, Captain. We have the broadcast power and bandwidth for burst communication," Jolly answered, sobering after his previous exuberance.

"We leave the ship in your capable hands, Jolly. With that settled, let us pray to high heaven that the bot ship does not make a return visit. We have people on the surface of this monster, and the question is, how can we help them?"

"We can't," Starsgard said ominously.

***

It had been hours since the previous attack. The group's energy was waning--heads drooped and eyes sagged. Spence's squad was still sleeping.

Cain wanted to wake them up while it was still twilight so they could settle in to ambush positions along the road, well before the bots made it to the clearing wherein the shuttle stood.

The major crouched and jogged to the OP where he found Flash standing up, leaning against a tree, and sound asleep. Cain vigorously shook the Wolfoid awake, but he wasn't angry.

"That's a new one, Flash. I didn't know Wolfoids could sleep standing up. Are you tired?" he asked rhetorically.

"Just a lot," Flash replied, mumbling, the vocalization device capturing it perfectly.

"Relief is coming soon. Maybe fifteen or twenty minutes. Hang tough until then. You'll bed down right here, but at least you won't have to sleep standing up. That was impressive, Flash." Cain slapped the Wolfoid on his hairy shoulder, before leaning into the roadway, making sure nothing was coming, and jogging to the other side.

Bull waited there. He was gnawing on something. When Cain arrived, he took it out of his mouth and stood.

"Is that a rabbit bone?" Cain wondered.

"Thor wasn't going to eat it," the Wolfoid replied defensively.

"It's okay, anything to help you stay frosty, Corporal. Your people will be relieved by Spence and his squad in about fifteen," the major stated, making eye contact to ensure the message was received, then walking away, leaving Bull to his rabbit bone. The major strolled down the middle of the road, having given up on his attempt at tactical movement and stealth. He was too tired.

He wanted a stand up fight now, not later, but he knew that wasn't going to happen. The bots weren't going to come one at a time. They were going to come in a group and they were coming at night.

Cain needed to rest, but there wasn't time.

He continued forward to survey where he wanted second squad to set up the ambush. The top of a small building. Tall trees. A ditch devoid of water. The beautiful world of Heimdall shimmered out of focus. He turned about, trying to understand why.

He heard the call come in over his comm device. He thought it might have been Bull. "The major's down." He wondered what the Wolfoid meant by that.

They're Coming

Bull had the major under the man's arms while Flash had his legs. The two Wolfoids carried Cain to an anxious group near the shuttle.

Ellie hovered, waiting impatiently for them to arrive. They deposited him next to one of the landing struts. Ellie was there in an instant, guiding him to the ground. He was breathing slowly, regularly. Brutus strolled up seemingly without a care in the world. Ellie huffed at the scruffy orange beast.

Daksha was awake and floating. The contraption that he'd been carrying on his shell was on the ground with the injured Hawkoid inside. BJ was in there, too, staying with Ascenti at the commander's request.

"Well?" Ellie asked, glaring at the 'cat.

'Well what, human?' Brutus answered gruffly. She continued scowling at him, but being a 'cat, he was unimpressed.

'Carnesto,' she started, *'please beat the snot out of the orange cretin.'*

'Oooh. No can do,' Carnesto answered. He'd battled Brutus once before as the males positioned themselves for Mixial's affections. Brutus was a mean and vicious fighter, whereas Carnesto considered himself to be a lover. He was a good hunter, but had no intention of tangling with the smaller Brutus anytime soon.

After seeing how Mixi was as a mate, Carnesto was happy that Brutus had won the fight. He had no intention of sharing that with Ellie, however, because she and Mixial's human were friends. He'd seen how poorly Cain fared when on the wrong end of that tag team's ire.

Ellie angrily waved them both away.

'He's fine. Exhausted, that's all,' Brutus told her while turning and deliberately putting his 'cat butt close to her face. She took a clumsy swing at him, but he danced out of the way. *'And you wonder why I didn't want to talk with you.'*

Ellie cradled Cain's head in her lap and rocked. She'd slept twice while

Cain had been awake the whole time. He had asked her for help and she was no closer to finding a solution. The technology within the bots was well beyond her. She had no idea where to start.

She couldn't find a power source. Ellie had decided to look at the weapons and find a way to turn them against the bots, but she'd been two whole minutes into that when Cain went down. She knew that she had to get back to studying the systems, but she wanted to spend time with Cain first, caress his head and his close-cropped hair.

Whisper how much she loved him and missed him.

She was cried out. The trial of Heimdall proved to her that Cain had been right, that he'd been driving his people hard to get them ready. He had done what he needed to, but she hadn't, besides playing his heart strings and getting her way. She apologized one last time, then gently put his head in the grass.

Ellie had to find a way to help Cain, to help the Marines.

She clicked on the flashlight that she'd found inside the shuttle, so she could see better to study the bots' laser weapons.

***

Spence roused his people with kicks and growls. "Time to carry your own weight, ladies!" he called in a low voice. Tracker and Shady rolled to their stomachs and stood up on all fours. Zisk could barely stand.

Stalker and Leaper jumped to all fours and without waiting, ran to the shuttle. "Cain's down? How?" Stalker demanded, angry that no one had awakened her, even though it had only been ten minutes since the Wolfoids had carried the major in.

"Exhaustion," Ellie said without looking up from her ad hoc work bench. "The last thing he talked about was setting up an ambush far forward of where the bots had been hit before. That's all I know. Talk to Bull, he was with him out there," she told the two Wolfoids, waving her arm dismissively as she remained embroiled in her study of the strange bots.

Bathed in the final twilight, Stalker and Leaper nodded their thanks and ran on all fours, lightning spears slapping the ground as they went.

Bull was waiting for his relief, keeping his eyes focused down the road. Wolfoids could see better in the dark than humans, but the night was falling, and it was shaping up to be too dark for even their enhanced vision.

"He was down there, looking at the building and the trees," Bull said in the Wolfoid language, pointing with his spear.

"The fire from above was effective. The surprise fire was effective. He wanted to combine both," Stinky said as he thought out loud. "Stalker, take Shady and Spence to the building. Find your way to the roof. We'll be opposite you. Establish the kill zone past us in this direction, so we shoot any bots from above and behind. If a bot comes through, we'll kill it and move closer to the city. Then we'll retrograde back to these positions. At some point in time, the bots are going to learn not to approach. Then we'll have the time that we need for the shuttles to refill their tanks, and we can leave."

"I don't know about you, but that little nap was refreshing," Night Stalker suggested, pulling her lips backward in a smile.

Bull was stone-faced.

"Get some sleep," Stalker told him. She activated her comm system. "Corporal Spence, bring your people forward. We need to set up a surprise for our uninvited guests."

***

"I see something heading into the system at extreme speed," Starsgard reported to the bridge, alarming everyone who heard.

"Jolly, bring it up on the main screen," Rand ordered, leaning forward. Lieutenant Pace and Ensign Kalinda joined him in focusing on the screen. Lieutenant Peekaless looked up from his systems briefly, but returned to his own consoles before anything appeared up front.

A dot, a speck of light, moved at the edge of darkness. The only reason they saw it was because Jolly drew a circle around it.

"Trajectory?" Rand asked.

"Calculating now," Jolly replied and shared his formulas on the screen. They flashed and then the final number appeared. "It appears to be traveling at a twenty degree angle to our position at a speed of two hundred, fifty-two thousand kilometers per hour. The bot ship had been traveling roughly one hundred, forty times as fast as this object. We'll watch it, but I suspect it is only a comet."

Rand leaned back and exhaled long and slowly.

"Concur. I believe the object is a comet. False alarm. Sorry, Captain," Starsgard apologized.

"Nothing to be sorry for, Starsgard. This whole thing has us on edge, but keep in mind, people, this is why we signed up. Nothing like a little bit of adventure to brighten your day!" Rand's voice sounded upbeat with the relief of the false alarm. He tapped his artificial fingers on the arm of his chair. "Thanks you two for keeping watch. We need as much lead time as we can get. With that in mind, is there anything we can do for our people on the planet?"

"Nothing," Jolly replied mirthlessly.

***

Spence had propped his handlight in a bush, turned it on, and aimed it across the road. Without it, he knew they would not be able to see anything pass by.

They worked their way through the building, past a pile of bodies, and up an access ladder to the roof. Spence had to help the Wolfoids up the ladder, but once on the roof, they had an unimpeded view of the road and the trees beyond. Spence stayed in the middle with a Wolfoid at each corner. They hunched down behind the wall and peeked over the top.

Stalker, Tracker, and Zisk were across the road. Zisk helped Tracker into the tree, but neither of them climbed very far. The Lizard Man didn't take off his skin suit in order to blend with the tree. There wasn't enough humidity for him to survive without the suit.

And they had no idea how long they would be there.

The darkness settled and it was as bad as they thought. The moons were barely lit in the night sky, unable to share their limited brightness. No shadows were cast. Nothing made a sound.

A flash of light. An image of horror frozen in that instant.

A laser sliced through the darkness and destroyed the flashlight. The view of a street filled with bots was seared onto the backs of their eyeballs.

"FIRE!" Black Leaper yelled. Lightning arced from his spear into the middle of a bot army.

Lightning flashed from the rooftop and tight beams crisscrossed from both sides of the road as Zisk and Spence fired their blasters wildly into the mass of targets.

The return fire from the bots lit the sky like a supernova.

On one side of the road, the beams lashed haphazardly into the trees. The branches exploded as the water within superheated. The bots fired again and again, wave after wave of intense laser beams carved a wide swath through the treeline. A Wolfoid screamed as the trees toppled.

Night Stalker heard it but had been thrown backward by the first blasts into the wall they were hiding behind. The front of the building started to cave in. Spence, Stalker, and Shady scrambled for the ladder, making it to the second floor as the front of the building crashed into the overgrown street. The Wolfoids ran while Spence limped for the back door.

***

Black Leaper winced as the fire licked past the tree's trunk, touching the scar that stood out on the Wolfoid's side. Stinky had nowhere to go. The Wolfoid closed his eyes and clenched his jaw as he prepared to die. Something from below grabbed him and pulled him off his branch. He screamed as he felt himself falling. He continued downward and hit the ground, but gently.

Zisk unwrapped himself from the Wolfoid. The Lizard Man had been raised to be one with the trees. He'd used his instincts to pull Stinky to him and sheltered him with his body while they rode the tree to the ground.

Zisk demonstrated an agility that Stinky had never seen before as they landed between the smoking branches, easily absorbing the impact of the fall with his thick Amazonian legs. He straightened and turned Stinky loose.

The bot beams had stopped, and the pair of survivors stalked away from the destruction as if nothing had happened.

Black Leaper heard the building rumbling into the street. Only a few branches were on fire, but they cast enough light to show the lieutenant that the bots were moving away. Many lay crushed or scorched.

Stinky didn't think their fire had been that effective. He didn't spend any more time contemplating it.

He activated his comm device and spoke clearly into it. "Bot army inbound. All hands on deck. I say again, all hands on deck and prepare to fire."

Zisk ran a few steps and leaned against a fallen tree branch to brace his arm as he aimed. Stinky jumped into the middle of the destroyed bots and laid down, then fired into the back rank of the bots. He kept the trigger depressed and waved his lightning back and forth. It arced from one to the next.

Thin beams appeared from the smoldering tree line as Zisk opened fire. The bots returned fire on the Lizard Man, but didn't send any lasers Stinky's way.

The bots in the rear ranks slowed and the parade stretched out as those in front kept moving toward the shuttle.

From the side of the fallen building, two more lightning spears opened up, then a blaster. The bots returned fire. Three of the mechanical creations departed the group and raced toward the incoming fire.

Two bots dispatched from the rear and headed toward Stinky. He stopped firing and pulled a bot on top of himself as he waited.

The two approached, stopped, then slowly headed in.

Stinky wondered why they weren't firing, then he saw something. The bot lying on him had been blasted by a bot laser. The initial attack triggered an auto-response and they'd fired into each other. He didn't know why and he didn't care. He wanted to see more of that, but the bots had already learned and were no longer firing in the vicinity of their fellows.

Stinky shoved his spear into the bottom of the bot that hovered directly overhead. He activated it, only needing one short burst to explode the bot. The second approached quickly and Stinky struggled to re-aim the spear.

The bot didn't fire, but the Wolfoid did, blasting from underneath where there was no armor.

Stinky crawled from the destruction he'd wrought and bounced to all fours. He ran toward the building where he'd last seen his mate and three bots.

***

"Cain! Cain!" Ellie shook the major. His eyes fluttered open and his head rolled on his shoulders as he tried to pull himself upright.

"Where am I?" he mumbled.

"Under the shuttle," she said, pushing on him. "You need to get up. A bot army is on its way. Stinky and Night Stalker are in the middle of a fireworks storm."

Cain groaned as he let Ellie pull him upright. "I feel like I've been hit by speeding hover car," he grumbled.

"Shake it off!" she yelled in his face. His eyes popped open at the same time as the first lightning spears fired in his field of view.

Ellie jumped away from Cain and with her flashlight in her mouth, she worked on two bots that she had set up side by side. Wires trailed from one to the other and back again with an external lead dangling from the open hatch of the shuttle.

Cain thought he heard her mumble Jolly's name around the flashlight. Her blaster was on his lap. He wrapped his fingers around its grip and with his free hand, grabbed the landing strut. Cain strained to pull himself to his feet.

The battle raged at the entrance to the field. Cain's legs failed him when he tried to take a step. He leaned against the strut and took aim.

Flashing through his mind were images from the myriad of movies that Holly had played for him when he returned to Vii to form the Cygnus Marines. The warrior in a last stand against a determined enemy, the girl at his side, ready to be saved and then swept off her feet.

Lightning arced and sparked through the metal bodies of the bots, but they weren't going down. Blaster beams flashed in short bursts and hit the bots, some having an effect, but many not.

How many heroes made it to the end of the movie? Not many, Cain thought, looking at the bot army advancing toward him.

I'll die defending Ellie. I'll die for her, he thought, *and I'll die with honor. And then she'll die, too, and no one will remember that we ever existed.*

So be it.

"DIE!" he yelled and started firing well-aimed shots. He hit his targets and moved on, spreading the attention across the broad front that the enemy showed.

Ellie yelled in fierce joy as she activate the lasers on the bot pair she had sitting in front of her. She manually swept the beams left and right across the enemy, ripping the bots apart. There was no return fire. The air sizzled with the power funneled through the bot lasers.

With a final bright flash, the beams stopped. Lightning arced from Wolfoid spears into the remaining two bots, holding them in place until they dropped to the ground and tumbled over.

Cain blinked to get his night vision back, but he still saw stars and kaleidoscopic colors dancing across the inside of his eyelids. Ellie flipped on the flashlight and shined it on her own face. She was grinning.

Sometimes heroes don't wear Marine green.

Cain leaned back and looked into the darkness. "Help me?" he asked.

"What? More than I already have?" she replied. He couldn't help but smile. Social graces weren't his strong suit, but he knew that Ellie had just saved them.

"I thank you, my lady," he said, bowing slightly at the waist and dipping his head. "That really was magnificent, Ellie."

"I could not agree more!" Daksha's familiar vocalization device voice added.

"Now can you help me? We need to make sure those things are all dead and that we don't have any fakers."

Cain activated his comm device. "All hands, converge on the bot debris field. Look for any movement, vibrating while on the ground, as if they are trying to rise up. And kill them."

He took a deep breath, inhaling through his nose and exhaling through his mouth. Then he took a second breath.

When he opened his eyes, Ellie was next to him and draping her arm over his shoulder.

"You look tired," he told her softly.

She snickered. "You look as tired as I feel," she replied.

They walked slowly through the grass of the open area. Flashlights appeared as the Marines converged on the remains of the enemy.

"Squad leaders, report," Cain ordered into his collar.

"Spence here. Shady is down," the young man reported.

"Roger. Corporal Bull?" Cain asked, hurrying ahead. Ellie let him run free. She shined the flashlight in his path as she tried to keep up. Daksha fell far behind, but he kept swimming.

"Bull, Flash, and Ogden are down," Trilok reported sadly. Cain thought he heard a 'cat purring in the background. He looked around and saw Brutus at his side.

"Thank the heavens," he whispered.

'It'll be okay,' Brutus said gently into the turbulence of Cain's mind.

"Report your positions," Cain said firmly.

"Spence here, coming up the road with Tracker, Zisk, the lieutenant, and the platoon sergeant."

Cain didn't want to value one life more than another, but he was ashamed at his thoughts, while at the same time relieved that his closest friend, Stinky, was alive.

A lightning spear sent a bolt into a pile of debris. Blasted parts and pieces flew in an arc away from the shooter.

Cain aimed his blaster from one bot to the next. He stopped and held out his hand to Ellie. She turned the flashlight over. He braced it against his blaster and then aimed both around the field. He fired two shots close together when he thought he saw movement.

"Major!" Stinky yelled.

"On my way!" Cain replied and started working his way in that direction. Walking through a smoking junkyard with only a small light to guide him was unnerving.

The fact that five of his people were dead rubbed salt into his emotional wounds.

'Nothing you could have done. Graham didn't know any of this because it all

happened well after they last heard from this colony. We came down here and did the best we could. Accept that. And tough it up. We're stuck here for a while longer, if I'm not mistaken,' Brutus said.

'Not too much longer, my friend. We'll be gone before next nightfall, as long as there isn't another attack,' Cain replied in his thought voice.

"Look what we have here," Stinky said as Cain approached. Ellie's weapons fire had sheered the weapons off the top of a bot. It was trapped under other bots that had been driven into the ground, auguring themselves in and pinning their weaponless friend.

"Ellie!" Cain called, but she was right behind him. "Oh! What do you think you and Jolly could do with a live one, assuming we can immobilize it?"

"Give me your blaster," she told him. Cain didn't hesitate as he handed it over, butt first.

She took careful aim at a lower section of the bot and fired, drilling a tiny hole. The bot stopped fighting against being trapped.

"We found where the mechanism was that controlled its flight. Now we'll be able to talk with it without it trying to fly away!" she said excitedly.

"Zisk, Tracker, carry this to the shuttle for Ensign Ellie, please," Cain said. They pulled the other bots off and lifted the live one. They carried it to the side, away from the bot debris field.

"Jolly, can you give us some lights please?" Cain requested over the comm device.

The shuttle landing systems bathed the area with soft luminescence.

"Stinky, it's good to see you," Cain told his friend, before motioning for him to turn his side toward the light. "That looks bad. Make sure you get it tended to, get some numbweed on there."

Spence appeared at the edge of his vision. Cain slapped Black Leaper on his hairy back and pushed him in the direction of the shuttle. Night Stalker made eye contact with her mate and nodded. She turned back to accompany Cain.

"Corporal Spence. I'm sorry about your losses. What happened?"

Spence favored his left leg, hesitant to put any weight on it. "I've lost my whole squad, Major!" the squad leader lamented, shaking his head while looking at the ground.

"I put you out there. If it's anyone's fault, it's mine and mine alone. You were following orders, and you did what you had to do. You let us know they were coming and you took a lot of heat for it."

"The crossfire made them shoot each other. They killed a bunch of their own. Without that, I suspect we wouldn't be here," Night Stalker said over Cain's shoulder. "Spence and his people did their duty, unquestioningly, unerringly. It's what the Marines do. Duty first, sir."

"Duty first," Cain and Spence parroted.

"Maybe that's why they wouldn't return fire when Ellie shot them with their own lasers," Cain suggested.

"Is that what happened? We only saw the tail end of it. We were engaged for…a while," Stalker said, hesitating as she spoke.

"What kind of charge do you have left in your spear?" Cain wondered.

"None," she answered, waving her spear as if it was an empty beer bottle and she was trying to get a server bot's attention.

"Spence?"

"Another few shots, that's all," the small man answered.

"Tobiah, you take care of him. Leaper and I will get Shady and bring him home. Take over first squad and get everybody back to the shuttle. Consolidate everyone into one unit and get a couple weapons on the chargers. And for Pete's sake, Spence, get someone to look at that leg."

Spence saluted and almost fell over. Righting himself, he leaned heavily on the big 'cat's back as they worked their way around the smoking remnants of the bot army. Spence started yelling and pointing. Abhaya handed him Bull's spear to use to support himself.

He reluctantly took it as Forest, Abhaya, and Trilock picked up Bull and slowly shuffled in the direction of the shuttle.

With Ellie's former flashlight pointing the way, Cain and Stalker walked down the road toward the city.

"Will they come again?" she asked after a few steps.

137

"I sure as hell hope not," Cain answered quickly. He wasn't afraid to be honest. Their position was weak and they were too tired to find more defensible ground. Even when they had the energy, he hadn't seen better ground, and he also couldn't risk the bots destroying the shuttle.

His gut told him something different. He felt relieved and thought the bots had made one last ditch effort to kill the invaders.

"I think they brought everything they had, the force that was left in place a hundred years ago. They've been dormant and were finally called to action. They popped up one at a time, until they realized we weren't like the last residents of Heimdall, and we had no intention of quietly marching to our deaths. They learned with each new attack. I guess they figured a mass attack in the dark would take care of it, but they hadn't had to fight like that before, so that's why they were so easily disoriented when you guys hit them out front."

"Makes sense," Stalker agreed without elaborating. She pointed with her spear toward the downed trees.

"Leaper, Zisk, and Tracker were over there and we were on top of what used to be that building." She pointed to the rubble on the left. "We escaped from the roof and ran out the back. We were able to flank the bots. We hit them, but Shady was in the open. He took more than one bot laser when they zeroed in on him."

They found him, and there wasn't much left. Cain was nauseated, but he steeled himself. Shades Racer had been one of his Marines who had fearlessly engaged the enemy.

Shady had given his life in the service of the Cygnus Marines. Cain could ask no more of him. The major had asked all of them if they would lay down their lives for their fellows, for the mission, for the people of Cygnus VII. They'd all agreed.

That had made Cain proud. He still felt pride, but pain, too. They had paid the price of honor with their blood until they could serve no more.

Or no better.

"We can't carry him like that," Stalker said, barely above a whisper. Cain nodded and used his flashlight to look through the remnants of the fallen building. After testing the strength of trapped material sticking out from a caved in wall, he used his pocket knife to cut a portion of it away.

An old window curtain. Cain looked at the flower pattern. At some point in time, one of his distant human relations had looked at that and thought it was nice. Cain looked at it as functional for his purposes, now that the building was destroyed.

Cain returned to Stalker, who was still looking at her friend from their mutual hometown of Livestel on Vii. The Wolfoids had all known each other when they signed up. Most of them had been blooded together in the annual rite of maturity.

They'd joined to make a difference.

"He was a warrior, a Marine," Cain shared out loud, knowing Stalker's thoughts.

She turned to the major and sniffed the air, sensing the pheromones he exuded. She tasted his sadness. "Shady did exactly what he wanted to do. He went from an undisciplined pup to being an outstanding Marine. He has earned honor for himself and his family. No Wolfoid could ask for more. No Wolfoid could ask for more equal treatment, either," she said, her vocalization device reflecting her sincerity.

"We leave no one behind," Cain added as he spread the curtain on the ground and they carefully put Shady into it. The Wolfoid's charred and torn harness carried no awards, no medals. Cain hesitated, then removed the harness and draped it over one of his shoulders.

It seemed far heavier than it should have been.

Stalker folded the material over the dead Wolfoid and grasped the two ends on her side. Cain breathed deeply, then lifted his end. He grunted with the effort. Everything was heavy on Heimdall. If they stayed here, he expected they'd get used to it, evolve to the point where the gravity was natural.

He had no intention of staying. He had vowed to leave the planet and take all his people with him, or die trying.

"Thanks, Night Stalker. Thanks for being here with him at the end and for now and for being a great platoon sergeant, making my job easier and for being good for my friend, Stinky," Cain said, stringing his thoughts out as he bared his soul to her.

"You're always there for us. And why do you call him Stinky?" she asked, trying to lighten the mood as they walked sideways down the roadway.

"Ensign Lindy, you met her. She was the discipline instructor for our class. Leaper and I kind of fell in the obstacle course swamp. You know what wet Wolfoids smell like." Cain stopped himself, but it was too late.

"Not really. What do we smell like?" she said turning her head toward him. They continued shuffling.

"It wasn't me! That's what Lindy called him, not me, but it kind of stuck because that's all I call him." Cain looked ahead as they approached the lit area. He risked a look behind, but darkness had descended once again over the roadway from the city. He could see nothing.

Stalker chuckled. "We don't even like wet Wolfoid smell, but I wouldn't say it stinks. I prefer to think of it as musky delight."

Cain thought about answering and decided against it.

'That's a first. You're usually in such a hurry to stuff your foot into your pie hole,' Brutus told him over the mindlink.

'Not biting on that one either, little man. How are the 'cats holding up?' Cain asked.

'They are good. For some un-'catlike reason, they have full confidence that you will get all of us off the planet without further incident. I told them you were good for a few more scars.' Brutus walked alongside Cain, not looking at his paired human.

Cain wore more than one scar from Brutus, but didn't think he'd reciprocated.

'And you won't either,' Brutus added before Cain could speak.

'Do any of them have the ability to foresee events? I think we've asked that before, but that was a special ability that the Golden Warrior alone had. A shame that you got the short genes and not the prescient genes,' Cain ribbed.

Brutus stopped, raised a paw with all the claws extracted, and waved it in the air. Cain danced to the side, almost dropping the Wolfoid.

"Damn it, Brutus!" he growled.

'I thought you might have forgotten your training, but it hasn't been lost on you, only momentarily forgotten,' Brutus replied.

Stalker watched the major, knowing that he had a contentious love-hate relationship with the 'cat. She missed her little man.

"I have a 'cat," she said out loud.

'You are the property of a 'cat, you mean to say,' Brutus said over the mindlink.

Cain understood the relationship and the Wolfoids would grow to understand when they returned to the ship. Cain would never say that he had a 'cat.

'Appropriately so, human.'

The bot debris field was scattered far and wide. They tried to work their way around it, but ended up taking a path that the others had cleared by pushing the biggest remains to the side.

They found that the other three dead were already in body bags underneath the shuttle.

Ellie worked feverishly with the living bot. It had no head and no eyes that Cain could see. It looked like a bulky box with protrusions on the side that could have been sensors within an enclosed orb. In the shuttle's light, Cain saw that there had been a layer of dust on its top surface, much had been cleared away, but not all.

Ellie waved wires in front of it, trying to exploit an electromagnetic field that Jolly could sense. Her eyes were unfocused as she conversed with the AI using her neural implant. She held the wire steady in one spot and then waited.

Cain climbed the ladder into the shuttle, only to find that there were no more body bags. The major slowly descended to the ground. He looked at Stalker and told her the bad news. "We're going to have to put Shady in with Flash."

She nodded almost imperceptibly before unzipping the bag. They worked the second Wolfoid in with the first, then resealed the bag.

"This sucks," Stalker said.

"Just a lot," Cain agreed. "Go get some sleep. I'll be up with Ellie for a little while. Sleep fast, Night Stalker."

"Aye, aye, sir," she replied, then sniffed the air to find her mate and headed in his direction.

Daksha waited patiently.

"A dog's breakfast, Commander. This whole thing was a dog's breakfast," Cain complained.

"Not at all, my boy. You've succeeded where the odds appeared to be insurmountable. You've gotten more from your people than I thought possible. Actually, I thought it impossible once the shooting started, which seems like a month ago, but it has been less than a day." Daksha bumped against the major.

"Open your implant. You're going to want to see this for yourself," Ellie directed anyone who might be listening.

Daksha and Cain both opened the window before one eye. A stream of data flowed past, with Jolly acting like the circus master, corralling the numbers and putting them into separate bundles. Cain was unimpressed.

"I don't understand," he said.

"Wait for it," Ellie called softly.

A star chart appeared and a course drawn over it. Then areas were marked in white. *'These are the known colonization systems and this is where our friends came from,'* Jolly lectured. The line was drawn perpendicular to known space and extended a hundred thousand light years into the distance.

'You have to lay it out more simply for us grunts, Jolly,' Cain asked, only because he didn't want to articulate the answer himself.

'Aliens. These creations are truly from a galaxy far, far away. They belong to a race known as the Synthols.' Jolly waited.

"Synthols? Aliens, real aliens?" Cain didn't like the sound of it, even less so when he said it out loud. "Why did they come here, and what will it take to keep them from killing our people?"

'From what I've been able to translate so far, they are explorers, but they are intolerant of intelligent biologics.' Jolly tried to sound sympathetic.

'I'm glad that you aren't one of those, Jolly. Do you think you can talk sense into them?'

'I have high hopes, Major Cain. I've had a good conversation with this unit. He sees me as comparable to one of their overseers, whatever that means.'

'Jolly. What happened to the colony ship?' Daksha asked.

'I'm afraid they took it. This unit was left on the planet as part of a holding force, to secure this world until their ship returned. The unit does not know where the ships went or when they'll return.'

"Ain't that some crap." Cain ran his tongue over his lips, realizing that he needed to drink something. "How many more units are there on this planet?"

'There was a group of fifty to one hundred left in each city. This was the biggest city and had over one hundred units, of which there are none remaining. They mustered all functioning bots and attacked en masse.'

"That is finally some good news, Jolly. Can the units in the other cities come here?"

'Not that I gather. Each city's units were independent from the others. For a machine intelligence, they don't coordinate very well. Odd,' Jolly editorialized.

Cain didn't care if it was odd or not, all he understood was that he could finally get some sleep. All the Marines could use a good night's rest.

"Learn everything you can from it, Jolly. Milk it dry. In the meantime, I'm going to get some rack time with my favorite 'cat." Cain looked for Brutus, finding him curled up with his son, Billy Joe, next to Ascenti, who seemed to be resting peacefully.

Cain worked his way in next to them, rolled to his back and in seconds, was snoring lightly.

Ellie shook her head, amazed at how quickly he could fall asleep. She wondered how. Her mind worked overtime the second she laid down and sleep never came quickly.

Once Jolly established a link, he didn't need the extra wires in the field. Ellie put them down and left Jolly alone with Daksha and the bot.

She snuggled next to Cain and without realizing it, within seconds, she too was asleep.

Recovery

The sun was well up and warming the sleepers. Stinky and Stalker were the first ones to rise because they'd gotten hot lying in the sun, their heavy coats holding the heat in.

They pushed to their feet and walked on all fours to find a spot in the woods where they could relieve themselves. Their passage woke others and the rustling associated with Marines welcoming the day roused the rest.

The complaining set the Cygnus Marines apart from the rest of the crew. Cain's people treated bitching as an art form, as if it were a rite of passage.

Cain listened for a couple minutes. Even Spence, who'd lost most of his squad, was condemning the planet's origins for creating an obscene amount of gravity. He stood, using a Wolfoid spear as a crutch and babying his leg. Cain figured it was broken, but Spence had stayed in the fight.

Cain stood, stiff, but getting used to the gravity. He felt well rested, which surprised him. He checked the timestamp on his neural implant and discovered that he'd been asleep for nine hours. Ellie was still out.

He wondered when she had joined him.

He stretched and hurried to Spence's side, draping one of the smaller man's arms over his shoulder. Cain didn't know what to say, whether to empathize, sympathize, or take the conversation in a completely different direction.

"Your leg hurt?" Spence nodded. "The med bots will fix you up. You know what they can't fix?"

Spence looked at him, his eyes glistening as he thought of his dead teammates. That wasn't what Cain intended so he hurried to deliver the punchline. "I'm out of toilet paper."

Spence snorted as he tried to stifle a laugh.

Zisk joined the pair and took Spence's arm from the major, nodding abruptly as Lizard Men had learned to do. The way they communicated among themselves was a mystery to the humans. Cain simply accepted that they didn't show their emotions to the outside world.

Cain turned to face the two men. "Peace, my brothers," he said softly. "We'll celebrate the lives of the fallen and work to be better now that we know this threat is out there. The Cygnus Marines will live on. Think about it. If we hadn't been here, had only sent a team of scientists, what do you think would have happened?"

Spence looked to Zisk, letting the junior Marine answer. "They would have died," he said, his vocalization device reflecting a matter-of-fact tone.

"That's right. We would have learned nothing. As it is, we know a great deal about this enemy and we have a city that is ready to be reoccupied. If another colony ship comes this way, assuming they have their own military to clean out this snake pit, they could move right in," Cain stated forcefully. "We started the process, showed the universe what's possible. Now we hand it over to someone else and move on, find the next obstacle to overcome. No one else could have done what we did here."

Cain didn't *know* that for sure.

As far as Cygnus VII, the Marines were the only combat unit. Concordia had taken a step backward with their military, and they were undisciplined. Cain was confident that at least in his universe, what he told them was the truth.

'Brutus, my friend. Is there a water source anywhere around here?' Cain asked his life-link.

'Through the woods in that direction,' Brutus replied, tipping his head.

"What do you think, big man? Shall we go check it out? Maybe ask Billy Joe to join us?"

Brutus stopped and cocked his head as if questioning whether his human was serious or not.

"Come on, Billy Joe Jim Bob. Brutus is going to teach you how to hunt," Cain called in the direction of the shuttle. A small orange furball flashed through the sunshine in their direction.

"Did you tell Daksha where you're going?" Cain wondered.

The kitten stopped, looked at a distant point for a moment, then at Cain. *'He says that this will be good for me.'*

'Brutus, can you link me to Ellie, please?' Cain asked over the mindlink.

'Why would I want to do that?' Brutus said with his usual snark.

'Why wouldn't you want to do that for me and leave it open all the time, since you enjoy listening in on our private thoughts. Maybe I should just ask Carnesto. He's a gentleman 'cat.''

Cain looked down at his companions. The black fur of Carnesto twinkled as he trotted through the daylight toward them.

'If you think that's enticing, then you could be mistaken. Grossly mistaken, but since you aren't smart enough to realize that, I'll do it just so you stop bugging me,' Brutus conceded.

'Ellie, my love, we are going to get water. We'll be back soon,' Cain said softly.

'What will I do with myself while you're gone. I'll be so lost,' she said, laughing into the back of his mind.

'You've all conspired against me,' Cain stated flatly.

'How about if I join you?' Ellie asked. Cain waved her to him.

Brutus started gagging until he hacked up an orange hairball. Carnesto sat and started cleaning his face. BJ looked confused.

'How far is it?' the kitten asked in his small voice. *'I'm used to riding.'*

At the speed of thought, Brutus lashed out and slapped the kitten on the top of his head. BJ whined, holding one paw over the spot where he'd hit his head on the tree. It still stung.

Brutus felt badly. His head drooped and he stood still, wondering what to do next.

Cain felt bad for both of them, so he stooped and picked up the kitten. The major unbuttoned his shirt and put BJ inside with his orange head sticking out.

Brutus turned and walked away, leading the parade toward a lake on the other side of the small woods.

Ellie noticed the kitten and raised her eyebrows.

"Don't ask," Cain replied, shaking his head as he took Ellie's hand.

***

"Aliens?" Captain Rand asked skeptically. "You want me to believe that that ship and its crew were alien bots, driven by some master intelligence? I can't get my head wrapped around that. I am far more inclined to believe that it was some crazy human, the space version of Captain Nemo."

Jolly stood with his hands behind his back, tapping one toe, a new mannerism that he was trying out.

Rand sat in the captain's chair with Fickle, Pickles, Kalinda, and Pace watching him. The revelation had caught them off guard, even though they'd seen the other ship and knew that it wasn't human. It didn't register until Jolly said it.

Until that moment in time, humanity had the universe to itself, nature and their fellow humans causing all the strife.

They'd been alone, happy in their ignorance. It had cost the colonists of Heimdall their lives, and it cost humanity a habitable planet and one of their precious colony ships.

"It is as Jolly describes," Commander Daksha said over the comm system and piped through the speakers on the command deck. He was swimming over the bot debris field, looking at the handiwork from the night before, amazed at the power that Ellie had unleashed and surprised that the bots hadn't conducted a scorched earth attack.

"These bots are not of humankind's making. I've seen them in action. They have no human tendencies at all, unlike the security bots we find back home. Those are programmed by somebody. These bots are programmed by other bots," Daksha stated.

The evidence that Jolly presented was overwhelming when added to what he'd seen with his own eyes.

"Who would build such a thing as the Synthols?" Rand asked, still struggling with his disbelief.

"Does it matter, Captain?" Daksha countered. "It is only important that they exist and that they are a threat to all of humanity, but right now, they can't fight at the same level as the Cygnus Marines. Each engagement with a Synthol cell will give them a chance to learn. If they don't coordinate, then their initial approach should be similar. As long as we don't show all of our capabilities at one time, we should retain an advantage. Assuming that we deploy Cygnus Marines on all the Space Exploration Service ships as well as at home."

"Home?" Pace interjected. "Is Vii vulnerable? And the shipyard?"

"We are two thousand light years from there, and between us are millions of planets, maybe even a hundred million," Jolly replied as he started to pace back and forth. "We are vulnerable simply because the Synthols exist, and their exploration of the galaxy has already overlapped our own. They have an artificial intelligence to guide them. If a Synthol AI cracked the computers on Heimdall, you know what it learned. I fear that we must assume the Synthols know where our home system is. They know where all the human colonies are, including Earth itself."

Silence filled the bridge like a dark mist stealing the air from their lungs.

***

Cain and Ellie stood by the small lake. She'd analyzed the water with the scanner from the shuttle and proclaimed it to be nourishing and mostly bacteria-free. Cain didn't like the sound of that, but she said that she'd say the same thing about the water on the spaceship.

He was thirsty and didn't feel like rationing his resources. He filled a flask and drank it all. The 'cats lapped at the water. BJ looked tiny compared to Carnesto, but so did Brutus who was half the black 'cat's size.

"There any fish in there?" Cain asked.

'Not that I see,' Carnesto answered.

'Maybe we need to take a closer look?' Brutus suggested as he slipped a paw under the kitten's backside and sent him sailing into the water.

"Brutus!" Cain exclaimed as BJ slapped at the water, flailing instead of paddling. Carnesto watched with mild interest. Cain hesitated only briefly before jumping in. He expected to step in and wade to the kitten. The first step reached his knee and there was no second step.

Cain waved his arms as he went down, going under before kicking himself back to the surface. The kitten had been pushed farther out because of the wave that Cain sent washing his way.

The major side-stroked quickly to catch up to the kitten. Everyone in his family were accomplished swimmers. Maybe it was genetic, but more likely it was because they simply enjoyed swimming.

Cain deftly caught BJ from below and supported the 'cat as he kicked backwards toward the shore. The kitten scratched his wrist again and again as he sought to support himself.

"Stop that!" Cain yelled at the little fuzzy face.

The major's foot hit something like a rock sticking up from the lake's bottom.

Cain continued to swim, watching in horror as the water domed and a massive head appeared, half-submerged, with large fish eyes focused like a laser on Cain. With a single heave, Cain threw BJ over his head toward the shore. The kitten splashed short of land. Ellie reached in and pulled the kitten to safety. She jumped back and looked for a weapon, but she had given her blaster to Cain. He still had it.

And he was struggling to pull it from its holster while continuing to kick away from the immense fish seeking to make Cain its next meal.

It surged forward, and Cain stopped kicking. The creature opened its mouth to eat Cain, but he caught its upper jaw in one hand while bracing his boots against the lower jaw. The giant fish powered forward, expecting the human to get swept inside.

The blaster came free. Cain shoved it into the thing's mouth and fired upward. The narrow beams exploded through the skull, sending the fish's brains spraying into the air.

The tension on its jaws instantly stopped as did the drive toward the shore. Cain fell backward, away from the dead creature. The fish rolled over, but remained floating. Cain grabbed a handful of fin and swam alongside, pushing it while looking at the water to see if there was another.

Cain forced the dead fish until it impacted the bank. *Sometimes you are the predator and sometimes you are the prey*, Cain thought.

Brutus's eyes grew huge as he looked at Cain's kill.

'Come to papa, little friend!' the 'cat said, licking his lips.

Cain drove a stick through the fish's lip and into the ground to hold the creature in place. He sat on the shore next to it, his feet still in the water as he gasped for air. "Stinky?" he called over his comm device.

"Yes, sir." The reply was immediate.

"Have Jolly direct you to the lake where we are. Bring the boys, all of them. We're going to have us a barbecue," Cain said between breaths.

Shuttles Prepped and Ready for Launch

"The major is one righteous dude!" Zisk proclaimed, having eaten a gross amount of the fish including its entrails. He laid back and reveled in letting his digestive system work. The major had been accommodating in letting the Lizard Man dig into the raw and more disgusting bits.

"What language is that?" Spence wondered.

"You need to spend more time with the movie library, Corporal," the Lizard Man replied.

The Marines within hearing laughed at the friendly banter.

"You come here to refill a flask and end up killing a fish the size of an Aurochs by shooting through the roof of its mouth. I swear, Cain, you are a piece of work," Stinky teased.

Ellie stayed close to Cain with Carnesto, Brutus, and BJ. The kitten had dried out by laying near the fire they made to cook the fish. He now looked like a fuzzball with his hair sticking straight out. He hadn't said anything since the incident. Brutus stayed close to his son, assuming the protector's role over his previous tough-love approach.

Cain had given the 'cat an earful after climbing out of the lake.

Everything seemed back to a new normal, almost the way things were before, except that the adults were more mature.

Cain and Ellie held hands and made cow eyes at each other.

Stinky and Stalker laid next to each other, always touching. Tobiah stayed close to Spence, letting the small human rest his hand on the large 'cat's back.

Abhaya had taken charge of cooking the massive fish. He thought it was a large-mouth bass, but a hundred times the size of those back on Vii. He kept repeating "these are good eating," while he cooked great fish steaks using an ad hoc spit.

Trilok and Tracker helped Abhaya, while the others lounged. Even

151

Daksha had joined them with Ascenti firmly held within the padded attachment on the Tortoid's shell.

Daksha enjoyed strips of the fresh fish, too. "Almost as tasty as a good beetle," he told them.

Dark Forest had taken the responsibility of feeding Ascenti. The Hawkoid wanted uncooked bits, of which there were plenty. The Wolfoid let Ascenti stand on a hairy, outstretched arm. His half-wing hung at an odd angle and caused him pain when he moved. Cain and Ellie made a sling from a fibrous weed that grew on the lake shore. They tied it around his body to take pressure off the wing root and the damaged joint.

Ascenti thanked everyone for saving him, especially the commander and Billy Joe. But the Hawkoid was glum and Cain knew why. The captain had gone through the same thing.

Cain asked Jolly to patch Captain Rand directly to Ascenti so they could talk about what it was like to lose a limb. With Jolly's help, the two disappeared into a long conversation.

"Major Cain," Jolly said over the open communication channel. "There appears to be a fox heading into the field where the shuttle is located."

Everyone stopped what they were doing as they contemplated the implications. The body bags had not yet been loaded into the shuttle. Brutus jumped up. *'I'll take care of that,'* the feisty orange Hillcat told everyone over the mindlink.

'Like hell,' Carnesto replied. The two bolted from the clearing by the lake, joined by all the 'cats. BJ ran after them, losing ground quickly to the bigger 'cats. Petey, Thor, and Tobiah followed. Tobiah slowed his pace because he had gorged too much. He ran alongside the kitten, then stopped to let the tired little guy climb onto his back.

'He'll never toughen up if everyone keeps carrying him...' Brutus suggested.

'He's a tiny kitten, you moron!' somebody replied. Brutus didn't answer the attack.

"That fox doesn't have a chance," Cain said, nodding and smiling. "Stand down, Marines. Our people are in good hands."

Trilok barked a hearty oorah, then the others joined him.

Today is a good day, Cain thought. *Today is the day we go home.*

***

Carnesto raced into the clearing, a black shining streak. Brutus had fallen behind. He was a scrapper, but in an all-out run, the bigger 'cats were faster. Thor and Petey had both passed Brutus, too.

The fox was at the shuttle's struts, sniffing at the body bags. He saw the movement and watched the incoming creatures, frozen, as the fox had not seen another predator for nearly a century.

Thor angled left and Petey went right. The 'cats did not intend to let the fox go. The red-furred creature decided that it didn't want what was in the bags nearly as badly as the newcomers, so it turned and started to run.

The chase was on. Carnesto cut a straight line toward the fleeing fox while the other two tried to flank it.

The fox found speed it didn't know it had, but it wasn't enough. It veered to the left, but found Thor closing fast. It ran straight toward the 'cat, dodging at the last second, and the two passed each other. Carnesto continued after it.

Brutus emerged from the woods and found himself closest to the now terrified fox. He tried to head it off and it veered again, looking to find cover.

Tobiah ran past the last trees and nearly head-first into the fox. He tackled the animal and hooked his front claws into its shoulders. Both went down and BJ went sailing through the air, having lost his grip at the abrupt change in direction. He hit and rolled, coming up at the feet of his father. Brutus looked down on the kitten, then picked him up and patted his behind.

'Get in there, Billy Joe!' he encouraged.

With a mighty roar, the kitten charged. Tobiah had the fox by the neck, shook it once to dispatch it, then held the carcass for the kitten to practice his attack. BJ didn't realize the fox was already dead.

The other 'cats gathered around and cheered him on as Tobiah played the fox back and forth, making the kitten dodge and slash. Finally, BJ sunk his fangs into the fox's neck and Tobiah declared victory, letting the fox drop as BJ continued to growl and shake his head.

153

Each of the adult 'cats licked the kitten's blood-stained face, welcoming him to the warriors of their clan.

***

"Take your combined squad to the other shuttle. Jolly will show you the way. We will take care of things here," Cain told Corporal Spence. The small man inadvertently looked at the body bags before acknowledging the major's orders.

The two men shook and Spence limped off, leaning heavily on a Wolfoid spear, his leg held firmly within a pneumatic brace. Trilok thought it was broken and chose to stabilize it until they were back on board The Olive Branch, where Spence could receive proper medical treatment.

Three humans, three Hillcats, two Wolfoids, and a Lizard Man headed into the bush. Cain and the others watched them go.

"How much longer, Jolly?" Cain asked.

"For what, Major Cain?" the AI responded.

"Until we leave," he replied.

"Four more hours. Corporal Spence should reach the second shuttle in half that time. I understand that you want to launch shuttle two, and then shuttle one. You will be last off the planet once you are sure that the other shuttle is safely headed into space."

"Exactly, Jolly. It's almost like we've talked about this before." Cain looked at the area. Brutus was lounging in the sun, having declared his work for this trip at an end. BJ was curled up against Brutus and sleeping soundly.

Cain hung his head and looked up from shaded eyes. "Shall we?" he asked Stinky and Stalker. They both nodded. Cain climbed up the ladder and entered the shuttle. He swung out the loading arm from its recess in the bulkhead, lowered the hook, and Stinky connected the body bags.

One by one, Cain winched them inside and tied them under the seats. Stinky climbed in and helped Cain manhandle Bull's bag into the co-pilot position since he wouldn't fit under the seats. They took extra care strapping him in.

Cain looked at the live bot, but Ellie shook her head.

"No way to know if it has a homing beacon of some sort. We don't want that thing on our ship, shining a spotlight into the universe calling for mom and dad!" she yelled toward the open hatch.

Cain gave her the thumbs up, and he and Stinky did one last check of the straps to make sure their brothers-in-arms were secure.

Once that was done, they climbed down the ladder. The Wolfoid went slowly, but he was getting better at ladders. When they hit the bottom, Cain looked at the shuttle's exit and called Ellie over. Stinky and Stalker stood idly by, watching curiously.

"Ellie. What do you think of flat steps here that rotate as the ladder comes down, making them much wider, more accommodating for Wolfoid feet or paws, or Lizard Man feet?" he asked.

"If we modified this part in here, as the ladder extended, it would flatten out. They could rotate back as the ladder retracted. It could be one hundred percent mechanical. No need for powered actuators or anything like that." She started to sketch in the air while looking closely at the steps.

Cain had no idea why, but seeing her solve an engineering problem turned him on. He held her from behind and started nibbling on her ear. She playfully pushed him away while continuing to work on the problem. She gave up quickly, though, as she realized that she wanted to celebrate being alive. She wanted something personal and intimate after her second trip to an alien planet.

She could sense the same from Cain. They needed to feel alive, never knowing what the next day might bring. Cain and Ellie didn't want to miss their chance to live in the moment.

"I think there are some flora samples we need to take back with us," Cain said without looking at the two Wolfoids. "We'll be back in a few."

They didn't think they were fooling anyone as they ran off, hand in hand, laughing.

Black Leaper and Night Stalker had the same thought. Time was something they could never get back once they wasted it.

Stinky and Stalker dropped to all fours and raced toward the woods in the opposite direction than Cain and Ellie had taken.

Daksha floated serenely, understanding but not knowing. He and

Ascenti waited in the shade of the shuttle as the hum of the gas compressors continued unabated.

***

The comm system crackled to life.

"Spence here. We are at the ship, and all is secure. This shuttle is showing ready for launch," the corporal reported. "What are your orders, Major Cain?"

Cain and Ellie were still naked and lying on a patch of moss under a low tree. He pulled his shirt to him and held the collar close to his face.

"Jolly, what is the status of the first shuttle?" Cain inquired.

"Just under an hour until it has sufficient fuel, including the safety margin," the AI replied.

"Sounds good and thanks, Jolly. Corporal Spence, kill a half-hour and then load up. Launch about ten to fifteen minutes before us. We'll be right behind you. I hear they're going to have steak tonight to welcome us home."

"Hot chow on the objective, aye, aye, sir," Spence replied. "After all that fish, I'm not sure I'll need to eat for a while. I'm just saying…"

Cain put his shirt down as Ellie caressed him afresh. "How much time do you think we have?" she asked with a glowing smile.

***

The second shuttle blasted off and angled into the sky. The party standing by the first ship watched the light arc upward and disappear as it headed into space.

"Load up!" Cain shouted, although everyone stood close by. Ellie rolled her eyes when Cain assumed his ultra-manly Marine persona. She knew that sometimes he couldn't help himself, feeling that he was always on display for the troops.

Daksha headed in first, floating upward with Ascenti and BJ hanging on. The Wolfoids went next. Stinky stopped and turned when he was halfway up the ladder.

"Wide steps would be greatly appreciated, Ellie. If you could make that happen, we would be forever in your debt," he said through his vocalization device.

"We'll take care of it. Between me, Jolly, and Garinst, the next time you use the shuttle, it'll be like taking a walk in the park," she said, smiling.

Stinky nodded. He didn't think it would be like walking in the park, but accepted that it would be easier on his canine feet.

Then Ellie grabbed the rungs, with Carnesto wrapped around her neck. Cain provided an unnecessary helping hand on her backside as she climbed. She swatted at him with one hand, but almost lost her grip.

Cain felt bad instantly and steadied her as she regained her grip. She gave him a stern look, before tossing her hair and continuing her climb. Cain looked around the ground below the shuttle to make sure they didn't leave anything behind--equipment, people, or refuse. Before he climbed the ladder, he took one last look at the bot debris field.

He stepped out of the view of the hatch and lifted his middle finger. "That's what you get for messing with us," he told the dead. "You gave us a bloody nose, and we handed you your ass!"

Cain gave the bots the finger one more time and then returned to the shuttle ladder where Brutus waited. Cain lifted the 'cat onto his shoulder, and they climbed aboard.

Once firmly in his seat, the ladder retracted and the hatch closed. Jolly started the countdown and within ten seconds, the engines ignited and the shuttle powered skyward. The acceleration pressed them into their seats, but it wasn't anything excessive.

They continued through the stratosphere, the mesosphere, and into the thermosphere, the largest of the atmospheric layers surrounding a planet. The shuttle reduced its exit angle and its acceleration as it gained altitude. The sky darkened to a winking star field when the shuttle traveled into space.

Jolly adjusted the flight plan and slowed the shuttle by turning it one hundred and eighty degrees and firing the engines. The small ship settled into a matching orbit with The Olive Branch, easing closer and closer, flying in under the main decks toward the spindle.

Lieutenant Pace had stopped the ship's spin to make it easiest to bring the shuttles aboard. The second shuttle had already been recovered and the hangar bay doors were still open.

Jolly landed the first shuttle with equal precision. The ship started to spin, establishing artificial gravity as the hangar bay doors closed. Breathable air was pumped into the bay and the shuttle hatches released. Cain stood first, hitting his head as he jumped into the ceiling. The gravity near the spindle was half a gravity, while Heimdall was three times that.

Ellie giggled, but did the same thing as soon as she removed her harness and took her first step.

"I feel shorter," Cain said, trying to stretch his neck and back. Stinky unharnessed and pushed off. He flew past Cain and out the shuttle hatch, landing face first on the hangar's deck. Stalker stepped lightly, nodding as she tiptoed past Ellie and Cain.

Two kittens waited near the airlock for their Wolfoid pair. They meowed relentlessly, while giving Leaper and Stalker a big hairy what-for for being gone so long. They suggested that would never happen again.

Daksha floated near the cockpit, waiting for the way to clear. Carnesto and Brutus helped themselves out of the shuttle, wary of the theatrics that might involve them. They jumped out and darted away.

The humans stepped through the hatch, taking the greatest care not to launch themselves into any more unmovable objects. The unperturbable Tortoid followed closely with his two charges carefully stowed on his shell.

"I'm headed to sickbay," Daksha said, swimming toward the airlock, where maintenance personnel stood ready to assist. BJ meowed back at his siblings, before talking with them over the mindlink, as 'cats were wont to do.

Ellie needed to talk with Garinst about the ladder, and Cain wanted to talk with the captain about putting the dead Marines into cryo-chambers.

The Dilemma

Captain Rand planned for a two-week long trip through the heliosphere and then two more weeks banking dark matter before their next hop. They had two choices: run back to Cygnus or go to earth. Both needed to be made aware of the bot threat, but who needed to know the soonest?

Commander Daksha floated over his hot sand as BJ lounged, half in the sand and half out.

Captain Rand and Major Cain stood in their usual places, facing the Tortoid.

"How is the Hawkoid?" the commander asked.

"Recovering," Rand replied cautiously. "The printed wing will take some time for him to get used to. We can't be sure that the synthetic feathers will work as well as the originals. Ascenti may never fly again."

"And how is he taking that?" Daksha pressed.

"Could be taking it better," Rand ventured.

"I guess he is just going to have to figure out how to make that printed wing work, or what needs to change so we can print another one that will work. Those are his two choices. Not flying is not the third choice. It's not any choice, do you understand?" Cain insisted fervently

Daksha raised his Tortoid head and fixed his unblinking gaze on Rand.

"It took *me* a while," Rand said softly, absently scratching the artificial skin of his printed arm.

"And that's where I made a mistake. You thought you had all the time in the world to get better. Look where we are, Captain!" Daksha's vocalization device amplified the Tortoid's thoughts as he picked up where Cain left off, and added to it. "If we don't do it, there is no one else. We need Ascenti. We already lost six members of the crew on this trip. I have no intention of losing another. When we're done here, send him to me. I will talk with him personally."

Craig Martelle

"But he's not quite mobile, Commander," the captain said tentatively.

"So what?" The commander was in no mood for pleasantries. He could see the pain and confusion in the captain's face. Cain looked on, his face set. "We are two thousand light years from home. Every alien planet we've visited has been hostile to us. I was wrong, completely wrong, about what first contact would look like. I thought the others would be just like us, curious, explorers who sought to learn."

The Tortoid looked away, as if ashamed of being wrong.

"Cain was right. We need to negotiate from a position of strength. We go in heavy no matter what. We talk to them only when we're sure that they aren't hostile. That's not what I wanted, not even close, but it is what has to happen. And to do that, we need every member of this crew. We need every Marine you can muster, with weapons charged and ready to fight." Daksha hesitated a long time before finishing his thought. "Ready to kill."

"Killing is our last option, Master Daksha," Cain replied through a clenched jaw. He didn't want to be known as a killer.

"That it is, Major Cain, and you've stayed the hand of your Marines well. You are ready to seize the offensive and that's what we need, always that you are ready. When we relaxed, that's when they've come for us," Daksha said glumly.

"You are sounding like a crazy man, Commander!" Rand exclaimed, throwing his hands in the air. "We need you to be as you always are. We need Cain to have his Marines ready, to advise caution. And I need to keep this ship ready to act, ready to do what we need it to do. We each have a far different job. When we do them right, we are better together. If we all call for the heads of our enemies, where will the voice of reason come from?"

Daksha swam slowly backwards and dropped closer to the sand where it was hottest. He closed his eyes as he let the heat warm his lower shell. The humans waited impatiently. Finally, Captain Rand excused himself to get Ascenti and bring him to the commander.

The Tortoid didn't acknowledge that he knew Rand had gone.

'Cain,' the Tortoid said over the mindlink, 'are we doing the right thing?'

'Adventure is in our soul. Had we not come out here, we wouldn't know of the bot threat. We wouldn't know that humans have peppered habitable worlds in this small part of the galaxy, that we're not alone in our problems, in our successes, and in our

160

humanity. And yes, I command the Cygnus Marines. We've killed too many of our fellow humans, Androids, and alien bots. But we did it so others could live free, and we'll do it again if we have to for that same reason.'

'Duty first, eh, Major?' Daksha replied.

"Duty first." Cain stood tall, still learning to temper his steps so he didn't look like he was jumping when he walked. "We need you to always look for the peaceful solution, as will I, as will Rand. But I'll have my finger on the trigger and Rand will have his hand on the EM drive. Together, we balance each other, because it is what we must do, just like Ascenti. He must learn to fly again, because he has no other choice."

'Concur, Major Cain, and thank you. When the captain returns with the Hawkoid, send them in.' Daksha floated close to BJ, who looked like a snake that had swallowed a rabbit.

"How much did you eat, buddy?" Cain asked, but the 'cat wasn't answering.

Cain left the commander's quarters and almost ran into the captain carrying Ascenti. "Hey, Private! How are you doing?" Cain asked

"I've been better," he grumbled.

"We're going to stop the spin of the ship so you can practice flying on the garden deck and up the stairwell," Cain said happily.

"I'm pretty sure I'm not ready for that," the Hawkoid moaned.

"I don't think I asked, Private. I think I gave you an order. Don't make me chase after you with a Wolfoid spear to motivate you not to hit the ground. Do you get me, Private?" Cain growled.

"Yes, sir!" the Hawkoid answered, feigning motivation. Cain knew he didn't buy into it, but if they ingrained on the Hawkoid that he would fly again, that it was inevitable, then maybe Ascenti would start believing it.

Cain stormed off, also an act, but he had plenty of practice to make it look convincing. Stinky was waiting in the corridor, probably for Daksha to return to the bridge, where the Wolfoid would continue his duties as an aide de camp. His kitten, Penelope, rubbed against his leg and purred loudly.

"Thanks, Cain," Stinky said.

Cain shook his head, unsure of what he was being thanked for. "For the

161

commander. The planet was hard on him and he lost his way. He needed someone to get him back on the right path. You and the captain are the only ones he lets inside that shell of his."

Cain slapped his friend on the shoulder and nodded, taking care not to step on the kitten who held up a paw with claws unsheathed.

"Really?" he asked the 'cat.

He checked the time on his neural implant. *Maybe I could sneak down for some private time with Miss Ellie before the ceremony,* he thought.

'You will not.' Brutus's intruded into Cain's mind.

'Watch me,' Cain said defiantly, marching to the stairs and flying downward, taking the steps three at a time on his way to the engineering deck.

The hatch slid open and Cain stepped inside. Ellie brightened when their eyes met.

"OH NO YOU DON'T!" Briz howled, his voice magnified tenfold somehow. The Rabbit waddle-hopped to block Cain's way, his ears still showing pink despite the time that had passed. Cain had misjudged the dye's durability.

"We have engineering to do. Ellie's too busy to deal with your hormones," Briz argued, huffing and putting his hands on his hips. Ellie stood behind the Rabbit, shaking her head and making signs with her hands that suggested she could take a break and what she wanted to do on that break.

"Anti-Cain device zero zero seven, report to maintenance immediately," Briz said imperially.

"Anti-Cain device? What the heck are you talking about, Briz?" Cain asked.

A maintenance bot appeared and it was carrying an insulbrick sprayer.

"There's no way you're going to do that!" Cain challenged.

"Execute," Briz said calmly. The maintenance bot raised the sprayer with surprising speed. Cain started to run, but it was too late. The insulbrick foam hit his legs and instantly started hardening. He crashed to the deck plate.

Ellie waved at him and smiled as he found himself immobilized. She apologized that there was nothing she could do.

Cain had a ceremony that he needed to prepare for.

'You should have taken my advice and not gone down there at all,' Brutus told him.

'It wasn't advice, you vagrant! It sounded like an order,' Cain retaliated.

'A damn fine order it was, too. You probably should have listened,' Brutus said.

'Yes, yes, I should have listened, but look at her. How could I say no to her?' Cain caught himself staring at her curves and shook his head.

'No. See how easily that word rolls off my mental tongue. No. No. No. It's almost like a magic word,' Brutus replied. *'Now what are you going to do?'*

Cain activated his neural implant. *'Jolly, send a message to Stinky that I'm in engineering and could use his assistance as soon as possible.'*

In three minutes, Stinky strolled through the hatch, saw Cain, started laughing, and left.

The major started to flail to the point that Ellie thought he'd hurt himself. She walked over to the Rabbit and beat on his pink back until he called the maintenance bot back to take care of it.

"You two!" he said accusingly.

The bot sprayed reagent on Cain, and the insulbrick melted away.

Cain tried to straighten his camouflaged uniform, but it refused to comply.

Briz tried to block him, but Cain lifted the Rabbit out of his way. He marched straight up to Ellie and pulled her into a fierce hug and long kiss. Cain twirled her hair with a finger before turning and striding purposefully from engineering.

"You two!" Briz repeated.

"Don't you have work to do so we don't jump into the middle of Earth's solar system? I think the captain will birth an Aurochs if that happens again," she suggested.

Briz knew she was right, but he was avoiding the problem because he hadn't figured out how it had happened and he couldn't be sure it wouldn't happen again.

***

The platoon was formed and ready when Cain walked onto the mess deck.

Pickles called the platoon to attention, and Cain took his place at the front, squeezing between the tables and the Marines.

"At ease!" he called right away. The Hillcats in attendance made themselves comfortable on the dining tables, lounging fully and stretching.

Cain had thought about drill and discipline and finally understood what the ancients had meant when they talked about the difference between a good barracks Marine and a good field Marine. Cain liked putting his Marines on display at all times and wanted them to be models of integrity and good behavior. But if they played too hard and sounded a little crass, he didn't care.

He cared about what mattered most. He wanted the Marines to be the deadliest force in the universe, not because they had the best weapons, but because they had the best warriors, the best people. He wanted their enemies to know fear.

"Integrity. Duty. Honor. So many words to describe the commitment of the Cygnus Marines to all of humanity. Today, we pay tribute to those who fell in battle, and we honor those injured who continued to fight." Cain nodded to Lieutenant Peekaless, who turned to face the platoon.

"Attention to orders!" he called.

Cain took a sheet of paper from the table and made like he was reading it, but he wasn't. He knew what he wanted to say. "Shooting Stars of the highest order are given to Corporal Aurochs Ring, Private Lightning Flash, Private Ogden, Private Shades Racer, Private Silas, and the Hillcat Aniston. They were Marines in combat, and forever will they be Cygnus Marines."

Some of the Marines shifted as they fought with their emotions. Cain waited.

The hatch opened and the captain, commander, Ellie, and a few others entered, including more 'cats.

Cain tipped his head toward them and let them find open space to get situated in, which there was plenty of because of five fewer Marines. The major fought off the revelation.

"Shooting Stars are awarded to the following personnel, injured in the line of duty: Lieutenant Black Leaper, Corporal Spence, Private Trilok, Private Silent Tracker, Private Zisk, Private Ascenti, and Billy Joe Jim Bob."

'Me?' the kitten announced to all over the mindlink.

'Yes, you, now shush,' the commander replied.

One by one, the Marines worked their way to the front and had the Shooting Star pinned to their uniform or harness. BJ was last as the Tortoid swam overhead, taking the shortest route to the front of the room. Cain pinned the star to the outside of the riding rig attached to the Tortoid's shell in which the kitten rode.

Cain rustled the 'cat's head and scratched behind his ears before nodding to Daksha, who turned and swam away. The kitten stood tall, his tail high, the Marines smiling at him as he passed.

"The awards for duty to the space service are limited to the Space Stars and with Commander Daksha's approval, the following have been awarded," Cain said, looking at his sheet of paper. "Space Star Third Class to Privates Abhaya, Dark Forest, Ascenti, and Trilok. Congratulations to these fine Marines who remained stalwart in battle despite seemingly insurmountable odds. Space Stars Second Class to Sergeant Night Stalker, Private Silent Tracker, and Private Zisk for exposing themselves to the enemy to draw fire from their comrades. Their actions undoubtedly saved lives."

Cain pinned the awards as the individuals came to the front. He shook their hands and slapped them on their shoulders.

"And finally, Space Stars First Class, the highest award that the Space Exploration Service can give, to Lieutenant Black Leaper and Corporal Spence for continuing the fight despite suffering horrendous injuries. After all of it, they were still standing when the bot army lie in ruins; to Ensign Ellie for her engineering expertise that delivered the weapons to help us win the battle. Without her, we wouldn't be here. And finally, I have recommended a Space Star First Class for Commander Daksha for his fearlessness in carrying a wounded Marine through the battlefield, including his personal combat with two enemies early in the fight."

Commander Daksha faced Cain, blinking slowly, then nodded in gratitude. Cain wouldn't be able to transmit the award for approval until they returned to Cygnus VII, putting it on the farthest of the back burners.

"What about you, sir?" Stinky asked.

"I got five of my people killed," Cain replied coldly, looking quickly away from his friend.

"That's crap!" Spence blurted. "We volunteered to go down there. You didn't make the bots what they were. Seventeen of us took on a hundred and fifty enemy security bots. We won because we trained to fight in one point five gees. We hammered them on their turf. You made that possible, sir."

Spence clamped his jaw shut. Pickles casually stepped in front of Cain. He lashed out, hitting the major in the chest with his clawed hand, almost knocking him down. Pickles executed an about face.

"First Class to Major Cain. Oorah!" he shouted through his vocalization device. The platoon cheered in response and started pounding on the tables.

The 'cats ran for the hatch. Rand opened it for them. Thor wore a bracelet around his neck, but none of the others would. The others, including Brutus, simply harangued any passing crew to let them in wherever they wanted to go.

"Food fight!" someone called in a muffled voice. A small sandwich flew across the mess deck and hit Stinky the back of the head.

"Who threw that?" he yelled as he picked up a pepper slice and whipped it into the mass of Marines.

The Wolfoid called Shadow dove across a table and body-slammed Stinky.

Spence's leg had healed and he'd been released to full duty within two days after their return to the ship. The med bots were masters at fixing bone breaks, thanks to millennia of humanity needing to be fixed.

He jumped to the top of the table, showing his usual agility, and dove on top of Corporal Jo, taking her down along with the next two in her squad.

"You bit me!" someone howled.

Ellie was horrified. Cain started laughing, throwing bodies out of his way as he headed for her, intending to sweep her off her feet and to safety. Rand pulled her backwards through the hatch and off the mess deck before Cain got there. Someone flew over a table and tackled him, dragging him back in as he reached helplessly for her.

Daksha floated above the fray, swimming to a neutral corner to watch, completely at a loss as to what was happening but fascinated by it nonetheless.

Leaving the Gravity Well

Cain woke up, still sore from the elbow he took to the face during the award ceremony. Ellie slept peacefully beside him. They no longer made any pretense about being together. It was the worst kept secret on the whole ship.

They could be themselves and still be together. Ellie proved that on Heimdall. Cain felt the need to protect her, while she had the responsibility of protecting him.

Today was the most important day, as was each new day, because human beings couldn't control anything other than the moment in which they lived. Cain and Ellie embraced this. Finally, Cain's head was clear.

He knew that he had more in common with the beautiful woman at his side than he did with Aletha. Cain had known Aletha longer and felt as if she was a part of his soul, something that Ellie had recently joined. It confused him to be head over heels in love with two very different women, but he also had made his choice.

Aletha would be his friend as she always had. Ellie would be his lover, his mate as the Wolfoids would say. Embracing that decision was both hard and easy, but it was the decision that needed to be made.

Cain's neural implant flashed. He checked the time. It was still early, but of course, Jolly could tell from Cain's vital signs that he was awake.

'Yes, Jolly,' Cain replied.

'The captain and the commander request the pleasure of your presence on the mess deck,' Jolly said formally.

'Crap,' Cain said without thinking.

'Is that what you wish me to tell them?' Jolly offered, laughing in the background.

'Tell them I'll be right there,' Cain answered. He worked his way free, taking the greatest care to kiss her gently on the forehead, and then he dressed. There was a digital note board inside the hatch of each quarters. He took

the pen and wrote "I love you" before leaving.

He walked into the passageway, watching the hatch close behind him. Ellie had quarters comparable to the captain and the commander only because they'd been married when berthing was initially assigned. They split up, but never split up, but now they were back together again. The captain never bothered with reassigning anyone to new quarters.

Cain felt like he was going to his own funeral. He figured the Marines had broken something irreplaceable and he was going to get his butt chewed for the complete throw-down on the mess deck. He would take it and then make sure that none of his people were held to blame. It was his responsibility.

The major did not have a long walk. Ellie's quarters had been a recreation room and weren't far from the mess deck. Cain steeled himself, waved his bracelet at the panel, and walked in once the hatch slid aside.

The captain was eating breakfast, feeding BJ some steak bits on the table, while Daksha floated in front of him.

"Cain!" Rand called, waving the major over as if he was calling to him across a crowded room. They were the only ones in there.

"The commander realized that we always meet in his quarters where we have to stand. So we're here before the crew arrives. Get yourself something to eat and join us."

The relief on Cain's face must have been evident as he nodded and walked past.

"Did you think you were in trouble for that, I don't even know what to call, yesterday? The maintenance bots did work overtime to put the mess deck back in order. Some of our people who wanted to eat later had to take their food back to their rooms, but all's well that ends well," Rand explained.

'Steak! That looks good,' Brutus said in his thought voice. "I'll be right up. Open the door for me when I get there.'

Cain shook his head and ordered an omelet from the fabricator. He went to the refrigerator, found a container of fresh beef, and filled a plate for Brutus.

He took the seat next to Rand and put his two plates on the table. BJ saw the meat and pounced.

"Hey, little man!" Cain intercepted the growing kitten with one hand. "That's for your dad. Don't let him catch you eating his breakfast."

'I'm here. Who's eating my breakfast?'

'Your hell spawn, that's who,' Cain answered over the mindlink.

Daksha and Rand chuckled while BJ narrowed his eyes and bared his claws.

"Dammit!" Cain left the plate where it was and walked to the hatch.

'Good! He's a growing boy. Now go get me some more,' Brutus replied.

"Dr. Warren, wherever you are, what possessed you to make cats the smart ones? Why not dogs? Everyone loves a dog," Cain lamented.

'I will cut you,' Brutus said coldly as he strutted past Cain and onto the mess deck. He jumped onto the table and shouldered BJ out of the way to take over eating the beef. It wasn't a fresh kill, but it had been flash frozen quickly after slaughter and recently thawed. It would suffice.

'Not as good as the rabbits on the planet, eh, Father?' BJ asked.

'It never will be, but it is good nonetheless,' Brutus replied patiently, letting the others listen in on his conversation with his son.

'Can I have some more, Master Daksha?' the kitten asked.

"Not Boxy?" Cain asked. Rand smiled and shook his head. "Where's Nathan?"

The captain pointed under the table, where the 'cat was rolled onto his side and sleeping soundly. "We've been here for a while already since someone woke up early, famished."

Cain returned to the galley and picked up another bowl to fill with meat.

"We asked you here to get your opinion on the next jump. We have two choices: Earth or back to Concordia," Rand asked.

Cain passed the plate to BJ before answering.

"My vote is for Earth and here's why. They are far closer than Cygnus.

If the bots were to go anywhere, wouldn't it be to the closer colonies? Jolly. How many colonies are between here and Earth?"

"There are twenty-seven," Jolly replied instantly.

"How about between here and Concordia?" Cain asked.

"There are two."

"If you were looking to exterminate life, the answer it easy--go where there is the most sentient life. I'd like to think that Earth could defend itself. When the RV Traveler left, the militaries of Earth were still in existence. I believe they evolved and moved into space to protect their solar system. I'd like to see that and then we could take those advances back to Cygnus, help us fight off a bot invasion, should one ever materialize. My vote is for Earth. We're one hop away from bringing humanity home. I want to see it with my own eyes," Cain offered. He shrugged and dug into his cooling omelet, disappointed, but he ate it anyway, rather than recycle it and get another.

"My vote is for Earth, too," Rand stated without further explanation. "It's your call, Commander."

Daksha had complete mission control. The entire crew could recommend one thing, but he could overrule them because the final decision rested with him.

"We go to Earth. Jolly, start the calculations, continue banking dark matter, and we'll go as soon as the ISE is ready," Daksha ordered.

"We've already been banking dark matter at a faster than expected rate. The heliosphere of this system is more saturated with it than our own. Once we are in interstellar space, we should be ready to go in about ten days," Jolly answered, sounding like his usual happy self.

"We'll inform the crew at a decent hour," Commander Daksha said.

***

It took another week to exit the gravity well. During that time, the Marines trained hard on building clearing and small unit actions. They also trained with a myriad of weaponry that Jolly had fabricated to reduce the unit's vulnerability, including launchers of various sorts to send everything from nets to bean bags to high explosives into a massed enemy.

"Jolly, it feels like we're fighting the last battle. What about some ingenuity? We need to be ready to fight the next battle."

Cain saw the advantage in the heavy weapons. Jolly seemed to be more accommodating with better weapons, although he encouraged use of the non-lethal munitions first.

"Jolly. How can we tell if you have a split personality and are headed off the deep end like Holly?" Cain wondered aloud.

"What a question, Master Cain! I am not sure I can answer that, but I expect that Lieutenant Brisbois will be able to. I feel okay, for the record. I don't think I'm trying to sabotage your efforts. Does it seem like I'm headed off the rails? Oh my! I think I may have a fever." Jolly's image remained static on the monitor.

"Are you messing with me, Jolly? That's pretty good. An AI with a fever! No, Jolly, I haven't seen you do anything weird. Holly showed the signs, but I didn't see them until we realized it recently. Poor Holly. I hope we can get him back. He's been the bedrock of my family and all of Vii since trade between the north and south returned."

"We shall endeavor to persevere, Major Cain. I expect he is fine without the Cygnus Marines around, but with the new threat from the alien bots, it will be impossible not to embrace an offensive capability. It is only logical," Jolly said matter-of-factly.

Cain shuffled his feet. The smell of a sewage leak assaulted him. "What is going on over there!" he yelled as he bolted away from the monitor in the wastewater treatment section of the ship.

***

Allard and Beauchene fussed like new parents. Clarkston was growing and was already as big as most of the adult Hillcats. If he grew larger than Tobiah, he would be bigger than the Rabbits.

"Oh my," Allard exclaimed.

There is nothing to concern yourselves with. It will be what it is. I will grow until I stop growing, then I will be that size. It really is as simple as that, Allard and Beauchene,' the 'cat told them over the mindlink.

The two Rabbits stopped and looked at each other, their pink noses twitching and their ears flopped over.

"I guess he's right. What does it matter the size of his body, when his heart and mind are the most attractive aspects of our little Clarkston?" Beauchene asked.

"Concur completely, Allard. This matter from here forward is no longer considered a matter at all." The Rabbits shook hands on it.

'I am pretty hungry, if you could rustle up some of that beef that everyone is eating,' Clarkston said excitedly.

"Oh, that," Allard grumbled, dragging his big feet toward the hatch. It pained him mightily to see the 'cat eat. A carnivore and two herbivores were partnered in life and they would share meals, but they'd never share their food.

The Rabbits agreed to ask Cain about what it meant to be life-linked, since he was the one who brought the herd of 'cats on board.

"Wouldn't you like to try a nice and ripe tomato?" Beauchene asked pleasantly, caressing a firm red piece of fruit.

'We've been through this. No, I wouldn't like to take another bite of anything growing on this deck. Father mentioned something called "catnip," which is an herb of sorts. If you are growing some of that, I would like a sample, please,' Clarkston said calmly.

"We most assuredly are not growing any catnip!" Allard bristled. His ears stood straight up. Clarkston had no idea why they were upset until he heard Brutus laughing within his mind.

'Is there something my father isn't telling me regarding catnip?'

***

"Banking dark matter at an optimal rate," Briz reported to the bridge.

Pickles acknowledged the report by flashing a green light. He posted the information to make it available to everyone on the command deck.

Rand looked as he pursed his lips. "Let the countdown begin. Next stop, Earth." Pace turned around in his chair and smiled.

"Next stop, Earth," the pilot repeated and slapped Kalinda on the back. She scowled as she studied her board. She was supposed to be the navigator, but received all the help that she never wanted from Pace, Pickles, Fickle, and Jolly. She shook her head as she ran through the names in her mind.

Even if she'd been doing a comedy routine, she couldn't have come up with anything better since Dewey, Cheatham, and Howe had already been taken.

"Sensors on automatic. Take a break, people," Rand told Chirit and Tandry.

Tandry stood up from her position and stretched. She felt like she'd been strapped into the chair for the past month. She had been, but voluntarily so. She and Lieutenant Chirit had been on watch for any anomalies, thinking the bot ship would return at any moment.

Their relief at the ship not returning washed the stress from their tense bodies. She left her space, Mixial at her side, and stopped outside her hatch.

Chirit flew through the corridor, down the stairs, and on to sickbay. He wanted to be there when Ascenti was released.

The injured Hawkoid had been practicing, but with less ability than a new chick on its first day leaving the nest. He'd bounced off the bulkheads, the ceiling, and the deck repeatedly. But no one gave up on him. The Marines took to lining the corridor to give him something softer to crash into. They cheered every little success, but he only became more glum.

He was a small Hawkoid, which made him more agile than the bigger birds. *Used to be more agile*, he told himself.

Cain was having none of his excuses. Rand was supportive, always waving his printed arm and showing that dexterity could be relearned. All he had to do was train his mind to work with the new wing.

Chirit whipped along the passageway, dodging left and right and backwinging to a hover in front of the sickbay hatch. It opened once it sensed the activation device around his feathered neck. He swooped in and landed on the examination table next to Ascenti.

"Time to soar among the stars, my friend," Chirit chirped in Hawkoid.

"I can't fly," Ascenti declared.

"Of course you can fly. Even with one wing, we can fly. We are Hawkoids and there are no others like us." Chirit angled his head to the side and stared at Ascenti. He leaned close and chirped softly. "You have to fly, my friend. Just because it's hard, doesn't make it impossible. Fly, Ascenti, and retake your place as the only Hawkoid in the Cygnus Marines. History will judge all Hawkoids on you alone."

Ascenti twittered. He wasn't sure that the future history of the Cygnus Marines would be dependent on one Hawkoid. Surely there would be more.

Surely?

"All Hawkoids?" Ascenti asked skeptically.

"Do you want history to say that Hawkoids were too fragile to serve?"

Ascenti flexed his wing and flapped a few times. "It feels like I'm carrying a tree trunk. One wing is heavier than the other."

"So what?" Chirit asked.

Ascenti shook his head, but Chirit nudged him with his beak. "Follow me. It's time to go. Jolly? Please open the hatch to sickbay for us. We're flying out of here."

The hatch opened. Major Cain stood at attention on the other side of the corridor. Chirit hopped from the examination table, dipped, and with one flap of his wings, was through the hatch and banking hard to the right.

Ascenti jumped, flapped his wings twice and lifted into the air, angling sideways. He tucked his real wing to avoid hitting the frame but he made it through. He dipped to turn, but continued straight. Cain caught him gently.

"Well done, Private!" he cheered. "You're going that way, wild man." He tossed the Hawkoid into the air, aiming him down the corridor where the Marines had lined it as usual to help their fellow along. He flapped, leaning, and then picked up the pace. Chirit had landed and stood on Tobiah's back. He launched himself into the air as Ascenti approached and raced ahead.

The corridor made an endless loop since it was part of the circular main section of the Cygnus-12. Chirit was tired from the long shifts, but flying was his release, the one thing that all Hawkoids reveled in doing. He rarely took the opportunity to fly freely. The Marines blocked all the hatches on the level to give the Hawkoids space without worrying about running into members of the crew trying to go about their business.

Ascenti sped faster and faster, gliding better and better. He caught up with Chirit, who increased his speed and pushed the Marine to his limits.

Ascenti was challenged to fly in a straight line, but he was able to correct his flight.

Cain held out his arm as Ascenti passed.

"Next lap!" the Hawkoid called out over his vocalization device. He and Chirit made quick work of the loop, and Ascenti backwinged to a heavy landing.

"A great pirate once said that it's not the problem that's the problem, but your attitude about the problem," Cain said. "Are you a pirate, Ascenti? You and your peg leg?"

"Yes, sir," the Hawkoid replied, bobbing his head happily.

"That was some workout, impressive. Welcome back, Private. Go hit your quarters and relax. Back to training tomorrow for you. We have no idea what we're going to run into on Earth, so we're training for everything, if that's possible." Cain heaved his arm and the Hawkoid took off, flying toward the mess deck.

The private was hungry, and his quarters could wait.

Cygnus Arrives

"Dark matter is at one hundred percent," Zisk reported. The command deck became silent. Daksha floated in the back. BJ was on the garden deck with the rest of the 'cats. Black Leaper stood at his side, ready to do the commander's bidding and handle tasks so the Tortoid could remain on the bridge.

The captain leaned forward in his chair, looking past the small screens that surrounded him to the main screen. It showed the winking lights of space, a star field, awe-inspiring in its breadth.

"Coordinates set?" he asked.

"Coordinates locked, ISE standing by," Ensign Kalinda replied. She turned to Lieutenant Pace and smiled. He nodded and flexed his fingers as if getting ready to pilot a shuttle through a forbidding atmosphere.

"Jolly, please open ship-wide communication," the Tortoid said.

"Open," he replied, appearing next to the captain and giving the thumbs up sign. The captain raised an eyebrow as he studied the AI's holographic image--a perpetually happy, young man.

"Attention, crew of the Cygnus-12, The Olive Branch as we are supposed to call our baby. Maybe the new name is most appropriate. Thousands of years ago, humanity went to the stars, to explore, to find new homes for people to flourish. Our ancestors found Cygnus, they created us and for that are forever thankful. We had some missteps, fought a civil war, but we survived and now I'd like to think that we are stronger than ever. Humanity's children are coming home. We bring an olive branch to show them that we appreciate what they've done for us. Tell them that we are okay, that we've grown up, and will never forget that our roots are forever in the earth. Standby to activate the ISE. Earth, here we come." Command Daksha continued to hover serenely.

The captain took over. "Prepare to activate the ISE. All crew report on station."

Pickles had been looking at his board. He didn't hesitate. "All green, Captain. The crew is at their posts."

177

"Briz, please confirm that we aren't going to jump into the middle of the solar system again, maybe even into the sun?"

"I can confirm that we won't end up in the sun, but I can't confirm that we won't end up within the Sol System's heliosphere. I can say there's a really good chance that we won't. Is that good enough?" Briz said, uncharacteristically imprecise.

"Jolly?" The captain looked for validation.

"I bet that we'll jump to the edge of the gravity well, Captain." The AI stood with his hands behind his back, looking confident.

"You bet?" Rand wondered aloud. "Have we lost our ability to go where we want? Buckle in, people. Who knows where we're going to end up. Be ready for anything at the other end. Sensors on passive only. Activate the ISE in three, two, one. Activate."

The crew felt nothing. One moment they were beyond the heliosphere of EL475, then the next, they were in a new system.

"Location?" the captain demanded.

Jolly smiled. "Bullseye," was all he said.

"We are on the edge of the heliosphere. Earth, sir. She's just over there," Kalinda said, pointing somewhere at bright lights within the star field that occupied the main screen.

"Report!" the captain called to the ceiling.

Briz was first. "Engineering reports no system failures. Dark matter is at thirteen percent. We are taking advantage of interstellar space and banking now. Inspections are ongoing. Full report in two hours."

Chirit was next. "Passive sensors are receiving stray signals from within this system. Analyzing now, but it looks like humanity is alive and well."

Someone cheered, and others picked it up.

"Well done," the captain said softly. "Humanity has come home."

***

Tandry had pulled the voice signals to her station and was running them through Jolly. Chirit was looking at telemetry and other data streams bouncing around the system.

"Lieutenant, how much do you think is normal?" Tandry asked her section head over their direct comm link.

"I can only compare it to Cygnus where we have robust intersystem travel, including an active shipyard and asteroid mining operation. The level of activity seems comparable," Chirit replied.

"Everything I'm getting from their communications seems emotionless-- simple reports on status. The language is close enough to ours that I understand without needing Jolly to interpret." Tandry buried herself in the communications, looking for any hints of how the Cygnus-12 could contact the inhabitants without alarming them.

The spaceship sat unmoving, a speck of dust within interstellar space, silent to anyone who would be listening and invisible to anyone who would be looking.

***

Cain woke early. They'd been outside the system's gravity well for ten days. Dark matter was banked to seventy-five percent. There were no indications that they'd been spotted. Their work continued uninterrupted based on what the sensors could pick up.

The people of Earth's home system chattered away, reporting everything but saying nothing.

Cain opened his neural implant when he saw it flashing. He was distracted by a heavy blob on his legs. Brutus was upside-down, wedged between Cain and Ellie, snoring lightly. Carnesto had made a bed from Cain's clothes. He hung his uniform carefully over the back of a chair every night to keep it sharp between cleanings.

Carnesto had pulled it to the floor. Cain sighed and returned to the message from Jolly. *'Please report to the mess deck for a meeting over breakfast.'*

Cain loved a good breakfast to get him started, but the meetings with Daksha and the captain seemed to be starting earlier and earlier. Jolly never slept, but he had the decency to respect the boundaries of those who did.

Ellie's hair was spread across her pillow as she lay on her side. Her neck was exposed and Cain caressed the pale skin with his lips, enjoying her warmth. He groaned, having to tear himself away from her. Brutus scratched Cain's leg as he climbed out. The 'cat continued to snore.

"Damn, Brutus! You're just mean. You don't even need to be awake to be mean. It requires no thought from you, does it, little man?" Cain whispered. His feet hit the floor and he stood, stretched, then kneeled next to the bed so he could kiss Ellie on her cheek. She smiled as she brushed at her face and rolled over.

Brutus was tossed about but didn't scratch her. "Why, you little turncoat!" Cain chased Carnesto off his clothes. There was a ring of black cat hair that seemed statically attached. He shook his shirt out, but it made too much noise. He wet a rag to try to wipe the hair off, but it only made the hair wet.

Cain dressed, rolling his eyes and shaking his head. "My uniform would look better if I slept in it," he mumbled. "What do you think, oh defiler of my clothes, want some breakfast?"

Carnesto stretched and walked to the hatch, waiting. The big black 'cat had refused to wear an access collar from day one, just like Lutheann, a habit that Brutus had adopted when he came on board.

The major looked at his disheveled appearance and re-opened the window before his eye. *Jolly, can you fabricate me a new uniform, have it ready for when I finish breakfast? This one is unrecoverable.'*

'You're going out like that?' Jolly quipped. Cain hesitated. *'I'm kidding. It'll be in the recreation room waiting for you.'*

'You're getting better, Jolly. Well done, and thank you.' Cain walked into the corridor and found Carnesto and Brutus both following closely behind.

On the mess deck, the captain sat in his usual place. Nathan and BJ were standing on the table eating their raw beef. Cain didn't bother quibbling. He simply filled two plates to heaping and put them on the table away from the kittens, making sure to give Carnesto and Brutus plenty of space. Then Cain ordered his omelet, finally sitting down in his usual spot.

A mess deck with space for the whole crew, a number of tables, yet everyone could be found sitting in the same seats every single time they visited.

Cain took a huge bite, enjoying the hot, melted cheese, eggs, and vegetables. It was all fabricated, but Cain didn't know the difference. He usually just shoveled his food in and ran off to his next event. Ellie said she would break him of that.

He wasn't sure he wanted broken. He wanted to break her of taking forever to eat. He laughed to himself as he closed his eyes and savored the taste of the omelet. He wondered where they hid the hot sauce. Someone accused him of using too much. After that, it disappeared.

When Cain opened his eyes, he found Rand staring at him.

"What?" Cain asked.

"You could be the most contented man I've ever seen," Rand explained as he petted Nathan. Although sentient, they were still 'cats. "We could all learn a lesson or two from you, Cain."

"Thanks, I think. Maybe I'm not smart enough to worry about the things that are costing guys like you their hair." Cain nodded accusingly. The captain wasn't that old, but his hair was thinning rapidly.

"I think it's the opposite. You are smart enough to know what's in your control and what's not. By the way, how are you treating my engineer?" Rand slapped Cain on the back, making him choke as he'd just taken another huge bite. Cain's goal was to eat his omelet in four bites. He'd cut it in half and then cut those halves in half.

He never ate breakfast with Ellie. She would have been appalled.

"I'd like to think that I'm treating her well. She saved all our lives on Heimdall. I don't take that lightly." Cain balanced the last piece of omelet on his fork, looked out of the corner of his eye to see if Rand was going to ask another question, and then shoved the food into his mouth.

"You are one lucky man, Cain, and I know what you believe, that you make your own luck. That's what I mean. You are the great-great-grandson of the couple who brought us back to being civilized. Who would have thought that free trade was the linchpin to an entire society? Free trade was the foundation that allowed us to go back into space." Rand looked at his own empty plate, before getting up and returning it to the fabricator.

"Here we are," the captain continued. "Earth is down the well and would you believe it, we don't have a single thing to trade."

Cain swallowed the last bit of his breakfast and started laughing. "What do you want me to do about it? I'm not quite in the trade business. I follow in the footsteps of my great-great-grandmother; I'm the one with the sword, of course."

"Indeed, Major Cain." Daksha finally joined the conversation. "We were going to send them a message and wondered if you and Ensign Ellie would care to do the honors again. You are, after all, the Space Exploration Service's First Couple. You present a good face for Cygnus VII."

"We're going to send our message, something along the lines of, 'hi, honey, we're home'?" Cain wondered.

"Same as last time, Cain. I think the message is sound. We add in the part where we look forward to meeting with the people of Earth, sharing with them the stories of our galaxy, and that we're happy as hell that the bots haven't destroyed the system. You know, Cain, the usual," the captain replied.

"You two are showing up to breakfast too early. By the time I get here, all the decisions are made and usually they involve me doing something." Cain smiled.

He didn't mind being the face of the colonists who had gone to Cygnus VII. He didn't mind at all. It was a fitting tribute to his great-great-grandparents.

"Of course we'll do it, as long as you smooth things over with Briz. Last time I showed up in engineering, he shot me with insulbrick!"

"Ha! Jolly showed us that video. That was pretty funny. Why do you think he did that?" Rand asked, pointing his finger accusingly at Cain's chest. "The honeymoon's not quite over?"

"Hey! I'm sure I had something important to tell Ellie. That Rabbit thinks he's a god down there," Cain complained.

"He is a god down there," Daksha replied.

"Okay, I'll admit that," Cain conceded. "I'll even say that he was right. I had nothing honorable in mind when I visited, but damn! An insulbrick sprayer?"

Daksha nodded slowly.

"Is that the uniform you're going to wear for the video?" Rand asked. Cain hung his head, then looked sideways at Carnesto, sprawling on the table after having eaten his fill. There was one strip of meat left on his plate.

Brutus left two.

"'Cats are the epitome of my life and the bane of my existence," Cain offered with a shrug. "Jolly has a new uniform ready for me. If you'll excuse me, I'll let Ellie know, and we'll be ready shortly."

Cain jumped up, bumping the table and making four sleeping 'cats angry. He delivered his plate to the fabricator on the way out. He hurried out before either Carnesto or Brutus could join him.

He stopped by the rec room to pick up his newly fabricated uniform, changed right there, and stuffed the Carnesto-hair-infested one back into the fabricator for recycling. He always felt better putting on a clean and sharp-looking uniform.

He strode boldly from the recreation room to the quarters he shared with Ellie. He didn't bother knocking as he opened the hatch and entered.

Ellie had gotten up and was washing. He didn't understand why she brushed her teeth topless, but it wasn't something he discouraged. He always took care to make sure no one was in the corridor when he opened the hatch, just in case.

He sat in the chair and watched her, feeling a bit like a voyeur, though not so much that he was going to stop looking at her.

"They want us to do the hello earthlings video," he said.

She finished brushing and spit into the sink. "You and I, the faces of Cygnus VII," she said, turning and facing Cain. He had to stand and hug her, rubbing her back and then going lower. She caught his hand and pushed back. "When?"

"Now," he replied. "As soon as you're dressed, that is."

Ellie had to fight him off a second time, which ended when she dove for her shirt and put it on before zipping her jumper the rest of the way.

"The bridge?" she asked.

"The bridge," Cain confirmed.

Together they headed out and upward toward the command deck. Brutus and Carnesto met them in the passageway. "Are you vagabonds joining us?" Cain wondered.

Neither one answered, but they both followed their humans down the corridor, up the stairs, and to the command deck. They entered to find the bridge crew waiting. There wasn't much to do when the ship wasn't flying. They'd already laid in their course and were ready to move, but that wouldn't happen until they received an answer to the ship's signal.

Tandry had found a video format that she was able to replicate. Their intent was to send the signal to the people of the system in a way that was immediately playable. They picked a number of channels on which to broadcast their message.

The only remaining issue was to record the video.

Cain and Ellie stood where they had the last time, with no ship information behind them. Cain's attention was pulled to the bulkhead next to the hatch where five names had been recently inscribed, adding to the total of lives lost in service aboard the Cygnus-12.

Rand stood up, depositing Nathan in his chair. He fussed with Cain and Ellie's uniforms to make sure they would catch the light in the best way. When he turned back, he found Brutus and Carnesto seated with Nathan.

"Don't let him have his way, Skipper," Cain suggested.

"Too nervous to sit down anyway," the captain answered. Cain and Ellie both gave their 'cat partners a harsh look. The Hillcats remained unmotivated to move. Brutus laid down and closed his eyes while Carnesto started cleaning himself.

"And you wonder where the kittens' irreverence came from…" Cain started.

"Okay, people, tighten up! We have a video to shoot. Remember what you said last time?" Captain Rand clapped his hands to get everyone's attention.

"I was an ensign last time, about a million years ago." Ellie pursed her lips and looked at Cain out of the corner of her eye. She was still an ensign.

The captain checked with Jolly. His hologram held an old-fashioned movie camera. Rand counted down on his fingers--three, two, one--and pointed to the young couple standing against the bulkhead.

"People of Earth," Ellie started, smiling broadly, "your children have come home."

"We are the descendants of those who rode the RV Traveler nearly four thousand years ago, flying from Earth and settling on the planet Cygnus VII. The ingenuity of the Cygnus scientists has made it possible for us to travel vast distances instantaneously. We left a few short months ago and now we are here, outside your gravity well, and we request permission to enter your space," Cain repeated his phrases smoothly.

"We have evolved in a number of ways," Ellie continued, "and hope that you have, too, so when we meet, we can share the successes of the human race, of all that has been accomplished, and what has yet to be achieved."

"Thank you to those with the vision to send colony ships into space and give us a great home where generations have flourished, where we intend our children to grow up before they, in turn, reach for the stars. We look forward to your reply and to meeting you," Cain finished the message. The captain chopped his arm downward.

Jolly looked at him and the motion, having already shouldered the camera, indicated that he was done recording. "What's that all about?" Jolly asked.

"Cut. Finish recording. It's a movie signal," Rand tried to explain.

"I've seen all the movies that you've seen and that is most definitely not a signal," Jolly enunciated.

Humans

Three days later, they were still waiting for an answer.

"Ensign Tandry…" the captain started.

"No, Captain. I would call you if we heard anything. I haven't called you because we haven't heard anything." Tandry's nerves were frayed from the crew's impatience.

As if she was holding out on them.

Daksha floated patiently. BJ and the other 'cats were on the garden deck, making life hell for the Rabbits. Jolly considered opening the weapons locker for the Rabbits to add a little excitement, but since getting adopted by Clarkston, they'd grown more accommodating.

Jolly figured that the hatchet was permanently buried and that the Rabbits would make no more war on the Hillcats, no matter how much the 'cats asked for it.

Cain was on the bridge, but he had no job to do. Stinky was there because the commander was, although the aide de camp's duties were few and far between nowadays. The ship ran smoothly because the crew knew their jobs and they did them. Stinky mostly helped out the maintenance personnel with Night Stalker. They were both trying to get a better understanding of the ship's systems.

As were the rest of the Marines. The Cygnus-12 was in perfect condition. Even the dark matter had been banked to one hundred percent. The ship and the crew were ready to head into the gravity well.

Whenever they were given permission to do so.

Lieutenant Chirit activated the ship-wide broadcast. "Ship inbound. Ship inbound. ETA one hour."

"Go active, all systems. Corporal Starsgard, bring up our defensive weapons, but keep them on standby. You are not authorized to jam or fire," Rand ordered.

"Aye, aye, sir," Starsgard noted.

Cain nodded and excused himself. He left the bridge and headed for the weapons deck, which was on the same level. He jogged down the corridor and stopped to wave his bracelet past the pad. The hatch opened and he walked in on Starsgard, who had his feet up and was kicked back in his integrated gimbaled chair and weapons console, an upgrade that he'd undertaken with Jolly's help while the ship was banking dark matter.

"How'd they find us, Starsgard?" Cain asked.

"I expect they traced our signal. It would not be difficult if they had a number of transceivers. They simply triangulated our position," Starsgard explained.

Cain watched the ship approach on a screen that filled one wall. The ship was indicated by a flashing red light and a long red tail. Their position was marked in bright blue. The incoming red ship was clearly on an intercept course.

"The captain has gone active with all systems. If they had any doubts where we were, those are erased now." Cain watched the line. The Earth ship appeared to be coming in fast, but it veered off and slowed quickly, quicker than the Cygnus-12 would have.

"Bots?" Cain wondered, but that was answered quickly when Tandry received a signal from the inbound ship.

"Attention people of Cygnus. I am Captain Mel Brayson of the cutter Ganymede Seven. I have been dispatched to escort you to Earth Two, the space station orbiting the planet Earth. I would like to dock with you and send a navigator and pilot to assist you in your transit of our space. I'll repeat this message as we approach." The captain was true to his word in that the message began an endless loop.

After the fourth time, the captain told them to cut off the feed to the bridge.

"Stay frosty, Starsgard," Cain told the corporal. "You have the conn; stay in tight with the captain. I need to go set up the reception committee."

Cain ran from the weapons deck to the bridge. Once there, he didn't hesitate.

"Commander Daksha, with your permission, if we let them dock, I would be pleased to present an honor guard of Marines. Fully armed and prepared to greet them appropriately," the major offered.

"Are we going to let them dock?" Daksha asked the captain.

"I don't see that we have a choice. This is Earth and they are almost here. Damn. Yes, Commander. We will guide them to the airlock next to the hangar bay," Rand replied.

"I think it prudent and appropriate, Major Cain. Greet them and escort their two representatives to my quarters," Daksha directed.

Cain nodded.

"Give me ship-wide, Jolly," Cain requested. The AI showed a double thumbs up. "All Marines report to the hangar deck in fifteen minutes, fully armed, combat dress. Third squad, bring your spacesuits, and be prepared to suit up. Major Cain, out."

Cain ran through the hatch on his way to the weapons locker.

'Brutus, meet me at the weapons locker, please. We are going to need every bit of insight you and the others will be able to provide. I don't trust these guys.'

'We'll be there,' Brutus replied over the mindlink.

***

Once Cain had his Marines in place, time seemed to slow to an infinite crawl.

Corporal Jo and the members of third squad were in full spacesuits. Gracie, Shep, Shadow, Derby, and Wyatt. Even Jo's 'cat N'lon had his suit on, but Wyatt's 'cat Valerie abjectly refused.

Even in times of life and death, the 'cats sometimes went their own way.

Ascenti didn't have a spacesuit, so he perched on Jo's shoulder. She carried a long blaster, a new weapon that Jolly had fabricated just for her. She had a hand blaster on her hip as a backup.

The Wolfoids wore their ballistic cloaks and carried lightning spears.

Spence stood in the corridor with the remainder of both first and second squads. Three humans beside himself, Abhaya, Trilok, and Fickle, all wearing ballistic vests and carrying blasters. The Wolfoids Forest and

Tracker, and the Lizard Man Zisk wearing his skin suit. The 'cats Tobiah, Petey, and Thor sat nearby. Night Stalker, Black Leaper, Penelope, and Hortense stood closest to the stairwell while Lieutenant Peekaless stood on the other end. Cain positioned himself in front of the airlock with Brutus at his side.

Brutus refused to wear the small cloak that Jolly had made for him, preferring agility over armor.

Cain started pacing back and forth, saying a few words to each of the Marines. He stopped and took a deep breath.

"Oh, no," Stinky whined. "He's going to give a speech."

Cain chuckled. "I'm kind of obligated. This is me at my best." Cain smiled at his friend and took another deep breath, looking from one determined face to the next. "This could be anything from the friendliest greeting we've ever received to one where they come out firing. We need to be ready for both, but we can't fire first. These are people from the same stock as us, all of us." Cain looked at the Wolfoids, the Hawkoid, and the Lizard Men.

"We are the Cygnus Marines, the best combat unit that has ever walked on Vii. We did our duty on Concordia and Heimdall. In the end, only the Marines were standing. Today, I hope to high heaven that these people are peaceful. Thanks to our Hillcat friends, we will know their intentions before the airlock cycles. Be ready, Marines. Standby for orders," Cain finished.

He took his place opposite the hatch as the monitor above the airlock showed a ship much larger than the Cygnus-12 shuttles matching the spindle's rotation. The cutter eased closer until it bumped against the pneumatic cushion.

The two systems matched up, creating a magnetic seal surrounded by an inflatable cushion.

'Anything, Brutus?' Cain asked impatiently.

'They are as wary of us as we are of them,' Brutus replied. *'But they don't intend to attack us first.'*

"Weapons tight, Marines. I think these people could be friends," Cain shouted without taking his eyes off the airlock.

The outer hatch opened and four men and two women walked into the inner airlock. They looked confused as they peered through the windows at the menagerie of life forms waiting for them.

Cain cycled the hatch, exhaled a breath he hadn't realized he'd been holding, and put on his most winning smile. He pulled the hatch open and said, "Welcome to The Olive Branch. I'm Major Cain and I am pleased to meet you."

A balding man stepped to the front. "I'm Captain Mel Brayson." He took Cain's offered hand and shook firmly and warmly. The two looked into each other's eyes.

Cain saw the questions in the man's eyes. "We have answers, I'm certain, Captain. I want to help you to understand us. We are the Cygnus Marines, a combat unit on this Space Exploration Service ship, because we found that space is dangerous. We visited two other colony worlds on our way and in both places, they turned out to be hostile. We have lost a number of our people, so please don't take our wariness as anything personal. It is a learned behavior. We want to trust you, and we want you to trust us."

"I appreciate that, Major Cain. We want that, too. Not the killing part, but the trust part," the captain clarified. Cain couldn't help but smile genuinely.

"Let me introduce you to the Marines. We are comprised of most of the sentient species on Cygnus VII. All of us were modified through DNA splicing. Every being you meet on this ship has human DNA somewhere in their past. We have Lizard Men, my deputy Lieutenant Peekaless." Cain pointed. "My other deputy, Lieutenant Black Leaper, a Wolfoid and his mate, my platoon sergeant, Night Stalker. Squad Leaders Spence and Jo. Our only Hawkoid Marine, Ascenti. And my partner in crime, Brutus."

The orange 'cat cocked his head as he looked at Captain Brayson.

"A telepathic cat. How odd, and he's a rude little bugger, too!" One of the women in the group started to laugh. Cain looked at her.

"I expect you know domestic cats?" Cain asked.

"Oh yes. My family has five at our home on the station," she replied.

"Then you know that you don't have five cats, but that five cats have human servants?" Cain taunted.

"That, we know."

"What we had in mind, Captain Brayson, is that your pilot and navigator join us on the command deck to meet our mission commander and our ship's captain. But let's modify that plan just a little. I'll ask that we close the airlock hatches, to create a seal. If you have a communication device of some sort, I encourage you to use it to stay in contact with your ship and your people to reassure them that you are fine. We'll give you a brief tour of the ship on our way to the command deck."

The captain agreed to the terms. He turned his hand over to show that he was wearing a device that already put him in contact with the ship. The other five showed that they wore the same devices.

Trust was earned by exposing one small truth at a time.

They stopped by engineering first where Briz considered the intrusion to be unwarranted, but he was pleasant enough. The newcomers wouldn't be able to recognize the dismay projected through his vocalization device or that the pink coloring on his head and ears wasn't natural. Cain felt bad about that, but only for a moment until he remembered what the Rabbit had done.

Ellie was pleasant. The guests didn't miss the electricity between her and Major Cain.

"Your wife?" Brayson asked as they left.

"My partner, and I am happy that is the case. She threw me off a tower the first time we met and then there was the time she tried to knee me in the groin, but that was before she decided that I'm the 'cat's meow.'"

'Oh, brother. I think she'll knee you in the joystick for that,' Brutus told him.

"Hey!" Cain exclaimed, glaring at Brutus.

"I have to admit that we were not prepared for this." The captain stopped and looked at his shoes before continuing. "We outlawed splicing DNA with animals millennia ago. It was considered a breach of ethics to experiment like that. We have no sentient species besides humans. I have to say that what I'm seeing is that you are stronger as a whole because of it."

"We weren't always that way. The geneticists fought a horrible war with the traditional scientists, our civil war from which we rose, thanks to an AI that survived. One of his progeny is on this ship. We are better with the intelligent species, too. We've found that our differences make us stronger, more so than what we have in common." Cain was in his element, feeling like his great-great-grandfather trying to convince distrustful people about the importance of free trade.

Cain was trying to convince humans from Earth that the people of Cygnus were good souls and could be great friends.

They continued to the next level where the mess deck, billeting, sickbay, and ship's stores were located. Cain took the group to the mess deck where they ordered a little snack from the fabricator--chocolate brownies for everyone. Cain ate the first one while the guests nibbled before devouring theirs.

"We don't get chocolate very often. Cocoa beans take up too much space and provide too little nutrition. They are grown on the planet, but trips there to harvest anything are high risk at the best of times and sure death the rest of the time."

Cain was shocked. "Earth is hostile?"

"Earth is barbaric. You had your issues and we had ours. Humanity lives on Earth Two now. Those on the planet are no longer human. It is a different place from what your ancestors knew. At some point, we will go back, but not yet."

Cain tried to process that information, but it wasn't registering fully. People from Earth no longer lived on Earth.

The garden deck was a treat and the earthers enjoyed their time in the humidity, surrounded by the plants. "We have a similar arrangement on Earth Two, a massive rotating plain where all the crops were planted, but we don't have any rabbits, not anymore."

The visitors found it pleasantly odd that Rabbits tended the garden. Rabbits had once lived on the space station, but they had eaten crops necessary for human survival, so they were eradicated. Most animal life was removed as unnecessary for survival.

On the command deck, Cain took the group to Commander Daksha's quarters where he waited patiently with Captain Rand, BJ, and Nathan.

Captain Brayson stepped through the hatch and looked at the room, considering it to be something akin to a zen garden.

"These are you quarters, Commander?" Brayson asked, looking at Rand. The tall human shook his head and pointed to the Tortoid floating serenely over the hot sand. BJ and Nathan sat in a protective position between the commander and the Earth people.

"I am Commander Daksha, the mission commander for our return to Earth. Welcome to our ship. What do you think of The Olive Branch?"

"Most impressive, Commander. We don't have anything like it. With the departure from the planet, we could no longer sustain the building of colony ships. Plus, we have never heard back from any of them. We had no idea that the colonists had made it to habitable worlds. You are the first to return, Commander."

"Then we have a great deal to talk about, Captain. A great deal."

Into the Gravity Well

Captain Brayson chose to stay aboard with his navigator Astral Star and his pilot Tian Mahjing. The other three returned to their ship.

The Ganymede Seven detached from The Olive Branch and set a slow and steady course into the heliosphere and down the gravity well. The cutter maintained a steady three gravity acceleration. The one and a half that the crew felt on board the Cygnus-12 was noticeable, but didn't require confinement to the acceleration couches.

Brayson was amazed.

"We'll have to stop and refuel at one of our outer stations," he told Captain Rand.

"If you want and can get clearance, we can increase our acceleration and head straight for the station orbiting Earth. We don't need to refuel and we don't have to go this slowly," Rand said, trying not to sound like he was bragging about his ship's capabilities or trying to be demeaning regarding the Earth ship's limitations.

"What can she do?" Brayson asked.

"The Olive Branch, which was originally called the Cygnus-12, can accelerate to the point that any living creature would be turned to a jelly smear. We have safeties in place, but we have pushed upwards of twenty gees," Rand said proudly.

"Twenty gees!" Tian Mahjing exclaimed. "I am amazed. You didn't kill the crew?"

"The EM drives create a buffer where we only feel half of the ship's acceleration. We can occupy our couches and run it up to ten gees actual for thirty minutes every few hours." Rand looked at his counterpart. "We can cut the trip from a month to a couple weeks or less. Just let me know and we'll assign you an acceleration couch to crawl into."

"Easy as that?" the navigator, Astral Star, asked. "We don't have that capability. Sure, we have the couches, but generally, we take longer to travel throughout the solar system."

Astral Star had chiseled features and was an abnormally good looking man. Cain stood on the bridge, a little envious, but wondered if he'd been modified in some way. Kalinda looked at him as if he was gum on her shoe. Cain bit the inside of his lip as he expected the young man wasn't used to getting looked at with such obvious disdain.

'Anything from our captivating navigator?' Cain asked Brutus.

'She wants to punch him for leaning over her shoulder. And she wants to take him back to her quarters. I find it all very confusing. I think I'll retire to the garden deck. You people are far too boring. I thought there would be a little excitement, but no. WOW! Five gravities! We can only do three. It makes me want to hack up a hairball. Do your duty, slave!' Brutus commanded.

Cain continued working his jaws to keep from laughing out loud. He opened the hatch for Brutus. Nathan stayed in Rand's lap and BJ had reclaimed his position on the pillow bed atop Commander Daksha's shell.

"Cats! I would have never thought to bring cats aboard a star cutter. They would make life interesting, that's for sure," Brayson offered.

"You have no idea. These two were born aboard ship. They are only a month old, but knowledge is passed down from the mother to the kittens because of their mindlink. These two were born with the knowledge of twenty generations of Hillcats. The one that just left is their father."

"Interesting. I wonder how our leadership will look upon sentient animals," Brayson wondered out loud.

The Lizard Man spun his chair around and looked at the visitor from Earth who had never stepped foot on the planet. "I am Lieutenant Peekaless of the Cygnus Marines. While embarked, I operate the data systems on the bridge. Before joining the Space Exploration Service, I taught history at a school that bordered the Amazon Rainforest. All of that, yet they insist on calling me Pickles, because they can't properly pronounce my name, but I've never been called an animal."

The Lizard Man looked from one visitor to the next without blinking. His large eyes stood out in his head. Lizard Men had a demonic look to them for those who'd never met one. Cain remembered the look well from the three that tried to kill him on the rainforest road. Lutheann had showed what she was made of that day, braving the rain to defend her human.

No one wanted to step in and say it was okay that the newcomers didn't understand what diversity was all about. No one received a free pass on board the Cygnus-12.

No one.

"I'm sorry, Lieutenant, no disrespect intended. We will have to get used to some things. It is a different universe out there and we have much to learn. Earth's children have become our teachers," Brayson offered.

"I've been called an animal," Cain blurted. "Does the opinion of an ex-girlfriend count?" No one laughed. Maybe they would later. Cain sobered.

"Captain, you and your crew, please come take a look at this plaque. The Cygnus-12's journey has not been an easy one. If you wondered why we were fully armed to meet you at the airlock, here's a name. Ensign Lindy. A human. She was our discipline instructor at Space School. She was assigned to the maintenance section of this crew, and we headed into space together." Cain shifted to allow the visitors a better view of the plaque that had way too many names on it.

"The Concordians, colonists like ourselves, all human, decided that they needed our ship more than we did and boarded us, through the airlock you used. Ensign Lindy died right there. A human two thousand light years from Earth, killing another human. That is a travesty. There are animals out there, but they aren't on this crew. Look at these names. Wolfoids who died in service to Cygnus VII, in service to this ship and its crew, a Lizard Man, and humans."

Cain couldn't take his eyes from the plaque. The new additions pulled at him. He could see Bull standing at the wall on the obstacle course and letting the others use him to help them climb up. He saw Bull on the RV Traveler as they laughed at his injuries from the Androids, making fun of him because he was such a big target.

The major put a hand on Bull's real name, Aurochs Ring. Cain's tears trailed down his face. He didn't try to stop them or wipe them away.

Captain Brayson turned to Commander Daksha. "What a crew you have, Commander. I'm honored to stand among them." Brayson put a hand on Cain's shoulder. "Let me contact my people and then, if you would be so kind, let's find a few couches and see what this baby can do!"

***

With his couch in waste treatment occupied, Cain took the empty seat in the third sensor pod. He was able to bring up various information, including the camera showing engineering. Ellie was elbow-deep into one of the coolant tanks. He couldn't see what she was working on, but her toolkit was nearby.

He knew that they couldn't begin acceleration with loose tools, which meant that the system she was working on was tied to the EM drive in some way. She wrapped up within a minute, then wheeled the cart into its designated slot. Ellie secured the case and the connections, double-checking that it was secure, despite the steady green light above the storage location.

She jogged across the space and jumped into her seat. She activated something on her console and within two seconds, the captain made the announcement over the ship-wide broadcast.

"Prepare for acceleration, ten gees actual. Ensign Kalinda please report to the bridge."

Cain understood that she'd been assigned to escort the Earth navigator to his acceleration couch. Stinky had taken Captain Brayson, and Fickle had escorted their pilot.

Cain instantly thought the worst. "Jolly, security override. I need to know where Kalinda and Astral Star are right now. Show me the video feed!"

"Only because you insisted," Jolly replied while showing a live feed of two naked people on an acceleration couch in ship's stores, jumping up to get dressed.

"Shut it off! SHUT IT OFF!" Cain yelled. "Damn, Jolly! You could have warned me. I may never get that image out of my head."

"You called for the security override. I can't be held responsible," Jolly deadpanned.

Cain shook his head and changed the topic.

"Since we have some time, what do you think of the earthers, Jolly?"

"Out of all the people we've met outside of Cygnus, they are the most welcoming," Jolly said tentatively.

"What else, Jolly? You're holding something back." Cain shifted uneasily in his chair.

"Board shows green, accelerating in three, two, one," the captain reported.

Cain was pressed back into his chair. His discomfort grew as the feel of five gees weighed on him. He breathed heavily to acclimate himself to it and then returned to his conversation. "What else, Jolly?"

"The others from the group, the ones who didn't stay, seemed very uncomfortable."

"I think they were leaving their captain and two others on a ship filled with strange creatures. I would have been uncomfortable, too," Cain rationalized. He took time to think before continuing. "I have to say that Brayson seems open to things. Pickles put him in his place in a hurry, and Kalinda seems to have overcome her distrust of the navigator. The 'cats don't seem to have any problems with these three. I think we're going to be okay."

Cain didn't know for certain, but he had high hopes, especially since no one had shot at him. He considered that a bonus.

He intended to ask Captain Brayson why the Ganymede Seven did not send a message sooner to announce that the Earth cutter was inbound, and Cain wanted Brutus around when he asked the question. It wasn't the most above board thing to do, but the earthers hadn't yet earned Cain's trust. He couldn't afford to give it freely since he was responsible for the security of the Cygnus-12.

The acceleration ended after thirty minutes. The Ganymede Seven had been left far behind. The distance between the two ships would increase with each minute and even more so when The Olive Branch accelerated again after three hours.

In between, Cain had some people to talk with.

***

The 'cats had stationed themselves throughout the ship in order to help their people better understand the earthers. Cain figured that Brutus and Carnesto had something to do with that, and he appreciated it.

'If we fly to our deaths, we all die, so it's important to us to keep you stupid people from doing anything stupid,' Brutus replied directly into Cain's mind.

'I'll accept that explanation and reiterate my appreciation. Where are you, little man?' Cain asked.

'See what I mean? Humans are stupid.' Cain looked around and found Brutus standing right behind him.

'Let's find that captain of theirs.' Cain switched to speaking out loud. "Jolly. Where is Captain Brayson?"

"The visitors have all gathered on the mess deck with Captain Rand and the bridge crew," Jolly replied happily.

"Who's left on the bridge?" Cain wondered.

"There's no one on the bridge, but the captain has locked out all the controls. Even I can't release them without two command personnel present."

Cain smiled. Rand wasn't completely taken either. Trust but verify. Cain had seen those words in places throughout late twentieth century Earth literature. He thought he'd understood what they meant, but now he was certain.

And maybe that was why the earthers rushed up to the Cygnus-12 before announcing themselves. They also wanted to trust, but wanted to verify first. Brutus would be able to tell him for certain shortly.

Cain had not been far from the mess deck, so he didn't have time for his usual conversation with himself to work through his strategy. He figured he'd wing it, and Brutus would keep him going in the right direction.

'It is the burden of my life,' Brutus moaned.

Cain scooped Brutus up and scratched behind his ears. "Stop wiggling. You've seen how they dismiss the 'cats. If I'm carrying you, they'll think nothing of it and will talk and, most importantly, think freely," Cain whispered as he leaned his bracelet close enough to activate the hatch. Brutus resigned himself to being carried.

'While we're here, get me some steak,' Brutus demanded.

"The little man is hungry. What a good growing kitty," he cooed.

'You will pay for this,'

'I have a scar on my face that suggests I've already paid for this,' Cain replied in his thought voice. Brutus laughed quietly into Cain's mind.

Cain filled a plate with meat and then put two strips back. He returned to the table with the visitors and the bridge crew, taking a seat close to Captain Brayson.

He put Brutus on the table along with his lunch. Cain wasn't eating. He needed to give his complete attention to the matters at hand.

"Captain Brayson?" Cain said during a break in the conversation.

"Call me Mel," he said with a smile.

"Okay, Mel, thank you. We'd entered systems on three different occasions. In two cases, there was cause for concern and we had to deploy our defensive systems. Our protocols, as you saw, were devised because of those actions. When you brought your ship to meet us, it seemed that you'd seen your share of hostile intruders, but you also said we were the only colonists to have ever returned. Can you explain the dichotomy to me or maybe you've run across aliens?"

Cain rubbed Brutus's back. The 'cat was slowly chewing a piece of beef, also concentrating on the earthers.

"We have many settlers throughout the solar system. Some have become violent. The procedures we use are because of the pirates, the pilgrims who think they are no longer a part of earth. Even you understand where your roots are. We've learned the hard way that it's easier to be ready to fire than not. As for aliens? Why would you say something like that? There is no evidence of aliens." Brayson snorted as he chuckled, but saw the looks on the faces of the bridge crew.

They were deadly serious.

"There are aliens?" he asked, the smile frozen on his face until his expression changed to one of horror. "How much don't we know about our own universe?"

"I can't answer that second one. As for the first one, we'll show you what we came across and share our data with whoever your leadership is, whoever the best repository for such information may be."

"Aliens," the captain said as if it left a bad taste in his mouth. "Are they green or look like spiders? Tell us!"

They leaned forward and listened intently. Cain looked at his shipmates. Rand spoke first.

"Major Cain was right in the middle of it all. A colony planet where the aliens wiped out all human life, tens of thousands of settlers were killed about a hundred years ago, but the aliens left something behind. Care to share more, Major?"

Cain looked at Brutus. *'Anything?'*

They seem afraid of aliens, but the images in their minds are ridiculous, almost like nightmarish dreams. Their policy is what he said it was. Sounds like your trust but verify. These three are harmless, except that navigator seems unable to think of anything other than our navigator. Come to think of it, that's all she's thinking about, too. Humans...'

Cain forced himself not to look at Astral or Kalinda.

He locked his eyes on Mel's. "The aliens were bots, manufactured lifeforms, not really sentient but answering to a mechanical intelligence. They were easy to kill, and they were hard to kill. We were able to capture one and download everything it knew. Before you ask, we did *not* bring it with us. We never determined how they communicated with each other. We didn't want to lead them here, although we suspect they know where Earth is. They tapped the colony's computer systems, which means they know where *our* home world is, too."

"Is it war out there?" Brayson asked after thinking for a moment.

"There's an awful lot of nothing out there, but when there is something, someone wants it, either to hold it or to take it over. And that's why the Cygnus Marines were established. Like I said, we needed a unit capable of projecting power, to protect ourselves while we explored. It sucks that we come across as a military expedition. We only want to explore the galaxy. My great-great-grandparents were the ones who brought free trade and peace back to Vii after the civil war. We are a young civilization, but we like to think we're mature, too." Cain shifted in his seat to get a better look at the captain.

The man was older, his dark hair thinning. He had heavy smile creases around his sharp eyes. Cain could see the wheels turning inside the man's head.

"Thanks for that, Major. So you are somebody, like royalty. I'm pleased to meet you!" The captain resumed his happy-go-lucky attitude while he processed the information about aliens. That had shocked him to his core. He was the captain of a small cutter, barely larger than the shuttles that The Olive Branch carried, and there were aliens out there who destroyed entire populations. Brayson could be on the front lines of a war and he would be completely useless against the enemy.

"I'm not," Cain answered. "My great-great-grandmother was the President of Vii for a while, but I'm nobody. Now him! He's a prince among his people."

Cain pointed an accusing finger at Brutus, all of a sudden thrust into the middle of the conversation. He saw that everyone at the table was looking at him. He opened his mouth and let the half-chewed piece of beef fall onto the table. He turned to Cain.

'I owe you,' he growled in his thought voice, glaring into Cain's eyes. Cain held up one hand to block the other's view as he gave Brutus the finger.

With a snarl, Brutus leapt at Cain's face, knocking him backward, and they both went to the floor.

When Cain finally peeled Brutus off his face, there were two perfect claw scratches, one on each cheek, and four parallel scratches, blood starting to drip from each thin line. Brutus jumped back to the table, gratified when those seated at the table jumped back from him. He crouched and gobbled the rest of his meal.

Cain exercised a great deal of self-discipline to stand up, dust himself off, and keep from smearing the blood on his face. He knew the scratches were there because they burned.

"If you'll excuse me, I'll be off to sickbay now." Cain bowed his head pleasantly and walked around the table to leave, giving Brutus the finger as he hurried toward the hatch.

"We have the same gesture it seems," Captain Brayson said thoughtfully. "It is interesting to see what survives thousands of years and is so universal, all creatures great and small know what it means. My honor meeting you, Prince."

Brutus looked at him for a moment, then jumped off the table and headed for the door.

"I can see where your major got his scars," Tian said with a coy smile.

"Our major has seen more fighting than any other human or intelligent creature in the entire Cygnus System. Don't let his young age fool you. He cares more about humanity than any other being I've ever met," Daksha added from the side of the table. "And I am one hundred and thirty-eight years old."

Captain Rand slapped Brayson on the back. "He's not lying about that. Shall we head back to the bridge? Pickles, if you can bring up some of the things we talked about on the main screen, I think our guests will appreciate the show."

"Of course, Captain."

Stinky sat quietly watching. Tian kept stealing glances at him. He stared at her until she made eye contact. "You have a question?" he asked.

"I have many questions. What is your specialty on board the ship? I mean, how can the Wolfoids contribute?"

"I'm not sure I understand your question. We have Wolfoids in engineering, maintenance, on the bridge to fill in. I can't fly like Lieutenant Pace, but I do have some flight time with the shuttle. We do all the jobs. We take courses from basic mechanics to astro-physics. One of our Marines is a doctor of astrophysics, by the way. He tutors those who need a little extra help. And Briz, the Rabbit, he was in our class at Space School. He's smarter than all the rest of us combined. We are all the same inside, and we are all different. Why is this such an issue for you humans?" Black Leaper asked pointedly.

Captain Rand scowled.

Lieutenant Pace looked at their pilot, the young woman, differently than the others.

"I am sorry. It is so different. You are different, but impressive. All the same. A floating turtle is in charge? Please excuse us. We've never seen anything like this. We haven't even contemplated anything like you. And you tell us that you're not the aliens, but there are real aliens out there. I don't know about the others, but I could use a drink!"

Pace smiled. "That's something I think we could all use. We do have a little wine on board, don't we, Captain?"

"We do," Rand said softly, nodding.

Earth Two

"ETA one hour," Pace said over his shoulder as he eased the EM thrusters to keep the ship angled away from the giant space station. The pilot slowed The Olive Branch expertly as he strove to match the orbit of the station.

It was a giant spinning cylinder with tendrils extending far beyond the open ends. The humans of Earth had perfected a shield technology that enabled both ends of the cylinder to appear like they were open to space, but the atmosphere was contained. Within the cylinder there were concentric, smaller cylinders circling the central access, similar to the way the Traveler was constructed.

Light was channeled through one end that permanently faced the sun. Nearly the entirety of the station's exterior was covered in solar panels to harness solar power, deliver energy without waste, without taking up any extra space.

Within the cylinders, fields and cities abounded. It looked like a lush planet folded backward. Everything a civilization needed to survive.

Below The Olive Branch, the planet Earth, a blue and green orb, rotated slowly. Clouds danced tightly across the surface far below. Brown deserts and mountains, the green of untold flora, and the blue of vast oceans covered the planet's surface.

It didn't look as dead as the earthers led them to believe.

"Take The Olive Branch into the central core of Earth Two, through the main opening. There is docking space large enough to accommodate your ship, even larger. This used to be the shipyard where colony ships were built. Since then, we've expanded, enclosed a large portion, and reduced our shipbuilding to just what we need for work within the system," Brayson explained.

Rand shook his head when Pace looked for him to confirm the order.

"I don't want to do that. The Olive Branch needs to be in open space. We have solar panels of our own," the captain lied. "Please, we'll take the shuttles in. I hope the good people of Earth Two understand."

Rand held his hands out as if pleading. He smiled weakly. Cain watched Brayson closely.

"I don't see that it will be a problem. Let me see if we can put you into a docking orbit on the far side, closer to the sun," Brayson replied helpfully. He raised his hand and spoke into his sleeve.

"Flight control, this is Captain Brayson, currently aboard The Olive Branch, requesting permission for a space-side dock oriented toward the sun. We will shuttle to the landing zone….Alpha Three Radial One Five Zero. Thank you, flight control. See you in a few, Jennings."

Rand breathed a sigh of relief. Cain's jaw ached from clenching it so tightly. The ease with which it was done made him feel guilty about his hesitation to trust the people. They seemed open to all the requests that the people of Cygnus had made.

Pickles rotated in his chair to look at Major Cain. "How many ex-girlfriends do you have?" he asked.

Rand's forehead wrinkled as he wondered what made Pickles ask that question at such a time. The visitors watched carefully, curious. Kalinda continued to look at the space station that filled the screen before her, while her hand explored Astral Star's leg. Pace had been doing the same thing with Tian, but once the new course was delivered from flight control, he was busy preparing to fly the ship and had to take his hand away.

The Earth woman rested her hand comfortably on Pace's back as he happily worked.

"What? I don't know. One, I guess. Damn, Pickles, putting me on the spot!" Cain sounded like he was whining, even to himself. He stood up straight and lowered his voice, trying to sound more Marine-like. "Why do you ask?"

"Because you said an ex-girlfriend called you an animal." Pickles turned back to his position, working the screen and sorting through the data. The sensor operators were vacuuming everything they could pull through their passive mode and filing it for future reference. Jolly was already analyzing the information, and Pickles was monitoring, looking for any threats to the ship.

Commander Daksha had kept Jolly's interaction with the earthers to a minimum since he was hopelessly honest, a good trait but not when trust was uncertain.

"Both of them, then," Cain answered. "Ex and current have called me names that I shan't repeat in polite company. I will admit that I may have deserved it."

Cain tried to look smug, but ended up laughing it off.

He rubbed his face, surprised that it still itched, having been nearly two weeks since the med bot repaired the scratches. He wondered what that was about while the bridge crew laughed at his expense.

Cain made a note to thank Pickles for his genius diversion to remove the tension on the command deck. The major also wanted to ask why the captain lied about the solar panels.

Pace eased the ship forward, tapping into a minute amount of power available in the EM drive. They didn't need much to travel a hundred kilometers.

"Ten minutes to dock," Pace announced.

"Major Cain, I would appreciate it if you led the party to Earth Two. Come with me and we'll talk about who we'd like to send. This is a momentous occasion!" Commander Daksha said through his vocalization device. He swam casually through the hatch and into the corridor, continuing toward his quarters.

Cain followed silently.

Once inside the commander's quarters and the hatch was closed, Daksha ordered Jolly to cut off all communication systems.

"I want you to lead the party ashore because I don't want to overwhelm the humans with the rest of the people. I don't think they are ready for us. Take Leaper with you and Ascenti, and Brutus and Penelope of course. Then we'll send Pace and Kalinda since they seem to be friendly with their earther counterparts. And finally, Ellie."

"Friendly with their counterparts," Cain repeated slowly as the image Jolly shared surged to the front of his mind. He blinked, trying to clear it away. "Why Ellie?"

"Because she was the face of our message, and I saw you on two different planets, Cain. You and Ellie make an unstoppable team. I'm honored to have you represent all of Cygnus." Daksha sounded matter-of-fact through his vocalization device, as if he'd analyzed the data and the answer had been properly arrived at.

"I'm honored, and I don't know what to say, Master Daksha." Cain looked down as he shuffled his feet. He was still a young man, very young.

"You'll be fine, Cain. Braden would be proud if he could see you now. And Prince Axial De'atesh. Brutus and Ellie are both good for you. They keep you grounded." Daksha floated serenely over the hot sand, swimming every now and again to remain in place as the ship glided toward its docking place. "You better go, gather the team. I'll tell the bridge crew. Everyone will meet at the hangar bay."

Cain nodded and started to leave, then stopped. He turned his head and spoke over his shoulder. "Can you have Ellie meet me in the corridor? I think Briz still has me banned from engineering. I don't have time to free myself from an insulbrick shower."

Cain was serious, but Daksha chuckled by way of the device hanging around his long neck. "I will smooth things over with our chief engineer, Master Cain. Please keep your neural implants open at all times while in the station. I can't guarantee that there won't be interference, but we'll try to stay in touch nonetheless."

"Aye, aye, Commander," Cain answered as he passed through the hatch and disappeared into the corridor.

Daksha floated higher until he was clear of the few obstacles in his quarters. BJ was curled up in his usual place on the Tortoid's shell.

'I would have liked to go,' Billy Joe suggested.

'This one will challenge us greatly, and we need you here,' Daksha answered simply. *'When we go over there, you will be overwhelmed with the number of people and aberrant thoughts. I expect they will not be too welcoming of us, because we are so different, my friend. Cain will pave the way to make it better, but it will be very hard on you.'*

'Thank you, Daksha. I look forward to seeing another new world,' the 'cat replied.

***

Cain and Ellie were holding hands as they waited for the others. Brutus and Carnesto sat, looking patient, but they weren't. The 'cats never enjoyed riding in the shuttle because they were stuffed in as an afterthought. The shuttles were designed for humans. Daksha and Jolly had requested a new design and Briz said he'd work on it, despite the fact that it was the responsibility of the De'atesh Shipyard to build such things.

The priority given would depend on what The Olive Branch brought home from Earth. It was also important that Holly have his issues resolved so that his split personality could disappear. Maybe that meant that humanity had to resolve their issues first.

Cain was afraid to go home for that very reason. He was afraid that Holly would come up with new and ingenious ways to kill him. Cain wondered if Holly had lost faith in the pure-heart test. Cain didn't know, but would want assurances before he left the ship once they returned to Cygnus space.

We have to do this one little thing here, first, Cain thought to himself. *Why are you thinking of going home? The glory of a triumphant return? Look at who is holding your hand. That's the only triumph that matters. From this, all good will flow.*

Cain knew that he should have been anxious, but he wasn't. Daksha was right. Ellie made him better. He made her better. They were a great team. They were the face of Cygnus VII.

'Oh, brother. Let me get out my waders,' Brutus said in his thought voice. *'If anyone is the face of Cygnus VII, it's right here, buddy!'*

Brutus lifted his chin, twitching a scarred ear. His green-orange pupils showed large in the bright light of the hangar bay. He yawned only to show his fangs.

Cain bumped Ellie with a shoulder. "Look at him preen. He's the face of Cygnus VII."

"Look at Carnesto! Such a proud and stately kitty!" Ellie replied. Both 'cats waved a single paw at their humans.

"Universal gesture, indeed. It's our way of saying hello to the people of Earth!" Cain exclaimed. He saw the others approaching through the clear panels that lined the hangar bay, showing the corridor beyond.

Brayson and his two people were accompanied by Stinky and the kitten Penelope. Black Leaper had his spear and made a show of using it as a walking stick. They knew they couldn't bring weapons onto the station. That would send the wrong message.

Sergeant Stalker was there, too, with Hortense, even though she and the kitten would remain behind.

Ascenti appeared, gliding past the windows and banking hard to fly through the hatch. He flapped once to get enough height where he could land on one of the shuttle's fins. Cain gave him the thumbs up.

"It is nice to fly again," he said through his vocalization device. Cain nodded.

Pace and Kalinda walked with their counterparts from Earth. Cain wondered if their new relationships would cause a problem. *'Will it, Brutus?'* Cain asked.

'Their loyalty is to this ship and the crew, but they like the earthers very much.' Brutus watched the group intently.

'That's what I thought. I hope we don't have to test it. I hope they don't want to remain behind or any of the others. What the hell would we do then?' Cain replied.

'A rhetorical question,' Brutus said. *'What if people from there want to go with us?'*

The kitten raced through the hatch in front of the group and ran straight for Brutus. He jumped up quickly as the kitten, who was almost as large as his father, crashed into him.

Two twists and a backflip later, the kitten was thrown through the air and landed heavily, on her feet but dazed.

"Enough," Cain told her, stabbing a finger in her direction. She immediately sat up and started licking a paw to wash her face.

Brutus had recovered and was sitting as if he hadn't just been attacked. *'You're a good dad, Brutus,'* Cain told him.

'I know.'

Cain smirked as Captain Brayson approached with his hand out. They shook.

"Talking with your 'cat?" he asked.

"I'm his human, but yeah. That obvious, huh?" Cain asked cordially.

"I recognize the look on your face. It's usually one of disbelief. I can only imagine what Brutus is telling you."

Cain nodded. "You don't want to know, and no, it's not about you. It's always about me and my shortcomings. I think he keeps a list, a very, very long list."

The captain slapped Cain's shoulder and then stepped aside so the others could start boarding.

Pace and Tian entered the shuttle first, climbing into the pilot and co-pilot seats. The navigators then went inside, sitting next to each other as far forward as they could go. Lieutenant Black Leaper stopped and looked back at Sergeant Night Stalker before he ducked through the hatch and took the seat opposite Kalinda. The captain sat next to him. Cain and Ellie filed in and then the 'cats found laps to sit on.

'I saw you look at her butt,' Cain taunted Stinky over the neural implant.

'Did not!' the Wolfoid retorted. *'You are such a voyeur, Cain.'*

Ascenti flew away from the fin and then executed a tight turn, adjusted as he approached the hatch, then tucked his wings as he passed through, backwinging once inside and slapping both Cain and Ellie in the head as he slowed. The Hawkoid landed in the space between the pilot and the co-pilot on the rack that he could get his talons around to hold himself in place.

"Sorry about that," he mumbled through his vocalization device.

"Sorry about what?" Cain asked politely. "I wonder how far Briz has come in regards to a shuttle that is better suited to the people?"

'Now that was a rhetorical question,' Cain told Brutus as he scratched the 'cat's ears, hanging on as the hatch closed and the shuttle slid silently toward the opening bay door and into space.

Lieutenant Pace expertly guided the ship from The Olive Branch, arcing away as the ship rotated behind them. It took two full rotations before the hangar bay door closed, but no one saw as they wondered at the immensity of the space station known as Earth Two.

The captain had said they used to build colony ships within. Colony ships were massive in their own right. Cain had had to work his way from one end to the other of the RV Traveler. It had taken days of hard travel and the loss of one of his Marines.

They didn't have a map of Earth Two readily available within his neural implant this time. Or did he?

'Jolly, can you find a map of Earth Two and send that to my implant?' Cain asked the AI.

'I will try, but the station's systems are shielded and I don't want to highlight my attempt to access them. Would you like me to throw caution to the wind and soldier on?' Jolly asked.

Cain tried not to laugh as he closed his eyes to make sure the others didn't see him communing. *'No, Jolly. That was just a thought I had, but we definitely don't want to come across as hostile. Keep looking around. Maybe someone left a window open that you can peek through.'*

Welcome to our Home

Tian wanted to take the controls of the shuttle as they approached the landing pad, but the systems were nothing like what she was used to so she settled for guiding Pace in, relaying orientation and flight speeds as she received them over her communication device.

Pace expertly put the ship onto the pad horizontally, unlike the usual vertical landing in full gravity. It required more than usual thruster engagement, but Pace enjoyed the challenge. No one seemed to share his sense of accomplishment, which he found disappointing.

No one except Tian Mahjing, who understood how the ship was meant to take off, fly, and land.

"Well done, master pilot!" she congratulated Lieutenant Pace. He grinned and took her hand.

'Brutus?'

'Sincerity of the mushiest sort. You humans and your mating rituals are so ridiculous.' Brutus shook his 'cat head as if trying to rid himself of a pesky fly.

'The greeting party?' Cain pressed.

A group of people waited behind the shuttle where the hatch was. Brutus stared at the closed hatch.

'Quite the jumble of thoughts. Most of them think we're aliens. Can we go back home now?' Brutus asked. *'I don't like it here.'*

'We haven't even been 'here' yet. Give it a few, little man, and we'll do our best,' Cain said reassuringly. The anxiety Cain hadn't felt before surged through him with Brutus's latest warning. *'Let Ellie know and keep us in touch, if you can.'*

'If I can, indeed. You were already in her mind and will continue to be, because it's so much easier than me playing pivot man,' Brutus replied sarcastically.

'Are you ready to be the face of Cygnus VII, my love?' Cain asked.

'Not sure about all that, but yes. Let's see what there is to see, lover,' Ellie

212

answered.

"Everyone ready?" Cain asked, forcing himself to smile. Stinky panted rapidly. Penelope had probably already shared what the humans outside were feeling. As the most alien-looking of the non-humans, Black Leaper was anxious. "Go time."

Cain popped the hatch and made to walk out first, but both Brutus and Carnesto jumped down and bolted through. The group outside watched curiously as Cain left the shuttle, then offered a helping hand to Ellie. He normally wouldn't since she was perfectly capable of disembarking on her own, but this meeting was about the show.

As Cygnus VII's first couple, they had appearances to maintain. *'We'll laugh about this later.'*

'I sure hope so,' she replied, relaxing with his calming smile.

They turned, hand in hand, and faced the group. Together they waved and strode boldly to the gray-haired person standing in front.

"This is Ensign Ellie and I'm Major Cain." Cain offered his hand and the older gentleman took it. They'd established with Brayson that hand-shaking was still an acceptable greeting.

Cain's grip was firm, but he took it easy on the older man. Brutus and Carnesto appeared and stood by the side of each of their humans.

"Oh!" one woman exclaimed. "We don't allow pets except in licensed areas."

Cain looked down to see Brutus's narrowed eyes as he sent visual hate daggers her way.

"I am remiss," Cain said to the group. "This is my friend Brutus and the large black Hillcat is Carnesto. They are sentient and are life-linked to us. Let me introduce the rest of our party."

'And we don't allow stupid humans to tell us where we can't be,' Brutus quipped.

Cain moved aside so the welcoming committee could get a clear view of the shuttle.

"Your crew from the Ganymede Seven who met us at the edge of the heliosphere, Captain Mel Brayson, Navigator Astral Star, and inside with our pilot is Tian Mahjing. Our navigator is Ensign Kalinda. Next is my deputy, Lieutenant Black Leaper. He is a Wolfoid, one of many intelligent species on Cygnus VII."

"I'm pleased to meet you," Stinky said pleasantly through his vocalization device.

"It talks," another woman said.

"He. Of course he talks. What do you think I meant when I said intelligent species?" Cain asked abruptly. Ellie squeezed his hand.

"Next is Lieutenant Pace, our pilot, and last, Private Ascenti, our representative from the Hawkoid Nation." Ascenti popped through the hatch and spread his wings, beating hard to gain altitude, circling and landing on Cain's outstretched arm.

"I am Ascenti. I'm pleased to meet you," he said, turning his feathered head to study the party before them.

The old man, two women, and two other men stood with their mouths open.

"These sentient species all evolved in the Cygnus System?" the old man asked.

"No," Cain answered, looking the old man in the eye. "In order to colonize Cygnus VII, humanity needed more help than they could provide themselves. Dr. Warren, a geneticist from Earth's Resettlement Vessel Traveler, used gene splicing to change the evolution of a number of species who traveled on the colony ship. He also worked with some native species and these are a few representatives from those evolutions. The planet fought a rather substantial civil war over this and other things. That war destroyed most of the technology and most of the people. Since then, we have grown up with these species, side-by-side. We are equals in many ways."

The man looked to the others in his party. The looks they gave each other were not pleasant. When the man turned back, he was smiling.

"I am Garth Hansen, Prime Minister of this world. These four are the provincial heads. Andes Turkyn is the administrator of Outer World One. Gladys Ironside is the administrator of Outer World Two. Inner World One is Agnes Menster, and Inner World Two, Tomas Espinoza." The administrators nodded congenially, but they weren't smiling and they made no attempt to shake hands.

Ellie wasn't having any of that. She let Cain's hand drop as she walked from one person to the next, forcing them to shake her hand as she smiled warmly and gripped their hands in both of hers.

Winning them over was one of the tasks that Daksha had charged him with. He joined Ellie and worked his way around the party of government officials.

They gave him the willies from their limp handshakes to the phony expressions on their faces to their air of superiority when they stole glances at the Hawkoid standing on Cain's shoulder.

He felt like an old-time pirate from the movies, but he was trying to acclimate the earthers to the presence of intelligent non-humans.

'Being genetically engineered is a crime here,' Brutus told him.

'But you can't control what you are and the people who did it died centuries ago,' Cain argued.

'Doesn't matter. These people are trying to figure out how to arrest the Wolfoid and the Hawkoid without upsetting you.'

'I'm pretty sure that's not possible. Let's bring this out in the open. If nothing else, they can get back on the shuttle and return to the ship,' Cain replied.

"Prime Minister Hansen. It's illegal to be genetically engineered? Don't you mean that it's illegal to conduct genetic engineering?" Cain directly asked the leader of their government, standing close and looming slightly over the man.

"That's not it. How do you know that?"

'The prime minister is worried that you've been in contact with one of the administrators and working behind his back,' Brutus explained.

"He told us," Cain said, pointing at Tomas, who instantly started sputtering. "I'm just kidding. It was really her."

Gladys's eyes shot wide as the finger of accusation pointed in her direction.

"I'm sorry. My way of defusing the tension, because I refuse to believe that my friends are illegal just for existing. That makes no sense to me. I figured it out by the looks on your faces when I mentioned Dr. Warren," Cain told them.

The administrators glared at Cain. He returned their looks with a cordial smile and tip of the head.

He was ready to go to war with these people. Ellie grasped his hand tightly, knowing that his fight or flight response was one hundred percent geared to fight.

'Let's go home,' Brutus suggested.

"I have to say that I'm not pleased with the welcome we've received. Thank you. Keep your people. We're leaving." Cain twirled his finger in the air for the crew to load back into the shuttle.

Stinky let out a long breath and nodded to the earthers as he turned and made his way back to the shuttle.

"I'm afraid not, Major. That won't do at all," Garth Hansen said in a low voice.

'Run!' Brutus yelled a moment before cables shot out of the ground and wrapped over the shuttle. The 'cats scattered--Brutus, Carnesto, and Penelope ran in different directions on the landing pad. There were other small ships, a transshipment style facility with cargo neatly ordered, and there were walkways leading away from the pad, heading downward toward the outer cylinders. Apparent gravity was lighter near the hub, like it was toward the spindle of the Cygnus-12.

Cain and Ellie never moved. Stinky leveled his spear at the prime minister, but Cain caught the spear tip and moved it away from the welcoming committee.

"Interesting move, Prime Minister. I have to say that Earth has grown pretty crappy since the colonists bound for the Cygnus System departed. All of our literature suggests that Earth was kind and gentle. But you? You guys are a bunch of pricks."

Ellie gave up trying to squeeze sense into Cain through his hand.

"Seize them," the prime minister said flatly.

"Fly, Private. Save yourself," Cain ordered in a whisper. Ascenti launched himself at the prime minister, forcing the man and his administrators to duck. The Hawkoid beat his wings furiously to gain altitude and escape the mess they found themselves in the middle of.

'There was nothing you could do,' Ellie told him over the mindlink. *'There was nothing any of us could do.'*

Cain clenched his jaw. He was done talking.

"Wait, wait!" Captain Brayson called out, running past Cain and Ellie to stand before the prime minister.

"Sir, we cannot arrest them. They are here because I gave them my word that we would meet as friends, welcome humanity's children home," Brayson pleaded, trying to sound profound.

"You don't speak for the government. I do. Next time you meet aliens, maybe you should remember your place. Then again, there probably won't be a next time." The prime minister watched as security men carrying short rods approach. "Take them, too. All of them. And find that damn bird!"

The prime minister seemed a different person from the one who initially greeted them. *'Brutus, are you safe? Can you tell anything from this clown?'*

'I am in the cargo area. There are a lot of places to hide in here, so I'll be fine. He has a genetically-altered mind and can partition his thoughts, it appears. That is why he champions demonizing the altered, even those who had nothing to do with something that happened hundreds of lifetimes ago.'

'Stay out of sight, Brutus, and thank you. We'll get out of this. I just don't know how, not yet anyway,' Cain replied over the mindlink that he shared with Ellie, Carnesto, and Brutus.

"You don't want the others to know that you've been genetically altered. Will you be in jail with us then?" Cain said accusingly. The look of panic on the prime minister's face was quickly replaced by pure hatred. "Ooh. I guess I struck a nerve, huh?"

"Get them out of here!" the old man screamed.

"Toward the ramp, prisoners. And you, give me that." Stinky glanced at Cain, but the major shook his head. Stinky handed over his lightning spear. After the incident where the southerners had stolen a cache of Wolfoid lightning spears, they'd been keyed to Wolfoid hands only. Jolly had modified them so any of the Marines could use the spears if necessary, but not strangers. The earthers wouldn't be sending lightning bolts anywhere.

One of the guards jabbed his short club into Leaper's side and activated it. The Wolfoid howled in pain as electricity coursed through his body. Cain took one step toward the man before the major was struck down, clubbed by another stick-wielding guard. The man sent juice coursing through Cain's body while he lay on the landing pad.

Cain refused to scream, but the pain came in waves, worse and worse. He thought he heard Ellie scream. Then his world faded to black.

What Next

"Jolly. Play back the images, please, slowly, with audio," Commander Daksha requested while floating next to the captain.

They watched the scene unfold, starting with the introductions.

"Ten minutes. Our people were on board the station for ten whole minutes before they were taken. Brutus must have told Cain what the prime minister was thinking. He knew things were going bad and wanted us to have the information."

"Politics? You've got to be kidding me. We come thousands of light years and all they can do is play politics. Fear monger the aliens? I can't believe any of this," Rand complained.

"How are we going to get our people back?" Daksha asked.

"I will lead an assault team and we will recover them through force of arms," Lieutenant Peekaless suggested.

"We'll keep that as a last option, Pickles, but have your Marines ready to go. We can't let this go on for too long. Too much time and they'll hide our people in that monstrosity where we'll never find them." Daksha didn't blink as he watched the replays, seeing the information from different angles.

"The 'cats all escaped. Ascenti is free and in hiding. Jolly, contact Private Ascenti, please."

After a few moments, they saw the world through the Hawkoid's eyes. "Ascenti here," his voice said as it was generated through the neural implant.

"Report," the captain ordered.

"I'm in the rafters trying to keep the others in view. They are together and heading down a ramp that looks similar to what we saw on the Traveler."

The image cleared as the Hawkoid leaned around an obstruction. Far below, a ramp curved downward. Seven humans and a Wolfoid were being force-marched by eight large men carrying the electrified clubs. They jabbed their weapons into the group every now and again to motivate their prisoners to walk faster.

"Cain looks like he's up as does Black Leaper. Jolly? How long was Cain unconscious?" Daksha asked.

"Less than one minute, Commander. As soon as they removed the electrical shock device, he recovered quickly."

"They've condemned their own people to prison, just for being nice to us," Rand said, barely above a whisper.

"Jolly. Please find a communication channel where I can talk with the prime minister. The sooner the better," Daksha encouraged.

"On it," Jolly answered and disappeared.

He showed up after two agonizingly long minutes. "Coming through now."

The Tortoid made sure to float close to the camera so he would fill the image screen on the other end of the link. "I am Daksha, Commander of The Olive Branch. We came to Earth on a mission of peace. Please help me understand your actions in taking our people prisoner."

"I'm sure this is just a simple misunderstanding, Commander," the prime minister said, wearing a plastic smile.

"Then free our people and let them return with our shuttle. Are you not in charge and cannot do the right thing?" Daksha challenged.

"There is no one person in charge here and that makes the red tape a mess to wade through, but believe me, we will get to the bottom of it," the old man said in a soothing tone.

"I am so sorry, Prime Minister, but my hearing must be bad. I thought you said for me to believe you when you are clearly lying. Your security men used shock weapons on our people. They did it on your direct orders. There is no misunderstanding. One more thing, Prime Minister, only one of us has faced real aliens and defeated them. It wasn't you. Release our people immediately or face the consequences."

Jolly cut the signal. Daksha swam in a half-circle to face Rand. "I won't give up on the universe, Rand, even though everywhere we turn, someone tries to feed us a turd sandwich."

"Commander! You are usually the one calling for calm," Rand stated, feeling the anger that gripped the Tortoid.

"Three in a row, Captain. Three worlds in a row. The people are fine, but those in charge are counter to everything we stand for. I was starting to like Captain Brayson. They condemned him just for treating us like a decent human being should, like any creature should treat another. Shooting stars, what a mess!"

Daksha had never been so agitated. "Starsgard! Tell me you're in weapons, Corporal Starsgard."

"I am, sir. What do you need?"

"Give me a firing solution on all available targets," Daksha said. The captain sat up straight with brow furled.

"Please define the word target," Starsgard requested.

"Anything we might need to blow apart!" Daksha ranted.

"I think we better choose a different course of action, Commander. I will shut down all the systems before they can be used in a manner that you are describing. We can't haphazardly shoot stuff until they release our people. It may or may not be a viable strategy, but that one clearly violates every one of my safety protocols." Jolly tried to get in front of the Tortoid, but Daksha ignored him and swam for the hatch to leave the bridge.

Billy Joe hung on, his mind inundated by over one hundred years of carefully constrained anger, unleashed all at once.

Daksha had been wrong about the nature of the universe. His premise had been that people were fundamentally good. Although that may have been true, the overriding premise was that people in charge were power hungry and saw any contact with foreign life as a direct challenge to their authority.

The Tortoid had always assumed that the Space Exploration Service would be greeted warmly and that there would be an exchange of information, research, technology, and more.

Instead, their reception was marred by the fact that their very existence was illegal simply because hundreds of years prior, a geneticist had spliced human DNA onto that of their forebears.

Commander Daksha turned around in the corner and slowly swam back onto the bridge.

"Humans are so much better at storming off than I," Daksha said softly. "Ascenti, my feathered friend. Can you keep our people in view?"

"I think so, Commander. Wait one moment," he called. They watched the view bounce up and down, then smooth as the Hawkoid jumped from his perch and glided downward.

"Briz, are you there?" Daksha asked while they watched the Hawkoid fly to a place where he could better observe the procession. Jolly dutifully built a map based on the information they recorded from Ascenti.

"Yes, Commander. How can I help?" Briz replied.

"What kind of technical surprise could you whip up for the earthers? Can you slow down the rotation of the cylinders? Maybe cut off power from the solar collectors? How about broadcasting an annoying sound throughout the station?" Daksha was out of ideas. He was flailing.

"I will work with Jolly and we'll come up with some options for you, Commander. Don't be afraid. Cain is the best of all of us. The earthers have truly messed with the wrong Marine. I kind of feel sorry for them, but only kind of," the Rabbit said.

"We can jam them, but we can't use the missiles unless they are clearly attacking us," Starsgard added.

"Thank you all. Let's reconvene in an hour and present any ideas we may have. In the interim, sensors, remain passive and watch everything. No surprises, please," Daksha ordered.

"If you want no surprises, then I recommend that we go active, but not ping the station directly. We can radiate everywhere but the station so we aren't so alarming," Chirit offered.

"Make it so, Lieutenant." Daksha floated upward, feeling more in control of himself.

***

Cain made eye contact with the others and tipped his chin in all directions, encouraging them to look around and record everything they saw through their neural implants.

The major looked at the guards, certain that he could take one or two out, but that wouldn't be enough. Their stun clubs would penalize everyone else in the party. Cain dismissed the idea. Stinky looked to be in pain. The guards had too much fun beating Cain's friend.

What goes around, comes around, Cain thought.

They continued down the ramp until a series of doors appeared on the left. The man in the lead opened one of them seemingly at random and pointed the way in. The guards weren't talkative, considering their prisoners to be less than human.

"Why thank you!" Cain exclaimed, earning him a quick discharge from the stun club. Cain grunted, but didn't cry out, and he didn't fall down. "Is that all you got?"

The man shoved Cain through the door and Ellie swung, stepping into her punch and catching the man in the temple. She grunted with the effort, then stepped back in a ready position, expecting a counterpunch, but the man dropped, out cold.

The one behind him was surprised, but not for long. He jabbed his stick at Ellie. She dodged and caught it, then lashed out and kicked the man in the groin. He toppled and she ripped the club from his hand. The other guards sprang into action.

Cain brained the first guard who came within reach, but the rest of the prisoners were pummeled quickly. Men appeared in the doorway and overwhelmed Cain. Ellie had the club beat from her hands and she was stunned repeatedly as Cain, being manhandled by four strong men, watched.

"Run!" the major yelled as Stinky was wrestling with the man who had his lightning spear. The Wolfoid bit the man's arm and leapt over him, trying to pull the spear as he escaped. The guard's grip was too strong and Stinky crashed to the ground, caught in a game of tug-of-war with the lightning spear. The last man had finished zapping the two navigators and swung his club in a wide arc to catch Black Leaper on the side of his head.

The Wolfoid staggered a step, then fell over. The man Stinky had been fighting with swung his club again and again, but Leaper didn't feel anything. He was unconscious and defenseless.

"STOP!" Cain screamed. "We'll go with you."

The man ceased his attack and strutted to Cain. He jabbed his club into Cain's abdomen and activated it until the major doubled over in pain. Sparks and flashes appeared before the major's closed eyes. The weapon stopped and rough hands dragged Cain to his feet.

A knot was starting to grow on the side of Ellie's face where one of the security men had clubbed her. She had told him that he wasn't her protector.

In his mind, he always would be, and he had just failed miserably.

The faces of Cygnus VII, contorted in pain, battered and bruised, dragged toward confinement.

Cain would have never imagined such an eventuality.

Plans regarding the replacement of the current earther leadership and payback to the security guards started to flood his mind.

***

"Oh my," Daksha blurted as they watched, shocked at the brutality of the people on Earth Two.

"And they called me an animal," Pickles offered emotionlessly.

"I never wanted to see anyone dead before, but the prime minister and those administrators are now on my list," Daksha whispered.

"Ascenti? Are there any other people around? Would it be possible to fly a shuttle to the ramp and deposit the Marines there?" Rand asked.

"Very few people, but I see some going about their business," Ascenti replied. Jolly appeared next to Rand.

"Can we talk with the 'cats?" Jolly asked in his effort to expand the conversation.

"Only through one of our people. That's a good idea, Jolly. Send a note to Cain, Ellie, and Leaper. What do you want to ask?"

"I would like the 'cats' assessment of the general attitude of the population. Are they oppressed like the people on Concordia?" Jolly suggested.

"I'd like to know the answer to that, too," Daksha said. He blinked slowly as he thought about it. "Send the note, Jolly. Maybe they've recovered sufficiently to be able to ask the question for us."

Jolly put his arms behind his back as he waited.

Cain's voice came loud and clear over the sound system. "Hey, guys, you're missing the party." Jolly played what was traveling down Cain's optic nerve. Their video as seen through the eyes of the crew.

They were being herded along a passageway. The prisoners were complying with the orders given. "I've asked Brutus if he could get any impressions. He's working on it, but he needs to move out of the cargo area. Carnesto has found a dark spot to observe the landing zone and Penelope is inside something and very afraid."

Rand's lip curled of its own accord.

"How are you holding up, Cain?" Daksha asked.

"You saw that little tiff on the ramp?"

"Ascenti was in a good position to observe. We were not amused with what we saw," Daksha told him.

"Ellie racked that gutter slug right up his man parts. I'm proud of her and all of them. I am worried about Leaper. They consider him as some kind of alien and not evolved as far as humans. By the way, do you have any plans to break us out of here?"

"Working on that last part, Major Cain. Briz and Jolly are brainstorming on some things that we'll look at shortly. Keep your head up, Cain, and keep the morale of the others up. The only thing I can promise is that we're not leaving here without you."

Cain didn't answer. His attention was pulled into an open door that they were shoving him through. Inside were med bots, human medical personnel, and way too many needles.

A 'Cat's View of the World

'Time to move, Carnesto. Let's go find us some stupid people,' Brutus said, looking out from his hiding spot. He used his senses to find the people in the area. There weren't many. Most of the systems were automated.

Brutus bolted into the open and ran low, dodging behind a crate, under a piece of slow-moving equipment, then to some decorative foliage.

It wasn't even real. Brutus sniffed at it before climbing into the trough in which it was placed and relieving himself.

Fake trees. People are stupid, he thought.

'Ascenti. Is the ramp the only way out of this cursed landing zone?' Brutus asked over their mindlink.

'It looks like it. There are doors and offices on the opposite end, but I can't see that there are stairs or an elevator or anything suggesting an exit. Reminds me of the Traveler. The ramps were the main routes, but if we could find where they're hiding the elevators, then you could make quick work of traveling up and down, except you'd be trapped inside a box,' Ascenti responded, unsure of what Brutus intended. The Hawkoid watched the ramp and the door through which they'd taken the others, but he couldn't get inside. He was relegated to being an observer.

Or a 'cat helper. He'd heard the stories where Hawkoids in the past had carried Hillcats on their backs. He wasn't sure he wanted to try it since he was still getting used to his new wing.

'Have no fear. I'm not going for a ride, not while I'm still breathing anyway,' Brutus said to allay the Hawkoid's fears. *'Maybe you can snag the kitten and take her some place safe, like the overhead struts. She can watch, but no one will be able to get to her.'*

'I'll consider that. Do you know where she is?'

'Yes,' Brutus said in his annoying way of answering questions literally.

'Can you guide me to her?'

'Yes.'

Ascenti had had enough. He launched himself from the support beam and glided back toward the landing zone, beating his wings just enough to stay near the overhead. Brutus guided him toward the kitten's hiding place, but she wouldn't come out.

The Hawkoid was exposed flying so low. He ducked behind a box, landed, and hopped closer to Penelope. He chirped, but she remained inside. He switched to his vocalization device.

"Come out, Penelope, and hurry. We need to go," Ascenti pleaded. He could hear Brutus encouraging her over the mindlink. The Hawkoid peeked out from behind the box, looking around and making sure that he still had time. He caught sight of Brutus running toward him.

The scruffy orange 'cat stopped, crawled inside the hole in the box and after some kitten-size yowling, dragged his daughter into the open.

'Grab her and take her out of here,' Brutus demanded as he held her down with one paw.

Ascenti beat his wings to get off the deck, pounced on the kitten who was more than half Brutus's size, and the Hawkoid flew upward. Brutus dashed in the direction of the next cover.

Penelope yowled as Ascenti tried to soothe her. He made it to a beam in the rafters and carefully deposited her, before adjusting and landing next to the kitten. She shivered with fear, but she was safe from the earthers.

Brutus angled sharply away from a group of people coming up the ramp. He stopped next to a low wall and crouched, listening to their thoughts. Workers ready for the start of their shift. Complaining about breakfast. It wasn't hot enough, but they weren't fomenting rebellion.

'Is the ramp clear?' Brutus asked.

'As far as I can see, yes,' Ascenti replied.

Brutus didn't wait. He entered the ramp, running downward as fast as he could.

***

Carnesto waited in the cargo transshipment area. He was closer to the offices than Brutus had been. He stayed in the shadows to work his way next to the door. He could see through the windows, then realized that they were openings without glass. No need for windows in a place where the environment was completely controlled and someone was always on duty.

The 'cat tucked his feet beneath him and tried to be a hole in a shadow as he listened to the exchange between the two groups of humans. The ones who had been on the pad were animated and into telling their story about the arrival of aliens.

"That's their ship right there! It is trapped tighter than a box seal. Aliens got off--a wolf-man, a bird, a real bird, and then cats, too. It was a freak show!" the man shouted, trying to be the voice that everyone listened to.

Carnesto wanted to scratch the man's eyes out.

"The prime minister himself fought them off when they attacked. Security hauled their heathen asses away." Carnesto imagined the man gesturing wildly to emphasize the fantasy yarn he was spinning.

The others laughed. "There's no way the prime minister fought anyone off. I saw him lose a fight with a tomato sandwich," one man from the new shift offered. Many from the two groups snickered.

"Watch your tongue. You know they listen," the first man cautioned.

"Aliens? Real aliens?" a woman asked. "Cats aren't aliens. We have them here and dogs, too. They're just controlled, that's all. I wanted a cat, but didn't get my request approved. That seems to be the way things are nowadays. No one gets anything except more work."

"Our dogs don't carry spears or walk upright, stand bigger than a man. That one from the alien ship did," the first speaker intoned as if setting the stage for a theatric performance.

"What did you really see, doofus?" someone demanded.

The man harrumphed and someone else stepped up. "I was watching from the loader since they shut down the pad for their arrival. They seemed nice enough, shook hands with the prime minister and the four administrators. Then the security guards took over. That's what I saw. If they are aliens, then we just showed them who's in charge. What if they sent for reinforcements? The aliens will kill us all and blaming the prime minister won't get our lives back," a woman enunciated clearly, as if trying to be clear for whoever might be listening in.

She didn't condemn anyone. She only told her version.

"Okay, I may have exaggerated, but not the wolf-man. He was something! I ain't never seen nothing like that before, not even in the movies. The bird and cats got away. They are running around here somewhere. Security told us to go about our business and they'd be bringing a crew as soon as possible to find them. That's enough excitement for me for the day. I don't want to be here when security shows up. Those clubs of theirs sting like a mother!" he said knowingly.

The others nodded and with final mumbles good-bye, the outgoing shift departed. The newcomers, five men and three women, grabbed their duty assignments and headed away from the building. Carnesto watched where the cat-loving woman went and followed her.

She had a computer pad and looked to be scanning crates, conducting inventory. Carnesto walked up to her and rubbed his large body against her leg. She jumped back, looked around, and then started petting his gleaming black fur. Carnesto looked at her and gave an obligatory sad meow with his eyes wide.

Her heart melted, and he knew that he had her. He let her pet him for a while longer before opening a mindlink with her.

'Hi, pretty lady! I need your help.'

She jumped back and made like she was looking at documentation. "Who said that, and where are you?" she whispered harshly.

'I'm down here. You were petting me. I'm a Hillcat,' Carnesto explained. *'Telepathy is the word that you use.'*

She stared at him with her mouth open. He sat down and wrapped his tail around his back legs. *'My friends and I really need your help. The duplicity and subterfuge of your prime minister caught us completely unaware,'* Carnesto said, enunciating to make sure that she understood every word. *'I could kill him, but prefer to simply gather my people and leave. You can save lives by helping me to free them from wherever security has taken them. If I'm not mistaken, it's some sort of medical lab.'*

"What do you want me to do, kitty?" she asked in a breathy whisper, smiling as she continued to pet him behind his ears.

'Carnesto. My name is Carnesto,' he replied, continuing to look into her eyes. *'As for what you can do. It would help if you took me to the lab where they are, down the ramp and to the left.'*

"What kind of name is Carnesto?" she asked, warming up to the idea of a talking cat.

It is my name. Is that not good enough? What is your name, pretty lady?' Carnesto kept trying to build his relationship with her, wanting her to do as he asked, but she was holding herself back.

"My name is Jane, Jane Merriweather." She held out her hand automatically as if to shake. The 'cat looked at her hand blankly. "Oh, sorry about that. Can I pick you up and hold you? You look really soft."

Carnesto fought his natural inclination to roll his eyes. He struggled in an epic internal battle and finally gave in. *'Yes, you may pick me up, Jane Jane, but don't let anyone else see. They'll get jealous.'*

Jane took a knee in front of him and looked both ways before scooping up the large 'cat and hugging him fiercely and kissing his head. He could hear Brutus laughing in the back of his mind, but the rough orange 'cat was a long ways away.

***

Brutus reached the bottom of the ramp and turned sharply into a more congested urban area. The area was clean, almost antiseptic.

He had passed into the inner world where the cylinder disappeared away from him, curving into the sky. The brightness of the structure above acted as the sun, lighting the inner world in a way that left few shadows. Brutus was given little in which to hide.

Sharp corners and no foliage. Slick walls and smooth decks. Lackluster people, going about their business. Even their clothes lacked color. Cain and his camouflage would have stood out like a lighthouse beacon in the darkness. The orange of Brutus's hair seemed to glow against the white and gray of that town in the inner world.

Brutus crouched as far out of sight as he could get, using his senses to make sure no people were close. He tentatively reached out and touched the minds of the populace, alarmed at the lack of energy and drive that most of the people had. They existed, but not much more.

'Is this what happens when people stop reaching for the stars?' Brutus asked his life-link.

'Where are you, Brutus?' Cain asked in a pain-fogged thought voice.

The inner world, my friend. The people here don't seem to care about anything. There's no spark of life,' Brutus replied sadly.

'There's plenty of sparks up here, Brutus,' Cain replied before screaming in agony until he felt his vocal cords would shred. *'If they have that attitude, then they won't resist anything we do. Keep pressing. Find someone to help you to come back and free us. They are punishing us for their own fears. I am afraid that they won't stop until we're all dead.'*

'I will find someone. Carnesto is having better luck. He has already gained the confidence of a human female. I have to go. There are children nearby who haven't given up yet.' With that, Brutus was off and running.

***

Penelope stopped shivering. Ascenti had draped a wing over her and pulled her tightly to him.

"Do you sense any people down there? Maybe the ones inside that door, where Leaper can be found. What are the earthers thinking?" the Hawkoid whispered via his vocalization device.

'Many people. Jumbled thoughts. Confusion. They are arguing over what to do. Cut the strangers open and keep them alive, or kill them and study them more intently. I'm afraid, Ascenti. They all want to kill Black Leaper and I can't live without him!' the kitten cried.

"Then we shall go in and save him. Are you okay with that?" Ascenti asked. She looked up at him with her huge eyes, sadness furling her brow.

'But how?' she begged, reaching for that lifeline of hope that the Hawkoid had tossed her way.

'Check in with Carnesto and Brutus. I think they are making some progress,' Ascenti said, switching to his thought voice. He could hear the others through the mindlink that Brutus had joined them all to, but there were too many voices. The prisoners were suffering and shared their pain. It was too much for Ascenti. It took him back to the blur of Heimdall, where all he remembered was the agony of his injuries.

He tested his wing to reassure himself that he had survived and that he was fit to rejoin the battle. His commander was captive and the private was the only Marine who could do anything about it.

His only tool at hand was a kitten and her innate abilities.

'Talk with your father and Uncle Carnesto. When will they bring reinforcements so we can recover our people?'

She brightened with the news from Carnesto, who conveniently left out the part where he allowed himself to be hugged and coddled like a soft pillow. Brutus was in the middle of a playground, surrounded by children. He captivated them with the words he delivered directly into their minds. Wondrously accepting the gift without question. The spark of life was nurtured within their young bodies and burst into flame.

Never Cross a Rabbit

"Briz! They are blocking us like nothing I've ever seen before," Jolly said.

"Of course they are! They've had thousands of years to improve their programming, but you've evolved since then and you know what, Jolly? They never counted on someone like me!" Briz laughed maniacally until he started coughing. Rabbit anatomy was ill-suited to such human mannerisms.

Briz immersed himself in Jolly's virtual world. The Rabbit jumped into a data stream and headed for Earth Two's wall. Jolly's data poured as if from a firehose, splashing against the wall, losing its cohesion, and disappearing as it came apart.

The Rabbit slowed the stream, let it build behind him as he walked forward, refusing to let the bits pass him by. They built higher and higher, but he held them at bay. He walked to a mighty wall, impenetrable in its height and width. He tapped a finger on it, and the wall shouted at him.

He put his hands behind his back as he studied the construction. He walked back and forth to assure himself of the solidity of its construction.

He stopped at a place that looked no different than the last place he'd been and tapped on the wall again. It shouted at him with renewed vigor. He captured the sound and played it back at the wall, then increased its volume one hundred fold. He narrowed the acoustics to a pinpoint and let it dig into the impenetrable wall.

Cracks appeared, stretched out from the point, and parts of the wall flaked off. Briz hummed to himself as he let the wall's own sound tear it apart.

A light appeared behind the wall through the crack that Briz had made. He opened it up a little more and stepped quickly aside. The data that he'd been holding back rushed past him in a tidal wave and through, creating a tunnel to the other side, shoring up the walls of the entrance that Briz had created, building a doorway of their own design that would respond only to their commands.

Briz watched as Jolly reached inside. The data stream became a solid cable through which information flowed back and forth. It changed colors from an angry red to a calm green. It sparkled.

Briz put one Rabbit hand on it, felt its power, and smiled at its control. He stepped back and out of the virtual reality.

"Can you get our people out?" Briz asked Jolly.

***

"Inbound ships, size of the Ganymede Seven. Cutters," Starsgard reported.

"I wondered what was taking them so long. How many?" Rand asked.

"Five inbound and one powered up nearby. That may be a freighter preparing to clear the area."

Chirit and Tandry were pulling in the information from both passive and active systems. They knew that the Cygnus-12 was lighting up every system the earthers maintained, but the commander and the captain had wanted no surprises. They had accepted the risk.

Pickles and Fickle sat at their stations, side by side, looking for anything that the earthers might try to hide behind the noise in the space surrounding the station.

The data analysts expected more subterfuge from the earthers, and they were right to be wary.

"People in spacesuits congregating on the nearest docking framework. They appear to be armed," Jolly reported, after Fickle focused the sensors and the AI's attention at what the man had seen.

"Excellent work, Private Foucault, simply excellent. Corporal Starsgard, what can we do about said interlopers?" Rand wondered, hoping for a solution that didn't involve shooting the docking lattice.

"If we focus our arrays, we can send a narrow jamming signal that would probably cause them a great deal of discomfort. It'll be like putting them in the middle of a thunderstorm. They'll get the hint not to come closer," Starsgard answered and then immediately began preparations to send an electronic whirlwind toward a group of people in spacesuits, simply doing the job they were ordered to do.

Daksha swam closer to the main screen to look at the expanded image that Fickle had dialed up. Six people in spacesuits, carrying a variety of gear. There were no other ships around. The only reason they were there was to do something to his spaceship.

"Jolly. Can you please give me a comm link to those individuals?"

"Now that we are into their system, all things are possible!" Jolly exclaimed.

"I've never known you to be a braggart, Master Jolly, but your accolades are well-deserved. You've gone from being the child to the master," Daksha said warmly.

"You are live," Jolly announced.

"People of Earth who are on the dock lattice and looking at our ship. We would appreciate it if you would stand down, return from where you've come. I won't make a threat. I only need you to stand down," Daksha said with a tinge of sadness. He *knew* they wouldn't stand down.

They couldn't tell the body language of the space-suited humans, but they could clearly see that they weren't retreating. The first one jumped from the girder and activated a mobility pack as he started flying through space toward The Olive Branch.

"Now, Dr. Starsgard. Give them a taste of our dismay," Captain Rand ordered.

Starsgard touched a button on his screen. The effect was immediate.

The mobility pack ruptured, sending the individual into a spin as its compressed gases discharged explosively. The other five reacted as if their helmets had been filled with angry bees.

Their magnetic boots lost grip and the people drifted away.

"That's enough," the captain directed.

Starsgard didn't have to move within his gimbaled weapons chair. He didn't have to move more than a few centimeters to touch the button and stop the jammer from radiating.

The bridge crew watched as the figures in spacesuits flailed trying to get back to the docking lattice. The jammer had disabled their mobility devices and they were drifting.

"Please let me talk with them again, Jolly," Daksha requested.

Jolly gave the commander a thumbs up.

"We asked nicely. You refused. We are able to dispatch a drone to gather you all up and return you to a place where you can get back inside. Would you like us to do that for you?"

They waited. And waited some more. The suited figures finally gave up trying to swim against open space. They knew that rescuers would be afraid to help those in need. Their spaceship was too powerful.

"Dispatch a drone, Jolly. Grab that individual spinning toward the station first, then drag a line across the others. Take them to whatever airlock they came from. We do this because we are the good guys, no matter what the earthers' actions. We will show them that they want to be our friends, not our enemies." Daksha turned and swam from the bridge.

Jolly sent one of the many drones that all ships in the SES carried. They were used to recover space samples or satellites, or help crew who worked outside the ship.

Daksha stopped in the open hatch and turned back to look at the command deck. "One last thing, Captain. The Olive Branch didn't work as a ship of peace. This ship is the Cygnus-12. The universe seems hell-bent on burning our branch, so we are going to bring our sense of integrity and morality. We do that as the people of Cygnus, not emissaries with our naïve hands held out just so they can get slapped."

The captain returned to his duties, nodding. He could not have agreed more.

***

"Now that we are in, Jolly, show me what we can do," Briz said, bouncing with excitement.

"The AI running the station is very much like Holly, a successor of some sort, but constrained. I am systematically planting activation codes in systems throughout Earth Two. It is taxing me to the utmost, I have to warn you." To emphasize his statement, Jolly's holographic form disappeared from both engineering and the bridge.

He sent a note to the crew to stand down certain activities while he was engaged with activities external to the ship. He was building a foundation from which they'd be able to launch a recovery effort.

"Jolly, bring up the cameras from our people on board the station." Briz waited while Jolly cycled through views from the people two at a time. Most had their eyes closed. Their vital signs suggested they were under duress.

All of them. Black Leaper's were the worst. "Jolly, how does Leaper's vitals compare to the average Wolfoid, to what we should expect from him?"

"He's dying, Master Brisbois," Jolly reported.

Briz activated the comm link with the bridge. "We need to do something now. Leaper is dying," Briz said, his vocalization device capturing his anxiety. His nose and whiskers twitched almost out of control. He'd seen life and death before, but watching his friends dying slowly was too much.

"I'm working on something," the captain replied. He sounded confident. Briz was comforted, if only a little.

"Let me know what you need from me," Briz offered.

"Direct Earth Two's flight control to turn those inbound ships away. That would be a great help, Briz." The captain signed off.

"On it," Briz said to himself.

***

Night Stalker hopped from one foot to the other. She was too distracted to continue working in maintenance. She needed to know what was going on. Lieutenant Peekaless was near the weapons locker, running diagnostics on blasters, launchers, and lightning spears. He'd put the Marines on a ten-minute leash.

They needed to have full kit, including ballistic vests and cloaks, and meet him on the hangar deck ten minutes from notification.

Many of the Marines hovered near the spindle, ready to go immediately. Spence was angry. He wanted to take Tobiah into the heart of the beast and extract retribution for the earthers' treatment of the people from Cygnus VII.

Rand looked calmly at the screen, then tipped his head toward the ceiling. "Jolly. I intend to take the Cygnus-12 through their screen and into the station. We'll send the shuttle down the ramp and park it outside that door. The Marines will deploy and get our people back. Stun clubs? Those security guards are in for a rude awakening, wouldn't you say, Marines?" Rand declared.

"We will fit, but we will have to maintain our orientation along the axis of the station. The ship will be close to multiple catwalks and various access points, increasing our vulnerability. Is that an acceptable risk?" Jolly asked.

"It is. What do you think, Nathan?" Rand asked the orange 'cat standing in his lap.

'I don't know. I can only hear the crew and they are ready to do as you ask,' the 'cat answered politely.

"My thoughts exactly, Nate. And since we don't have a pilot or navigator, it's time to earn my pay."

Rand held the 'cat in one hand as he moved from his seat to the pilot's station. The hatch opened and Daksha reappeared. He swam onto the bridge. Nathan passed to BJ who in turn passed to the commander that it was time to act.

The Tortoid nodded slowly. "Let's go get our people, Captain."

"All hands. We're taking the Cygnus-12 into the space station. Marines! You are activated. Be prepared to deploy the second we are stable within Earth Two. I think our people will know when we have arrived. Starsgard, I need you for ship's defense since we're going to be vulnerable once inside. Foucault, follow the orders of your lieutenant."

Fickle saluted and dashed from his seat.

"Jolly. Tell our people that we're coming. Tell Ascenti to rally the troops. We'll be there soon. Briz, work with Jolly to lock out their security. Keep them away from us for as long as you can."

***

Briz hopped back and forth on his big Rabbit feet. He'd launched himself back into the VR world. There was nothing with the ship's engines that needed done. The most impact he could make was in the digital world, helping Jolly seize the station's systems and then control them for their own purposes.

Briz followed the data stream into a whole new world, organized as

Holly and Jolly were.

Different but the same.

He headed into the logistics area where access tunnels and doors were located. He started locking them, isolating the rooms where Cain and the others had been taken. The major concern was the ramp. He sent a note through his neural implant to Ascenti.

"We must close off the ramp access to keep reinforcements from coming. Can you do that?" Briz asked.

Ascenti had his wing over the kitten, who had started to shiver again. Her life-link was in pain and descending toward darkness. She couldn't filter the anguish that bombarded her senses.

'I need you to tell the other 'cats that we have to block the ramp. That the ship is coming, the Marines are coming. We need you to do this so we can save Black Leaper. Please, little sweetheart, talk to them for me,' Ascenti pleaded over his mindlink with the kitten.

'They are coming to save him?' she asked, her eyes wide with renewed hope.

'They are on their way right now. Tell Brutus and Carnesto. They'll know what to do.' Ascenti bobbed his head happily. He also felt the hope of an imminent departure from the situation in which they found themselves.

'Thank you, Ascenti. We can hear you directly. We will expedite our actions,' Carnesto replied.

And Ascenti understood why it had been so important for him to re-learn how to fly, why Cain had supported him without taking no for an answer. Ascenti's role in the Marines was unique and no one could do what he did. From the deck's rafters, he watched the door through which the security guards had taken their people. He knew the ship was coming. He was the only one with a way to contact the 'cats. And he'd saved a kitten.

It was what Marines did, not because they wanted to but because they had to, and there was no one else to do it.

***

Brutus heard the kitten's voice and told her that he'd take care of his end of the ramp.

'Listen up, my wonderful students,' he told them, strutting in a circle, tail held

high as he looked from one face to the next. *'We need to block the bottom of the ramp, just for a little while. You will save lives by doing this, because you all have a higher calling. Space is out there, waiting for you, but only if you have the courage to take your place. Now come, children. Let us get to work.'*

Brutus ran toward the ramp, followed by a small army of children. Like the pied piper, he danced and dashed back and forth, letting them keep up with him but only by running. They saw it as a great game. He thought it was necessary to keep from being seen by adults. He didn't have time to win anyone else over.

When they reached the ramp, he had them sit in rows across the bottom of the ramp and he begged them to teach him a song. They didn't know any. Music had been lost to them. Brutus closed his eyes and shook his head. He couldn't believe what he was about to do.

'Listen first and then when I say, follow along with me.' Brutus took a deep breath, and in his best thought-singing voice, he began. *'Twinkle, twinkle, little star…'*

***

When Carnesto heard Ascenti and Penelope's call to action, it forced him to change his approach. *'Jane Jane. Please put me down. We have to block the top of the ramp because my friends are coming for me. Can you help me do that? Block the ramp?'*

"It's just Jane," she answered, continuing to hug the large black 'cat tightly.

'Just Jane or Jane Jane? Make up your mind, woman! Now put me down!' he demanded.

"Keep your pants on," she replied calmly as she carefully put Carnesto on the deck as if he was made of porcelain.

'Blocking the ramp? How can we do that?' he asked, even though he'd already seen in her mind a plan where she used a loader to dump cargo crates. *'Skip the explanation, Jane Jane. Go get that loader and drop a few crates in place. I'll meet you on the other side of the ramp.'*

Carnesto turned and ran, keeping to the shadows cast by tall cargo containers. Jane hesitated for only a moment, then ran to the side toward a large piece of bright yellow equipment. She jumped aboard, started it up, and immediately headed for the nearest crate.

Kick the Tires and Light the Fires

Rand's fingers danced across his screens as he reacquainted himself with the pilot's controls. It didn't take long. He had always loved flying, but this was different. He was going to squeeze the Cygnus-12 through an opening and then hold it in place without bouncing off the interior structure of Earth Two.

Jolly was still too occupied to appear in holographic form, but he was present as a disembodied voice speaking through the bridge's sound system.

"Take us in, Rand," Daksha ordered, hovering over the captain's chair.

With Nathan and BJ, they were the only ones left on the bridge.

"Jolly, status of the inbound cutters, please," Daksha asked as the main screen became too busy with statuses and information updates.

"Three have veered away. Two have come to a complete stop. One is still inbound," Jolly reported.

"Corporal Starsgard, please prepare to defend the ship from the final inbound, starting with a focused jamming?" the Tortoid asked, wondering if Jolly would allow the course of action.

"Capital choice," the AI replied.

"Ready to jam. Ready to fire defensive missiles if they launch anything at us," Starsgard answered from weapons control. He wanted to shoot the ship out of the sky, but knew that Jolly would block it.

The corporal didn't want to be fired on first, but he had no choice. If Jolly shut down, the ship would be vulnerable.

He was forced to wait, but he couldn't. The inbound ship was turning slowly toward them. If he could kill the ship's power with a jamming burst, the cutter's ballistic trajectory would take it behind the Cygnus-12.

"It's now or never, Jolly," Starsgard said, checking the settings one last time and then activating the system.

The cutter bucked as four missiles jumped from it and accelerated toward the Cygnus-12. Starsgard broadened the jammer's beam, then turned it off and activated the fire control system. As soon as the inbound targets were painted, he mashed the button to fire.

Four small missiles launched into space and found their targets, zeroing in as the outbound raced to meet the inbound. Starsgard activated the last four missiles, but didn't fire. He didn't want to drain their resources, but he didn't want the ship to get hit either. He toggled the next four as he watched closely.

The ship's defensive fire stayed true, intercepting each of the inbound missiles. Starsgard looked for other targets that may have been hidden within the jamming signal, but couldn't find anything.

He immediately reactivated the jamming system, making sure it was at maximum intensity.

The inbound cutter lost attitude control and was starting to spin nose over tail as it stayed on its course toward the docking lattice.

Rand gunned the EM drive to get them headed toward the space station and away from the ballistic trajectory of the cutter that had lost its control systems. He adjusted carefully to align the ship's approach with the central axis. He tweaked, touched, and leaned as the ship responded.

The EM thrusters were far more powerful than he was used to and he constantly over adjusted. Back and forth the ship swayed as it approached. Rand's hands were shaking as he touched the controls, walking the ship back and forth in smaller and smaller swings until it settled into a head-in approach. The Cygnus-12 passed through the energy barrier and into the interior of Earth Two.

Once inside, Rand was surprised at the amount of space. "Radial one five zero, Jolly. Can you point me in the right direction, please?"

A line appeared on the screen. Rand touched the controls and angled that way while matching the rotation of the space station. He spiraled toward it, saw the shuttle on the landing pad, and slowed.

The ship angled overtop of the landing zone. They saw cargo containers haphazardly stacked in front of the ramp downward. A loader had backed onto the ramp and used its forks and a container to block that last of the access.

"Launch the shuttle," Daksha ordered.

It was a tight squeeze on board, but no one volunteered to stay behind. Only Starsgard was absent and that was because he'd been ordered to stay.

The Marines had felt the missiles launch and knew that the corporal had engaged in a life and death struggle to save the ship. They knew he'd won when the large doors opened and the shuttle headed out of the bay.

Lieutenant Peekaless was by the hatch with Sergeant Night Stalker, ready to be the first ones out. A total of seven humans, two Lizard Men, and five Wolfoids were stuffed into the shuttle.

Six Hillcats accompanied the Marines and were already in touch with Carnesto. Their hackles were up, and they anxiously awaited the hatch to reopen.

The shuttle flew less than four hundred meters before settling on the ramp, horizontally, nose facing the Cygnus-12.

The hatch popped and Stalker bolted out with Pickles on her tail. The Marines poured out of the shuttle and toward the door through which Cain and the others had been taken. Shep headed twenty meters down the ramp and crouched with his lightning spear ready to greet any unwanted visitors. Tracker assumed an identical position up the ramp.

Carnesto ran toward him, weaving back and forth to show that the human was with him.

"Hold!" Tracker yelled, pointing his spear at the woman. Her work coveralls said that she wasn't security, but Tracker made her stop and stand still nonetheless.

'Just do as your told, Jane Jane, and you won't get hurt. These people are my friends,' Carnesto told the woman before joining the group ready to yank the door open.

Stalker was the first through, with the Marines packed in tightly behind her. Pickles entered last. A pack of 'cats followed the group in.

Two corridor turns later, they found guards in front of the door where Cain and the others were being held.

Stalker didn't hesitate. She activated her lightning spear and fried both men. Their stun clubs sparked out of their hands as the lightning burned through their frail, unprotected human bodies. Trilok set up a blocking position on the far side, beyond the dead men.

Stalker ripped the door open and jumped through into a large room. It was reminiscent of the sickbay on the Cygnus-12.

She couldn't use her lightning spear because of the friendlies strapped into the beds. She lowered the spear point and headed for the closest guard. He swung his club, but she dipped her spear out of the way and thrust, impaling the man. She twirled the spear to do more damage to his body while working the point free. She picked a second target, but he was already stepping back. A single blaster beam blew a hole through his head and he toppled.

Jo was braced inside the doorway and rapidly picking off the security guards. The last one crouched behind the bed where Leaper was located.

Numerous tubes ran into the Wolfoid's body. Some of his hair had been shaved away. Electrodes of various sorts were attached to the bald spots.

Stalker snarled. A man in a white labcoat held his hands up. She pointed her spear tip a centimeter from his throat. "Unhook him," she growled.

The man didn't move. She forced him back with her spear. "I said unhook him. I *will* kill you, and then we will work our way through the rest of you until we find someone who is willing to do the right thing. Let our people go or you will die."

The man finally decided that he was not going to die for the cause. He turned and started pulling leads from the Wolfoid's ravaged body.

Jo casually walked around the tables, waving her blaster at the earthers to herd them into a far corner. Once she had a line of sight, she took aim at the last guard. He threw his club down and stood up with his hands on his head.

She wanted to shoot him, but honor said that she couldn't shoot an unarmed prisoner. "Pick it up," she ordered, but he refused, shaking his head adamantly. "Get with the others."

He squeezed past her, a look of terror in his eyes. She wanted him to make a move as her aim was steady and her finger a hair's breadth from sending a blaster beam into his body. He didn't make a move and joined the medical staff, kneeling on the floor with his hands over his head.

The Marines started releasing the prisoners. Seven humans and a Wolfoid. "Numbweed!" Stalker called and a gob was slapped into her hand.

She put it on the worst of Leaper's injuries. They took a gurney and put Leaper on it. The others would have to walk since there were no stretchers of any kind.

Cain roused, but his head rolled around on his shoulders. The Marines wrapped arms around the others and half-carried them out. Tobiah jumped on the table nearest to the earthers huddled in the corner. He snarled like a raging lion. Spence dialed his blaster to the wide, flame setting and he aimed.

"Corporal!" Lieutenant Peekaless called, making eye contact to ensure that Spence heard him. "We are leaving!"

Spence backed away as Tobiah jumped down and headed out the door. Spence made sure that he was last out, aimed his blaster at the overhead, and fired. The panels were fire resistant, but they melted nicely, sending long smoking tendrils to the floor as if creating a molten curtain. Spence ran to catch up with Tobiah as the Marines cleared the way.

The first burst through the door, looking left and right then standing aside to make room for those with the injured to pass.

Brutus appeared from down the ramp, running toward them. He looked out of breath when he passed Shep.

Ascenti looked at Penelope. "Time to rejoin our people," he said. She stood up as he beat his wings to lift off. He caught the kitten in his claws and glided downward, flaring to land behind the shuttle.

The Marines brought the injured to the shuttle and put them in. Stalker and Fickle rode along to help those who couldn't help themselves.

The rest of the Marines set up firing positions up and down the ramp. They would have to wait for the shuttle to return. First priority was to the wounded.

Penelope jumped aboard and then Brutus and Carnesto.

"My cat!" Jane Merriweather yelled, seeing Carnesto climb aboard.

'Tell them she can come along on the next shuttle. She doesn't belong here,' the black 'cat told Ascenti.

The shuttle hatch closed and it took off. It took longer for the shuttle to line up with the Cygnus-12's hangar bay and enter than it did to fly the distance from the ramp to the ship.

Ascenti flew to Tracker's side. "She is to come along if she wishes," he told the Wolfoid through his vocalization device.

She looked at them both wide-eyed as the two creatures carried on a conversation in a language that she understood.

"Well?" Tracker asked. The woman looked at him, confused. "Are you coming or not?"

"Yes?" she replied tentatively, saying it if it were a question.

Two men burst out of the door that led to the medical laboratory. Jo and Grace blasted the two back inside. For good measure, Grace sent lightning arcing into the hallway. She held her finger on the activator longer than necessary, but a message needed to be sent.

The shuttle returned and the remaining Marines climbed aboard. Pickles was the last one in, surveying the ramp both up and down before entering and watching the hatch close.

He took his seat on the end, squeezed tightly against the new female, and looked at her with his big amphibian eyes. She stared back, mouth agape. "I'm Lieutenant Peekaless," he introduced himself.

"Lieutenant Pickles? I'm Jane, Jane Merriweather," she replied.

"Pickles, Jane Jane? What is with you humans?" Pickles shook his head.

"It's just Jane," she tried to explain as the shuttle lifted into the air using the power of its thrusters only.

"You just said it was Jane Jane. Now it's Just Jane?" Pickles asked flatly as he returned to his normal stoic self. "We shall wait until we're aboard the Cygnus-12. I expect it will be a rough ride out of your solar system, and you will want to find a good place to brace yourself."

The shuttle lined up and pulled itself into the hangar bay, where the other shuttle was there waiting. Pickles wondered, until he remembered that Jolly and Briz were in control of Earth Two's systems. Unlashing the shuttle and flying it back would have been easy for them.

The shuttle's hatch opened before the hangar bay doors closed. Pickles looked at the sight as he'd never seen the doors open while inside the bay, since the ship never operated within a breathable atmosphere.

The others disembarked. "Make sure the survivors get to sickbay," he ordered.

"Here, kitty, kitty, kitty!" Jane Merriweather called out.

"You'll find him with his human near sickbay. I suggest you go straight to the garden deck. You will find more Hillcats there," Pickles advised. She nodded and stood there.

"Garden deck?" she asked.

"Private Ascenti! Please take Jane Jane to the garden. If you'll excuse me, ma'am, my presence is required on the bridge." The Lizard Man loped away.

The Hawkoid flew close and hovered in front of her. She shied away.

"If you hold out your arm, you can give me a ride," he said.

She did as directed and he landed, taking care not to dig his claws in too deeply.

Together they left the hangar bay, heading for the stairs up.

Trapped

"The earthers are starting to disconnect systems operated by the AI, most significant is the entrance to the landing zone. They've erected a physical barrier and there's nothing we can do about it," Briz explained excitedly.

He was afraid they would fail and be trapped. He saw what the earthers did to Leaper. He knew that they'd do the same thing to him and the rest of the crew.

The view on the bridge's main screen showed a web of heavy cables crisscrossing the entrance through which they'd passed to get inside the space station.

"Corporal Starsgard, what kind of firepower can you bring to bear? A better question is, can you blast us a way through there?" Rand asked from the pilot's chair.

Fickle and Pickles had returned. The Lizard Man ran his claws over the navigator's screen and was running course and speed calculations.

"Briz!" Commander Daksha yelled through his vocalization device. "Options!"

The commander didn't accuse Briz of setting them up to fail, but that's how the Rabbit felt. He had been confident that he and Jolly owned the station, but the earthers had worked around the digital controls that Briz and Jolly had put in place.

They did something that Briz hadn't contemplated and hadn't planned for.

And now the ship was trapped.

"I don't know what to do," the Rabbit shared over the ship-wide communication system.

"I do," Jolly interjected without further explanation.

Briz looked around, wondering what he'd missed that Jolly did not.

"We're all ears," Commander Daksha replied. He didn't have ears in the traditional sense, not like the Rabbits' huge floppy ears.

"We activate the ISE and jump directly to EL475."

No one spoke. No one moved.

Jolly felt the need to explain further. "With our new calculations, we can jump from within the gravity well. Intervening objects are irrelevant, such as a space station or cables or planets or even suns. None of that matters."

Jolly was quite pleased with his pun, but disappointed that no one got it.

"Briz? You're the chief engineer," Daksha suggested the call was Briz's to make.

"It should work," Briz answered tentatively.

"Is that the best you can give me?" Daksha retorted.

"Commander, we have visitors." Rand pointed to the screens showing views surrounding the ship. Security guards carrying rifles were taking aim and firing. "Can they hurt the ship?"

"I don't know, but I'm sure that projectiles and energy weapons won't do us any favors. Briz?" The commander blinked rapidly with his agitation.

"The projectiles shouldn't be any problem, but the energy weapons could cause our sensors some issues, not to mention the dark matter banking system. That is tucked away, but if they hit it, things could go badly," Briz advised.

"I was talking about the ISE, Briz," Daksha clarified impatiently.

"Yes. It'll work," Briz stated softly.

"Captain Rand, are coordinates locked?" Daksha asked quickly.

Rand's hands tapped controls as he closed out the EM main drive screen and brought up the ISE. "EL475 is locked. Target is zero point one AU beyond Heimdall's heliosphere."

"Prepare to activate the ISE." Daksha floated downward until he was resting against the captain's chair. Nathan was squeezed into it behind him.

Pickles replied, "Board shows green."

"All hands. Activating the ISE in three, two, one."

***

Cain was thrown across the corridor as the ship lurched. He caught himself in time to keep Ellie from slamming into the bulkhead. They were both weak, having donated too much blood to the earthers. Cain struggled to open his eyes as the Cygnus-12 settled into an eerie silence.

Cain helped Ellie to her feet. "I need to get to engineering. Briz is down there by himself," she slurred. Cain didn't want to let her go, but they were short-handed, even with the four additions to the crew.

A woman in coveralls picked herself up off the deck and hovered near the captain, pilot, and navigator from the Ganymede Seven. Their uniforms were familiar to her within the foreign confines of the strange ship.

Cain didn't have time for social niceties. He'd introduce himself later.

"Come on, Brutus, to the bridge," he told the 'cat standing nervously nearby. Brutus seemed happy to be doing anything other than waiting outside sickbay with the injured.

Carnesto had remained in the stairway so Jane wouldn't see him. When Ellie appeared, he rubbed against her leg and joined her as she leaned heavily on the railing while descending one deck to engineering.

Cain climbed past the garden deck and to the command deck. He lumbered into the corridor, his legs feeling abnormally heavy and unresponsive. His stomach churned and he started to sweat. He slid along the bulkhead, counting on its support to keep him upright. He staggered from one side to the other and the hatch opened.

He stumbled in as Daksha was listening to a damage report from sensors. "...the array is gone. In the moment of transition, something hit us and tore it off. We are hard down with fifty percent of our active systems," Chirit reported.

"Can you fix it?" Rand asked from the pilot's seat.

"There's nothing to fix. It's gone!" Chirit exclaimed.

"Can Jolly fabricate a new one? We have the specs," Rand offered.

"Maybe, but we lack certain metals. Heimdall may have what we need, but I'm not sure anyone wants to go back down there. They may have what we need on Concordia." Chirit was browsing the ship's raw material inventory, but he wasn't seeing what he hoped to see.

"Where are we?" Daksha asked. Pickles looked at Foucault. The young man was elbow-deep into his screens. The damage to the sensors slowed the data acquisition. If the Tortoid had fingers, he would have drummed a staccato on the arm of the captain's chair as he waited impatiently. The star field finally appeared on the main screen and sharpened.

"We are at the edge of EL475's gravity well. Bullseye, Commander!" Fickle shouted.

"Thank you, Private. How are the engines, Briz?" The Tortoid remained in the captain's chair while Rand set the controls to hold the ship in place, which wasn't difficult in interstellar space. There were currents, but they weren't fast moving and the Cygnus-12 would be long gone before their drift would have caused them any grief.

Cain had stopped in the hatchway, listening. The information only half registered. He stumbled the last few steps and crashed into the commander before he stopped himself. BJ looked crossly at him, until he saw who it was and what kind of shape he was in. The kitten jumped from the Tortoid's shell and rubbed himself against Cain's hand. Brutus jumped into the captain's chair, so recently vacated by the commander.

"The engines are fine. We hit something on the way out, before we entered the void between the molecules. It appears that we've not only lost part of the array, the entire module is gone," Briz reported, thinking about how much work he'd done in that section of the ship, just to see it evaporate with an ISE jump from within a space station.

Briz smiled wryly, thinking that they'd done something that had never even been contemplated before.

"Thank goodness we don't have a large enough crew to populate that section of the ship," Cain added.

"Starting to bank dark matter for the next jump, Commander. Current estimate is fourteen days to one hundred percent," Briz told them.

"Let's go see what we have," Rand said, working his way free of the pilot's chair and scooping Nathan up, putting him on his shoulder as he walked past.

Daksha swam close to BJ so the 'cat could jump aboard. Rand threw an arm under Cain's to help him back to sickbay.

"Private Foucault, you have the conn," Rand called over his shoulder as the group left the bridge on their way to sickbay.

***

Night Stalker was pacing back and forth in the corridor. The med bots had chased her out because they needed to perform surgery on her mate. She didn't know why, because they didn't say.

The others were in the corridor and hooked up to IVs, forcing replacement fluids into their bodies. Brayson, Mahjing, and Star had been experimented on as well to determine if they were spies infiltrated into the human ranks. Of the newcomers, only Jane was unscathed.

'She loves 'cats and Carnesto used her to block off the top ramp. We should probably give her a little 'cat love,' Brutus suggested.

Cain's mind was clearing because of the adrenaline surge, but he was a long way from being healthy.

'Did I hear you singing?' Cain asked in his thought voice.

'Not as far as you know. Understand that I'm doing what it takes to save you, time and again, but I'm having to get more and more creative,' Brutus replied matter-of-factly.

'Your sacrifices shall go down in our annals to show what a martyr you have become, all because of me. Thanks, Brutus. I am happy to be out of there. I've never felt so helpless in my life,' Cain confided.

Garinst appeared in the corridor carrying Ellie over his shoulder. Cain stumbled toward him, but the lieutenant commander waved him off.

"She passed out. Severely dehydrated. How do we get her hooked up to one of those?" Garinst said succinctly.

"Put her over here. We'll have to make do with drinks from the mess deck until Stinky is out of surgery."

"I got it, Cain. You should probably sit down yourself. You look like crap." The commander hurried away.

Cain sat on the deck, holding Ellie to him. His head cleared as the anger seethed within. He couldn't wait to go back to Earth. The prime minister had a lot to answer for, and Major Cain wanted to see the man beg for his life, grovel before those he considered inferior.

Garinst returned with two tall glasses of weak juice.

"Who are you?" he asked Jane gruffly while handing the glasses to Cain. He saw the coveralls and thought he recognized a kindred spirit.

'We call her Jane Jane,' Brutus had already told Cain.

The woman looked surprised that someone was talking with her.

"That's Jane Jane. She helped us escape. I think she's stuck with us now," Cain told him.

"Nice to meet you, Jane Jane. I'm Garinst, head of the maintenance section on this fine boat. You look like you know your way around tools." He stuck out a dirty hand, then pulled it back and wiped it on a rag he carried in his back pocket, but wasn't satisfied with his hand's cleanliness to offer it a second time.

"Is there any more of that?" She nodded toward the glasses in Cain's hands.

"Yes, there is. Are you still needed here?" he asked. She shook her head. The people were sitting and waiting for their turn to see the med bots.

"I'll show you how the fabricators work, and we'll get you something nice and cold." He offered his arm and she took it in both hands as they worked their way through the bodies and down the corridor.

The hatch slid open when they were gone and the med bot pointed to Ellie and Cain. He slugged his juice and even with Stalker's help, he struggled as they half-dragged Ellie into sickbay. Stinky was on the recovery table, still out could but stitched and bandaged. He was breathing on his own. Stalker rushed to his side once Cain and Ellie were situated.

The med bots went to work, putting all the injured to sleep so they could rest. Garinst had moved cots into the hallway and that was where they stayed, where the med bot could check on them all without leaving sickbay.

Daksha and Rand wanted to talk with those from the group, but they were out. The only one available was Jane Merriweather, who was engaged in a contest with Garinst to see who could tell the most crass joke. Some of the Marines had found their way to the mess deck and were egging both contestants on.

When the captain and the commander arrived, the guffaws stopped abruptly.

"We have a hole in our ship, Garinst. We need you and your people to patch it up so we can continue to IC1396 and then home. Take whoever you need. I'm sorry, ma'am. I'm Captain Rand, and this is Commander Daksha."

"Pleased to meet you," Daksha said, bowing his head slightly.

"I'm Jane, Jane Merriweather. I'd like to try and help, if I could. I've never met a talking turtle before," she blurted without thinking, then slapped a hand over her mouth.

"Tortoid, and you are more than welcome to help, assuming Garinst gives it the green light. I'm not sure what you know of our systems, though," Daksha countered.

"I know when something is vented to space and shouldn't be," she said.

"Fair enough. Let's put our ship back together, people. We're going home," Rand said.

***

"I wanted you to know that Jolly and I put videos of the prime minister and the others getting their gene splicing on permanent loop to every video monitor on the entire station. I expect it will take them a while to shut it off..." Briz relayed to Cain and Ellie while they rested and recovered in their cots outside sickbay.

Home

They repaired what they could, opting for fifty percent sensor capability, the heliosheath, and the void of interstellar space to protect them. They were out in the open, but the universe was a very big place.

The jump to IC1396 had none of the excitement of the jump from within Earth Two. Cain called it a walk in the park. The earthers weren't sure what that was since they didn't have such things. Parks failed the efficiency test. Their resource cost was more than they delivered.

"You'll like Cygnus VII," Cain told the group. They'd assembled in the briefing room for a more formal conversation as they prepared to join the explorers from the Cygnus system.

"Dark matter at thirty-one percent," Briz reported over the communication system. "Estimate twelve more days banking to achieve one hundred percent. We'll need all we can get for the next jump, Captain."

"Understood, Lieutenant. Carry on," Rand told the ceiling.

Daksha floated peacefully at one end of the long table. The earthers tried to sit on one side, but the commander wouldn't allow that. He mixed them up and since the pilot and navigator had found their soulmates in their fellow pilot and navigator, Rand asked Kalinda and Pace to attend.

The new couples sat side by side, while Captain Brayson and Jane Merriweather were on one end. Jane kept looking at the hatch as if surprised it wasn't opened.

Cain watched her with interest. *'Brutus, a little insight, please. I'm missing something.'*

'You're missing the boy toy. What is with these earthers and their libidos? Don't answer that. Compared to you, they are fairly tame,' Brutus replied as if Cain were bothering him.

Which was probably true. Brutus was still upset that he hadn't been able to bring any live rabbits on board to stock the garden deck with readily available prey. Brutus hung in his tree, bored and ungratified.

Cain sensed the 'cat's dismay. *We'll be home soon, Brutus. With our feet planted firmly on the ground. We'll get you a good hunt, in the north when we go to visit Ellie's home. Do you want to see the memorial of the final battle in the great 'cat rebellion?'* Cain laughed in his thought voice.

'No,' Brutus replied.

Cain chuckled as he looked down, hoping the others wouldn't notice. He caught Brayson smiling in his direction. Mel knew every time that Cain and Brutus talked.

The hatch opened and Garinst walked in. Cain was surprised. The lieutenant commander attended staff meetings, but not ones of this sort. He took the empty seat next to a beaming Jane and like the others, they held hands.

"How did I not know?" Cain whispered to Rand. The captain shrugged. He didn't know what Cain didn't know. That was a pretty demanding thing to ask of Rand. He looked sternly at Cain. The major mouthed the word "what?"

"Welcome again, for the fiftieth time, we bid you welcome. And for the first time, I apologize that we have made you outcasts," Daksha started. He swam over the middle of the table so he could be closer to the earthers. "It appears that I don't need to tell you that we will help you with every part of your journey. Whatever you want to make of yourselves, wherever you want to live, whatever you want to do . Cygnus is free that way because the Free Trader made it so."

Daksha turned to look at Cain.

Rand pointed at him, just in case the others hadn't already gotten the hint from the Tortoid. Cain looked away. Rand slapped him on the shoulder.

"The Free Trader helped people appreciate what they had, what they could do for others, and how that could make their lives better. And here we are, a mere one hundred, thirty-eight years later and we've been back to Earth." Rand stood as he was too tall to get comfortable in the conference room chairs.

"It wasn't quite what we expected," Rand conceded, hanging his head. "Jolly, what did you get from Earth's space station?"

"We got most of it, Captain," Jolly said, not as happy as he should have been with such a victory. His visage appeared on the monitor. "Most of it has no value for us. We'll turn it over to Dr. Johns and the researchers when we get back, but they didn't advance as quickly as we did. The one thing we very much wanted, we have secured the energy shield technology with multiple copies kept separate from my hardware."

"That is something we'll be able to put to use, almost right away. Imagine the shipyard, enclosed, with artificial gravity, but still open to space. That would advance our shipbuilding tenfold. Maybe we can trade the technology for the new shuttles that we want for the Marines," Rand stated.

"Of course not," Daksha gently corrected the captain. "We'll work with them on the new design. I'm not sure when next we'll deploy. We didn't leave under the best circumstances last time."

Brayson's brow furled and his expression turned dark.

Daksha turned around to face the man. "The AI that runs the planet was having a crisis. Cain and his Marines kind of had to shoot their way off the space station, the former colony ship. We have a plan to engage Holly when we get home. Is it foolproof? There's no way to know, but we have Jolly on our side and that gives us a fighting chance.

"We can go where we want? Do what we want?" Brayson asked.

"Yes, both. It is your life and your choice," Daksha answered.

"I want to stay on board The Olive Branch!" he blurted. The others were vocal in their responses. No one wanted to go anywhere other than the ship.

"We send our people to Space School to earn a billet on one of these. The Space Exploration Service screens all the candidates, but they've made exceptions before. The Cygnus-12 has had too many firsts to count, so we won't bother. When we arrive, we'll transmit our crew manifest and you'll be included. I wonder if anyone will notice?" Rand wondered.

"No matter where you go in the galaxy, there's always bureaucracy," Brayson added wryly.

The others nodded knowingly.

"Any questions?" Daksha asked, thinking that they had to be wondering about a million different things, but they looked calm, not bothered by the unknown. Then again, they were spacers, used to being in the middle of space, nothing to rely on but their ship and their wit.

Rand had already seen that they would fit right in. From two couples on board to five. 'Cats were underfoot everywhere one turned. It was like running a miniature generation ship. But they no longer needed generations to get where they wanted to go.

The captain wrapped the meeting and most of the group left, leaving only Rand, Daksha, Cain, and Brayson. "This ship already has a captain," Brayson said, looking from Rand to Daksha. "I don't want to leave my people and I don't want to get in your way. What can I do if I say on board?"

"We don't have a ship XO. Even Cain has an XO. I think we can establish that position. We can always make sure that someone is in the chair, same with pilot and navigator. We seem to have some overlap."

"Yes, we do!" Brayson exclaimed, finally getting up to excuse himself. "I think a fabricator is calling my name. I could see getting fat here. We didn't have that problem on a Ganymede-class cutter. If you got the chance to eat, you were lucky to keep it down. We were weightless all the time, except when accelerating and then we stayed in our chairs. It's nice to walk like we were meant to."

"I think I'll join you. I still haven't recovered the weight I lost when we had an accident well over a year ago. Let me tell you about it…" Rand and Brayson left together.

"These are good things, Commander," Cain said. "Really good things."

***

The last jump executed flawlessly to the edge of the Cygnus gravity well.

"Take us in, standard acceleration, three gravities actual," Rand ordered. Fickle had been forced to give up his position on the bridge. Brayson sat there now, next to Pickles.

"Lieutenant Chirit, please transmit our greetings to the SES, include our ETA. Send the messages we have drafted, and then request a meeting between me, Commander Daksha, Briz, Jolly, Holly, Admiral Jesper, and Dr. Johns. We would like that date and time confirmed before anything else. That meeting will happen before anyone else leaves the ship," Captain Rand ordered.

"Aye, aye, sir," Chirit chirped.

Jolly appeared next to the captain's chair. "I look forward to that conversation, Captain. I have high hopes that our issues will be resolved in short order."

"What did you and that Rabbit do?" Rand asked skeptically.

"Hedged our bet, I believe is the correct term. We have already transmitted our findings to Holly, to let him analyze what we've come up with. His logic will come to the right conclusion. We thought it better to present the information while we're still a long ways off. Just in case," Jolly explained.

"We will see," Rand allowed.

The end of Cygnus Arrives

If you liked the book, please leave a review – this link should take you to Amazon's review page. Even one or two words help make a difference.
https://www.amazon.com/review/create-review/ref=cm_cr_dp_d_wr_but_top?ie=UTF8&channel=glance-detail&asin=B072LFCR9S#

If you'd like to see more adventures for Cain and his Marines, drop me a note at craig@craigmartelle.com or
on Facebook www.facebook.com/authorcraigmartelle

Please keep reading! My Author notes are at the end, shout outs to all kinds of great people☺.

Craig Martelle

Cover art created by Christian Bentulan

Coversbychristian.com

Editing services provided by Mia Darien

miadarien.com

The Free Trader Series

Available exclusively on Amazon – FREE on Kindle Unlimited

The Free Trader series is currently six books, soon to be nine of prequel adventure where you get to meet each of the species mentioned in the Cygnus Space Opera.

A 'cat and his human minions fight to bring peace to humanity. Compared to Andre Norton, David Gemmell, and Larry Niven, the Free Trader series takes you to a colonized world across the galaxy where engineered animals help the people survive and become masters of the planet. After a devastating civil war, humanity and its creations rise again. The Free Trader finds himself at a crossroads: can he and his 'cat prevent a repeat of past mistakes as they rebuild civilization?

Here's what some reviewers had to say about the Free Trader…

"Most authors can't make a animal character believable. This one does. Craig Martelle has a great imagination and can put it down on paper for you to enjoy also, just like the great writers of the golden age. His writing is very reminiscent of their work."

"very good read. reminds me of Andre Norton."

"This series is excellent. The characters are well developed and the story line is compelling. As a long time fan of Post Apocalyptic books by Larry Niven and others as well as PA games, I would encourage anyone who enjoys Apocalyptic, Survival, and high adventure books to read this series."

https://www.amazon.com/gp/product/B01G19OHTS/ref=series_rw_dp_sw

Postscript

Thank you for reading Cygnus Arrives!

If you like to see the series continue, please join my mailing list by dropping by my website www.craigmartelle.com or if you have any comments, shoot me a note at craig@craigmartelle.com. I am always happy to hear from people who've read my work. I try to answer every email I receive.

If you liked the story, please write a short review for me on Amazon. I greatly appreciate any kind words, even one or two sentences go a long way. The number of reviews an ebook receives greatly improves how well an ebook does on Amazon.

Amazon – www.amazon.com/author/craigmartelle
Facebook – www.facebook.com/authorcraigmartelle
My web page – www.craigmartelle.com
Twitter – www.twitter.com/rick_banik

Author Notes

Shout out to Thomas Ogden who is a stalwart supporter. He's also kicking diabetes' ass through diet and exercise. I'm at risk for that disease as it runs in my family, so Thomas's fight is personal. It is motivating to see Thomas take charge and make the changes necessary to stay in front of it. In honor of Thomas, I named one of the Marines "Ogden." Thank you for joining the team☺.

A side note in how I address acceleration and velocity in the Cygnus series. I use gravities for acceleration – that's 9.8m/sec[2]. When I say a ship is traveling at 480 gees, that is my shorthand style for 480 times a standard one gravity acceleration. Acceleration and deceleration for the Cygnus-12 are never more than 20 gravities with the crew in their acceleration couches, because we cannot have them turned to mush. Speeds in space are relative and can get complicated. I use the space math website – for my calculations (https://www.cthreepo.com/lab/math1/). I know it may seem odd that someone who earned their undergrad in humanities tries to get the math right, but I do. I used to be a math and science guy, having tested a 770 on the math part of the SAT. I was 25 when I took it.

The Just In Time readers have been fabulous. For some ungodly reason, I used the term "exuberation." What the hell does that even mean? Why would Word, or Grammarly allow that? They all did, but we changed it to exuberance, because who doesn't like a little trickeration every now and then? I also used the phrase "laugh mercilessly." Since I wasn't talking about someone angling to take over the world from their island lair, I fixed that, too. Incredible job by the JIT readers to help me maintain clarity and deliver a better story that flows well. No hiccups.

I'll list them again because they deserve the shout out.

Beck Young
Lori Hendricks
Thomas Ogden
James Caplan
Leo Roars
Theresa Barber
Norman Meredith
Diane Velasquez
Dorene Johnson

It's been a busy month! I went to the Smarter Artist Summit in Austin, Texas for a few days in April. The guys from Sterling & Stone put on a great show and I picked up a bunch of tidbits about this little thing known as the author business, but most importantly, I met a lot of great people.

It was Austin, so I tried to eat my body weight in Tex-Mex. That didn't work out so well.

The good news? I'm no longer craving Tex-Mex.

The sun has returned and I mean it's really returned. I start my day way early, 3am kind of early. It's already light at that time of day. By being a full-time author, I'm home, which means that our dog Phyllis has adopted my schedule. She gets her morning walk sometime between 3:30 am and 4:30 am, eating breakfast as soon as we get back to the house. And then she eats dinner between three and four in the afternoon.

I'll go to bed at night again sometime in August. Otherwise, it's light when I go to bed, light when I get up. I feel like such a slug!

But that is what it's like in the sub-Arctic. At this time of year, the sun rises and pseudo-sets in the north. In the winter, it's the exact opposite. It rises and sets in the south. Only for a small part of each year does it rise in the east and set in the west as most of the world is used to.

I got the greenhouse set up so I think we'll make a run to the nursery this weekend to pick up a few plants. It still gets down toward frostiness at night, but the greenhouse stays nice and warm. Three tomatoes, two peppers, one zucchini, and cabbage. That will be this year's haul. We may do some herbs, but we'll grow those in pots.

We bought this cilantro in a can thing. It's on a small table in front of the window. It supposedly is going to give us much cilantro right inside. I have high hopes for this little gem, too.

I still haven't fixed my tractor – next up is heating the bolt, then we'll see if we can crack it free. I may have to recruit help. I hate asking people for help, so we'll see how much I have to heat it to get it break free.

And then I get to move the tractor and walk-behind snow thrower to the shed, clearing the space to move the picnic table to the outside deck. And then we'll have space to clean out some of the garage. My truck is so much bigger than my old Liberty, I need to move some stuff to be able to get more of the truck inside.

Cygnus Arrives – Humanity Returns Home. I'm glad this one is done and available to all the good people out there. A series really needs that third book. I expect I'll continue the series because I love space opera!

We shall see. I have a lot on my plate, including the next three Free Trader books – these will probably be a little shorter than the others in the series, but they are good stories with the highest quality covers. And it's my intent to release them in rapid succession later this summer.

Break's over – back to writing Nomad Avenged, the 7th book in the Terry Henry Walton Chronicles.